BLOODLINES

Also by
Chris Bishop

The Shadow of the Raven series:
Blood and Destiny
The Warrior with the Pierced Heart
The Final Reckoning

BLOODLINES

CHRIS BISHOP

Red Door

Published by RedDoor
www.reddoorpress.co.uk

ISBN 978-1-913062-52-1

A CIP catalogue record for this book is available from the British
Library

Cover design: Patrick Knowles
www.patrickknowlesdesign.com

Map design: Joey Everett

Typesetting: Jen Parker, Fuzzy Flamingo
www.fuzzyflamingo.co.uk

Printed and bound in Denmark by Nørhaven

To all my windsurfing friends with whom I've shared so many great times over the years – particularly the members of the RBISC (may they never act their age!)

A glossary of some of the terms used in this story can be found at the back of the book

The Author's Impression of the Burh at Wareham

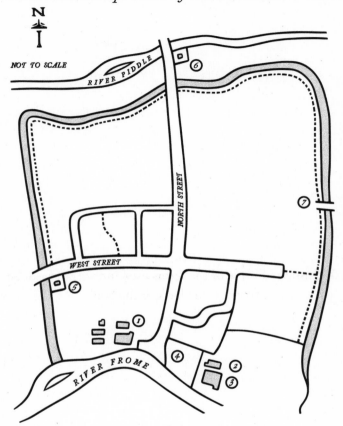

NOT TO SCALE

RIVER PIDDLE

NORTH STREET

WEST STREET

RIVER FROME

THE BURH AT WAREHAM

Most of the people would have lived around the crossroads and the quay

KEY

- - - - FOOT PATH

① THE VILL WITH ANCILLARY BUILDINGS AND STABLES

② MINSTER OF THE LADY ST MARY

③ NUNNERY

④ THE QUAY

⑤ WEST GATES

⑥ NORTH BRIDGE

⑦ GATE TO PASSAGE AT BELL'S ORCHARD

Your bloodline flows not from your heart, but from
the very core of your existence

The screams emanating from the birthing chamber were every bit as piercing as any Aelred had ever heard, including those of the men he'd seen wounded and dying on a battlefield. He glanced at the nun whose name he didn't know but whose job it was to keep him from entering. Like everyone else at the nunnery, she had assumed that he was the father of the twins being born and, given that Ingar was unmarried, treated him with the disdain she thought he deserved. He was thus obliged to wait outside the chamber which, although part of the nunnery precincts, was little more than a lodge devoted to the care of the sick and infirm. What remained of the other buildings stood within a gated enclosure a little way off, though were, for the most part, still in a very poor state of repair having been ransacked during the time of the Vikings' occupation of Wareham a few years earlier.

Looking anxious, Aelred fingered the small knife he had hidden under his cloak knowing that he would soon need to use it. 'Is it yet her time?' he demanded, almost dreading the answer.

'The child will be born when the good Lord sees fit!' said the Holy sister, scolding him for his impatience.

Ingar screamed again; this time the sound of it was even

more shrill and seemed to last for much longer. In the end Aelred could stand it no longer. He roughly pushed the nun aside and forced open the door.

He found himself in a dimly lit room which reeked of an incense which, whilst seeming vaguely familiar, was not one he recognised or could name. There was a workbench along one wall laden with numerous pots and jars and yet more pots were stored on shelves above it from which were hung bunches of dried herbs. A large wooden crucifix was pinned to one wall but Aelred ignored that and instead looked to the far corner where Ingar lay on a cot, naked but for a shawl draped across her shoulders and with her legs parted and drawn up towards her swollen belly. Three nuns attended her. One was trying to force her to drink something, another was mopping sweat from her brow whilst the third was peering anxiously between her legs.

'Get out!' screamed one of them.

Aelred ignored her. Instead, he went to stand beside the cot. Instinctively, all three nuns stepped aside, for everything about Aelred told them that he was not a man who would be readily denied.

Ingar looked up at him but her eyes were half closed as she endured the pain. Then, between the intensity of her contractions, she managed to smile when she realised who it was. He reached out and put his hand on hers. 'Is it time?' he asked softly.

Still in great pain, she hesitated for a moment then nodded.

Aelred dreaded even the thought of what he was about to do but was determined to keep his word. He leaned across and gently kissed her forehead and, as he did so, pulled the small knife from beneath his cloak without her seeing it. Taking her hand in his, he turned it over and, holding her gaze to distract her, drew the blade across her wrist.

He knew where and how to cut so that she barely seemed to feel it or even know what had happened. She simply relaxed and lay back, smiling up at him as the blood drained from her body.

The three nuns looked aghast. They could barely countenance what they'd just witnessed, for it seemed to have happened so quickly and yet so tenderly that there'd been no time for rebuke. Then, as they looked at the blood-soaked bedding on which she lay, they all realised what he'd done.

'Holy Mother of God!' exclaimed one of them as she crossed herself.

Aelred ignored them all. Instead, he held Ingar's hand until he was certain she had passed beyond pain, then turned to face them. 'Show me where to cut!' he demanded, still brandishing the knife.

None were in any fit state to answer.

'I have to free these babies! Show me where to cut!'

Still they were all speechless.

'They won't live long now she's gone, so show me!' he demanded again. 'And don't look at me like that. I'm no monster come to steal her babies! I've done only that which she asked of me as a friend.'

Two of the nuns turned and fled from the chamber, leaving the door ajar so that Aelred could hear their sobs and screams as they ran along the cobbled walkway towards the safety of the nunnery itself. The other one seemed to be made of sterner stuff. She stepped nearer to the cot and pointed to Ingar's belly, drawing an imaginary line across it with her finger.

Aelred made the incision then stepped aside as the nun set about the task of lifting first one baby free from the womb and then the other. Having cut the umbilical cords and dealt with the afterbirths, she then cradled them lovingly as they spluttered and screamed their way into the world.

Aelred gave the babies no more than a glance, then bent down and tenderly kissed Ingar's head before turning to leave. Already an alarm bell had been sounded somewhere and he knew he would have to hurry if he was to make good his escape.

Outside, the abbess was already waiting, looking pale and shaken at the news the nuns had brought her about all that which had transpired.

'Dear God, what have you done?' she asked, crossing herself.

'I've done only what I promised,' replied Aelred. 'She was not of your faith so bury her in the woods beyond this place, for that was her wish.'

'But to kill your own…' She stopped short of saying 'wife' recalling that Ingar had not been wed.

'She was not my woman, nor are the babies mine. Like I said, I was her friend and did only what she asked of me.'

'Even so, to murder her when…'

'When what?' asked Aelred. 'Are you saying she would have survived the births?'

She looked at him, unable to refute what he was saying, for they'd already concluded that Ingar would not survive delivering even one child, never mind two. 'May God have mercy on your soul,' she said crossing herself again and clearly still regarding what had been done as nothing short of murder.

Aelred was slow to answer. 'God will understand, but others may not. I must leave these babies in your care and be gone from here. It was Ingar's wish that the girl should be called Ingrid and the boy Coenred. They are of different blood and must be reared apart or one will surely kill the other.' He hesitated for a moment, then felt the need to say more. 'Trust me in this,' he continued. 'For Ingar knew the way of such things and you would do well to heed her wishes. The girl will one day become a healer like her mother, whereas the boy is the bastard spawn of a Viking slaver who forced himself upon her.' With that he started towards where his horse was tethered.

'Where to?' she called after him. 'Where can you possibly go to avoid God's judgement?'

He stopped and turned to answer. 'To Winchester,' he said. 'There to confess what's been done to Lord Alfred in person. He'll understand that I did only what was needed even if others do not.'

'Then you'd best hurry,' warned the abbess. 'For I've already sent for the Garrison Commander.'

Aelred knew what that would mean. The settlement at Wareham was set between two rivers and was served by just two roads, one to the west and the other to the north. The one to the west was nearest but the northern one would enable him to reach Winchester soonest, even though it would mean using the bridge there to cross the river. He knew that would be guarded but, once across it, he was certain he could make good his escape. Having untethered his horse, he took one last look at the abbess before mounting up and riding hard through the settlement and down towards the crossing. Even as he reached it, he knew he was too late – already there were men forming a line in front of the bridge with their spears raised to bar his path.

Undeterred, Aelred rode straight at them, forcing them to let him pass for fear of being knocked down and trampled underfoot. As they parted, he rode on and was all but halfway across the bridge before an arrow struck his mount, bringing both horse and rider down. Aelred found himself trapped beneath the weight of his horse but was able to struggle free. Limping, he then continued on foot but managed only a few steps before he too was struck by an arrow which took him full between his shoulders. He grasped the rail of the bridge for support as the pain surged through his body and even managed to stand long enough to turn as he prepared to face his attackers.

Two of the guards were upon him almost at once, holding back from actually engaging with him but with their spears raised and pointed directly towards him. Having lived his life without fear of dying he intended to pass in that same way so made no attempt to move. Besides, he knew that if they took him alive he'd hang – particularly as his 'crime' had been witnessed by three others, all of them women whose integrity was beyond reproach. He'd seen men hanged often enough and had no intention of dying with his hands tied and his body twitching like a fool as he pissed himself in his final agonies. He therefore resolved to end matters there and then rather than await that fate. Using all the strength he could muster, he roared his defiance and, even though unarmed, lurched towards the guards.

The first of them reacted in the only way he could, driving

his spear point hard into Aelred's belly whilst the second waited, ready to finish the job if needed. For a moment, Aelred just stared at them both, then, as the spear point was jerked free, he looked down at the wound. He briefly tried to staunch the flow of blood with his hands but realised it was much too late for that. Instead, he turned to face the rail once more, leaned forward and toppled over it into the river below. He floated there, face down as his body drifted slowly downstream leaving a crimson shadow on the water behind him.

Chapter One

Winchester, Fourteen Years Later

The doors to the Great Hall at Winchester were flung wide open. So sudden was the intrusion that every Saxon nobleman there present stood up, pushing aside benches and trestles in their haste to do so. In deference to the presence of their King, Lord Alfred, none, save the two guards stationed just inside the Hall, were armed. Some grabbed a knife from the table and held themselves ready whilst others simply stood their ground, defiant and with their eyes fixed hard on the old man who now stood in the still open doorway, his staff held tight across the throat of a man he was holding captive.

Both guards inside the Hall raised their spears but seemed unsure of what to do. They were sworn to protect the life of their King even at the cost of their own and had every intention of doing so. Yet, even as they stepped forward to bar the old man's path, they recognised at once that his captive was their comrade who had been stationed outside the doors.

Although no longer chief of the King's personal guard, old habits die hard and thus Governor Osric stepped away from the table and stood ready to cover his Liege. Only then did he recognise the old man and so hurriedly motioned for the two guards to lower their spears. Both men were reluctant to do so and looked back awkwardly towards the King as though awaiting orders from him in person. When he gave no response, they finally acknowledged Osric's seniority and followed his lead, stepping back though keeping their weapons poised.

For a moment there was silence. Then, as others began to recognise the old warrior as well, the name of Lord Ethelnorth was whispered between them. Few could claim to know him personally though almost all knew him by repute.

In fairness, it was hard to think of the old man, now bent and withered, as the warrior he had once been, but he was still much revered even though it was said by some that his mind had become addled and confused in his old age. Even so, he was still not a man to be taken lightly, especially when roused.

Lord Ethelnorth barged his way deeper into the Great Hall, pushing his unfortunate captive before him. 'Sire, this wretch was asleep at his post,' he bellowed, forcing the man to his knees. He then gave Alfred a token bow before pushing his hostage with his foot so that he lay fully prostrate on his belly, his face half buried in the rushes which were strewn across the floor.

'Sire, give me leave to deal with him as he deserves,' shouted Ethelnorth, one hand placed on the hilt of his sword. He had stopped short of drawing it knowing that to do so in anger in the presence of the King was a crime for which the punishment could be death, even for such a trusted warrior as himself. 'You can't afford to have men idle at their posts!' he scolded. 'Particularly in such troubled times as these!'

Alfred seemed unmoved and motioned for Osric to step

aside and for all the others to be seated. 'My Lord Ethelnorth, what I can't afford is to have you execute one of my guards every time I summon you,' he said calmly. Then he looked at the guard still lying flat on his belly on the floor. 'Asleep you say?'

'Aye, and drunk too I'll wager,' said Ethelnorth, prodding the man with his staff.

'Ten lashes,' announced Alfred. 'Ten lashes then two days continuous duty. And if during that time he so much as closes his eyes, give him another ten strokes to help keep him from his slumber.'

Ethelnorth looked disappointed. 'Sire, both you and I have cause enough to know the danger in having men asleep at their posts...'

Alfred waved his hand and the other two guards stepped forward and hauled the prisoner to his feet then dragged him off. He made no protest knowing he had got off lightly. Given that it was, as Ethelnorth had said, such a dangerous time, sleeping on duty could have ended with his head being placed on a spike from where he could keep watch until the flesh melted from his skull, his fate thereby serving as a fitting reminder and as a warning to all.

The Hall settled back and Lord Ethelnorth hobbled forward to take his rightful place at the table beside the King. Men, including Governor Osric, shuffled along on the benches to make room for him, knowing that his rank entitled him to sit closest to their Liege. Alfred greeted him warmly and called for food and drink to be brought even though the feast was finished.

'You've journeyed here alone?' he asked.

Ethelnorth shook his head. Although old, he remained

every inch a warrior. His silver hair, now thinning, was still long and braided but he carried his tall frame with a stoop and walked with a limp, probably from one of the many wounds he had taken whilst fighting for the Saxon cause.

'Your message said to come in haste, my Lord. So I brought just two guards,' he confided. 'One is stabling our horses and the other has taken the place of that idle wretch who was sleeping.'

Alfred smiled to himself, remembering that in such troubled times there were few men of note who would dare to travel so far with such a small escort. It was typical of Ethelnorth that he should do so, although perhaps it also showed that his mind was not as clear as it should be, for it was an unnecessary risk and one which a wise man would have avoided. 'I'll see that your men are looked after but must speak with you and Osric in private to explain why I've summoned you both here.'

Lord Ethelnorth acknowledged the point. 'I assumed that you required us to attend the Council of War with all the others here,' he said.

'That's true in part, but I've a more urgent matter to discuss with you both.'

With that Alfred hammered the table with his fist and called for order. Remaining seated, he spoke to all those assembled, which included several Governors and other nobles who had been individually summoned, but mostly it comprised of those whose job it was to command the forces at the various burhs – a series of fortified settlements which formed the backbone of Alfred's defence system against further Viking attacks. 'I welcome Lord Ethelnorth as indeed I welcome you all,' he said. 'I need hardly tell you why I've called for a Council of War tomorrow. As you will all know by now, the prospect of a full Viking invasion hangs above our heads like the sword of Damocles. We must therefore prepare ourselves to meet whatever challenges that brings.'

There was silence even though what Alfred had said was not news to anyone. 'Tomorrow, when others have arrived and all are rested, I would have you attend me that I may learn what remains to be done at each of the burhs so that we may present a united front, each seeking and providing whatever support is needed. In the meantime, there are other important matters I must first discuss with Lord Ethelnorth and with Governor Osric, for which purpose we must take our leave of you for now.'

With that he rose and every man in the Great Hall did likewise, all of them silent. Alfred then led Lord Ethelnorth and Governor Osric towards a small chamber which he sometimes used for private meetings or to escape the constant attentions of his court. His two guards followed him but, just as he was leaving the Great Hall, he turned and spoke again to all those assembled there, clearly feeling he'd not stressed the huge importance of the Council of War to which all had been summoned. 'I need hardly remind you that the threat we now face is perhaps as grave as anything we have ever encountered before, even during those dark days leading up to our great victory at Edington. I therefore urge you not to treat it lightly, for we ignore it at our peril.' Satisfied that his point had been well made, he entered the small side chamber then dismissed the guards with an almost cursory wave. 'Tend to Lord Ethelnorth's men,' he ordered. 'Relieve the one on watch and find them a bed for the night.'

'My men will sleep with our horses,' said Ethelnorth

curtly. 'I've trained them to be ready at all times. Unlike others I could mention…'

Alfred took no offence. 'Then give them food and ale,' he said to his guards. 'And have young Edward the stable boy attend us.'

The two guards looked surprised at the last point but knew better than to question an order. Instead, they bowed as they backed from the chamber, leaving King Alfred, Lord Ethelnorth and Governor Osric alone. Alfred took his rightful seat in the large carved chair which had once occupied pride of place in the main part of the Great Hall but had since been replaced there by an even grander and more impressive throne. Having made himself comfortable, he motioned for both men to be seated as well.

'There is a matter of some weight which I would discuss with you both,' he said. 'Something which concerns us all.'

'What is it, Sire? You look worried,' asked Osric.

'I am,' said Alfred. 'And perhaps with good cause. In a few moments you shall both see why. But tell me, do you both fare well?'

Ethelnorth sneered. 'Old age is a curse. I keep myself battle ready but struggle to remember things I used to recall with ease. The faces of my men I saw slain haunt me in my dreams but I no longer remember their names. Perhaps I've lived too long and should have died in battle like so many others before me.'

Alfred nodded consolingly. 'And you Osric. How are things with you, my friend?'

Osric gave a little laugh. 'You know what they say, my Lord. No rest for the wicked in this world nor precious little for the righteous. I find all my labours harder now than when

I was a younger man and, when I call upon it, my strength is not what it was. You remember how I used to carry my sword in a sheath strapped across my back? Much good would it do me now for I can scarce reach back that far without that it pains my shoulder. Yet you look well, my Lord.'

Alfred shook his head. 'I'm still much troubled by the inflammation in my gut. There are remedies that ease it but always it returns sharper and even more persistent.'

With that a boy appeared. He was a puny lad who was obviously unused to service and struggled as he tried to carry three beakers at once, not having had the wit to use a tray. He served Alfred first, then tried to bow awkwardly as he went next to Lord Ethelnorth and set a beaker down on the table in front of him, spilling some of the mead as he did so. Ethelnorth pushed him aside impatiently as he tried to mop up the spillage but otherwise paid the boy no mind. Then, as he reached to pick up the beaker, he suddenly caught sight of the lad and was astonished. Although small and slight, his appearance was at once familiar, stirring memories of a time they all had cause to remember only too well. 'Dear God!' he said.

Alfred watched in silence.

For a moment Osric was not sure what had caused the reaction but then he too noticed the resemblance. However, before he could say anything, Ethelnorth reached out and caught the boy's arm, twisting it to draw him closer so that he could peer deep into his vivid blue eyes. 'What are you called, boy?' he demanded.

'My Lord, I was christened Edward.'

Ethelnorth looked at Alfred. 'This cannot be!' he exclaimed.

Alfred nodded. 'Oh, it can. And shortly I will tell you how.'

'Edward, you say?' demanded Osric, turning his attention to the boy as well. 'Then who is your father?'

'My Lord, I never knew him.'

'Then ask your mother, boy!' bellowed Ethelnorth. 'Or does she not know him either?'

'My Lord, my mother is dead. She died giving life to me and...'

Lord Ethelnorth released Edward's arm and took a long drink from the beaker.

'How old are you?' asked Osric quietly, as the boy clumsily placed the third beaker on the table in front of him, clearly made nervous by the close attentions of three such senior men.

He shook his head. 'My Lord, I do not know...'

Alfred spoke for him. 'He has but fourteen years of age,' he confided. 'As he said, his mother died giving birth to him. Her name was Emelda.' At mention of that name both Ethelnorth and Osric were stunned.

'Then no wonder he doesn't know who his father was!' sneered Ethelnorth.

With that Alfred dismissed Edward, then waited to ensure he'd fully left the chamber before saying more. 'This has to remain a secret between us,' he said firmly.

'But is he not the very image of...'

'Which is to be expected,' said Alfred. 'He is Matthew's son, conceived whilst we were at Athelney, or soon after.'

Both Ethelnorth and Osric were silent.

'But Emelda was a whore,' said Ethelnorth at last. 'Any man in the camp during those dreadful days at Athelney could claim to be the boy's father.'

'I know it, and I feared to admit the truth of it myself. But come my friends, you've seen him. Were you not struck by the resemblance in an instant?'

Ethelnorth gulped some more mead, then wiped his beard on his sleeve. 'That's not enough. If you plan to recognise him as Matthew's son he'll need to do more than share his features.'

Alfred nodded. 'All I can say for certain is that he is Emelda's son. When she told me she was with child I sent her away to a nunnery. There she died giving birth to this boy. She assured me Matthew was the father...'

'She could not be certain of that!' accused Ethelnorth, still not convinced.

'Well, she was. Though I grant you there are grounds for doubt.'

'Even so...' protested Osric.

Alfred raised his hand to stop him saying more. 'There is yet more you should know. Soon after the battle at Edington, Matthew came to me and asked for my consent to wed Emelda. Of course I objected. She was still a whore at that time and her father had been a traitor to our cause so she could never be a wife to one of such a noble bloodline. But Matthew was determined so I sent him away to allow him time to reconsider.'

'That was when he was wounded by that arrow in the chest?' confirmed Osric.

'Aye, it was. When he at last returned to us I told him Emelda was with child and he remained intent on marrying her, something I was, of course, most anxious to avoid. I therefore advised him to leave her be. Lord Ethelnorth, you'll remember that as well, for you were there at the time, were you not?'

9

Ethelnorth nodded, recalling a meeting at which it had been discussed.

'As you know, to keep them apart I then ordered Matthew to secure and defend the settlement at Leatherhead. To my regret, he did not survive the ensuing battle, most likely having been slain by Arne, that treacherous Viking boy whose father was cruelly tortured and killed by Matthew's brother, Lord Edwin.'

'Do we know all this for certain?' asked Lord Ethelnorth.

'We do, but only because after the battle Matthew's friend, Aelred, came to me and told me what had happened. He said that he'd buried Matthew in an unmarked grave but refused to say where. He also gave me Matthew's sword and, knowing that by then Emelda was dead, he offered to provide and care for the child himself. I refused him, saying that I'd fostered Edward with a woman who was barren and who desperately craved a child. As it turned out, when the boy was five or perhaps six years of age, the woman and her husband were blessed with a child of their own so I took Edward in and found him work in my stables.'

'Dear God. And now you fear that the truth must come out!' said Ethelnorth.

'I do. I shall carry the guilt for all that which transpired to my grave, for I fear that on my account Matthew perished without ever seeing his son and is therefore not at rest. Many times I fear that I see him in my dreams, so feel compelled to make things right and honour the promises I made to him. If you recall, whilst we sheltered at Athelney he gave a great fortune to our cause which I pledged to repay. I intend to recognise that and also restore all the lands that would have been his by right by bestowing them on this lad who, had Matthew and Emelda wed as they intended, would have taken his rightful place as heir.'

'Perhaps,' said Ethelnorth nodding wisely. 'But we cannot be sure of his parentage, whatever you may think.'

'The boy is his, of that I'm certain.'

'You'll need to be,' warned Ethelnorth. 'For if he is heir to Matthew's entire fortune that could make him one of the wealthiest men in all Wessex, perhaps second only to yourself.'

'Aye,' added Osric. 'And bastard or not, he's the last of his father's line, a bloodline to which we and all Wessex owe a great deal. As of right he would merit the rank of a nobleman at least. In fact, with all he stands to inherit, there are those who might even propose him to succeed you, my Lord, when the time comes.'

Alfred was suddenly silent. 'I'm all too well aware that he could be used to usurp me, if that's what you imply,' he said at last, acknowledging the possibility. 'Which is why this must remain a secret between us. Having no one to protect and advise him, he could be easily taken advantage of by those who would befriend him and use him for their own advancement.'

'Also, he has no schooling or training,' observed Osric. 'Yet his claim to certain lands might be seen as a threat to those into whose hands they've since passed. As he stands now, he would be like a lamb to the slaughter if your intentions towards him became known.'

Ethelnorth drank again, this time draining the beaker. 'You're right. A fool and his money are soon parted and there are rogues and cheats enough even here at court to ensure that a mere stable boy is quickly relieved of his fortune. So, what have you in mind?'

'I want you to take him away from here,' said Alfred. 'He must be secretly schooled and tutored in the ways of a noble Saxon. You know that I require all young noblemen to learn to read and write, let Edward be as one with them. He must also learn all the skills of a strong and noble lord. Then, when the time is right, we shall tell him of his bloodline and of his true station in life.'

Ethelnorth looked doubtful. 'Pah! You'll need to make a warrior of him if he's to keep all that's his secure,' he warned. 'Though if he truly has the blood of Edwin and Matthew in his veins that should come to him as natural as breath itself!'

Alfred considered that and could see that it did make sense. 'Osric, you have men training to serve in the fyrd at Wareham?'

'My nephew Oswald trains them now, my Lord. As Garrison Commander he is also head of our permanent guard.'

Alfred seemed pleased at that. 'Good. There could be none better, especially with you on hand to ensure that the boy fares well. Teach him what he needs to know then, when you feel he's ready, bring him back here to Winchester. I will reimburse whatever costs you incur.'

'My Lord, if he is indeed Matthew's son then I shall require no payment,' said Osric simply. 'I owed Matthew much as it was he who cleared my name when others suspected me of being the traitor who opened the gates at Chippenham on that fateful day on which our cause was all but lost. Thus the boy shall be as a son to me and I a father in place of his own.'

'No, you must show him no favour until we're sure,' advised Alfred. 'Let it be known that I send him to you as a gift in recognition of all your great services to me, a lad to tend that wanton stallion I gave you. I gather the beast is still so wild that it's yet to carry a saddle, never mind a rider. Edward is well suited to that task for, having worked in my stables, he's shown that he has a particular way with horses. His appointment should therefore not arouse suspicion. Besides, who pays any mind to a stable boy?'

Osric nodded his agreement. In fact, he was grateful, for it was true that he badly needed someone who understood horses. The stallion was indeed wild yet his one wish was that it could be tamed that he might one day ride it, but his own stable boy had proved useless in doing more than riling the horse by trying to beat it into submission.

'My Lord Ethelnorth,' continued Alfred. 'You were also a friend to Matthew when he lived, and especially to his brother, Lord Edwin. Whilst I know that as an Ealdorman you have many urgent duties of your own, I would charge you to watch out for this boy where you can.'

'I will my Lord, though I'm not as easily convinced as you that he is Matthew's bastard. And even if he is, I question the wisdom of placing so much wealth and responsibility on such puny shoulders.'

'Trust me,' said Alfred. 'If I'm right his blood will out and leave none of us in any doubt as to his true lineage. If not, by keeping what I intend a secret, neither he nor anyone else need be any the wiser.'

'And what of that pagan healer?' asked Ethelnorth. 'I recall that she also claimed that Matthew was father to one of her children as well.'

'You mean Ingar? Well, that may be true,' admitted Alfred. 'Though I didn't believe her for I've never before heard tell of a woman bearing the children of two different men at the same time. Besides, Matthew claimed that they'd lain together but once and even that only as part of some pagan ritual he was duped into attending, whereas that Viking slaver took her often enough.'

'They look to be twins,' observed Osric. 'They both share their mother's red hair.'

Alfred looked surprised. 'You know of them?' he asked.

'I do, my Lord. They both reside within the settlement at Wareham. It was before I took up my duties there but I'm told that Matthew's friend, Aelred, came to attend Ingar whilst she was giving birth. By all accounts, seeing her struggling and in great pain, he killed her then cut both babies from her womb that they might live.'

Alfred nodded. 'Yes, I'd heard something to that effect. I gather they took him for a murderer and he was killed whilst trying to leave the settlement in haste. But what of the two babies?'

'They were separated at birth as was Ingar's wish. No doubt it was just as well, for I'm told that even in the crib they would scream and cry out if placed too close together. The girl is called Ingrid and remains at the nunnery attached to the Minster of the Lady Saint Mary where she follows in her mother's path and tends the sick. The boy is called Coenred and is an idle wastrel who sweeps out the horse shit from my stables.'

'Then what do they know of their parentage?'

'Very little,' said Osric. 'They each believe that their mother died giving birth to them but have been told nothing more, though I understand that Coenred knows that his father was probably a Viking. Other than that, I'm certain neither of them knows anything of the other's existence, for Ingar's dying wish was for them to be reared apart.'

Alfred seemed worried. 'Then Edward must be told nothing either.'

Both men agreed that made sense.

'So, is that Matthew's legacy – secrets and suspicions?' asked Osric.

'It would seem so,' acknowledged Alfred. 'Now, rest tonight then, come morning, I would have you both attend my Council of War. After that leave at dawn the following day and take the boy with you, for the sooner we remove him from court the better.'

Ethelnorth glanced at Osric then nodded. 'Then we should leave together,' said Ethelnorth. 'I'll escort you and the boy back to Wareham then journey on to my Vill in Somerset from there.'

'Good,' said Alfred. 'But remember, only we three know of this boy's true bloodline and we must ensure that it remains that way, at least for now.'

* * * * *

As Edward began to clear away the beakers he'd used to serve the three great men, he was not sure what else needed to be done as it was not work he was used to. Also, it was growing late and he still had Lord Ethelnorth's horses to attend to yet had been ordered by Alfred's Reeve to remain in the separate lodge where food was prepared as he wanted to speak with him, something which the young boy dreaded. To be summoned by the Reeve usually meant he'd done something wrong and that would often end in a beating.

As he waited, he stood beside the fire trying to keep out of the way whilst being grateful for the warmth. The stables where he normally both slept and worked were damp and draughty, with nothing save some handfuls of straw stuffed under his clothes to ward off the cold night air. Almost anything was better than returning to that, so he stood there with his head bowed in anticipation of what might follow, fearing the worst.

At least six or seven other servants were busy preparing food needed for Alfred's important Council of War the following day and when the Reeve eventually arrived he spoke first to the cook, giving final orders, then to several others before he at last turned and deigned to speak with Edward. What he said came as a complete surprise.

'Boy, you're to leave us the day after tomorrow,' announced the Reeve. 'Gather what's yours and quickly so, for you're to go with Governor Osric to tend his horse.'

'Why?' asked Edward.

Never a patient man, the Reeve erupted at once. 'What? Would you question my orders? Should I have the King of this mighty realm consult with the likes of you before deciding what's to be done?'

Half expecting to feel the weight of the man's hand for that alone, Edward readied himself to duck, but nothing came.

'Don't press me boy. I take my orders as do we all,' said the Reeve.

'Sir, then how long will I be away?'

'Till he's done with you,' the Reeve explained harshly. 'He has a horse which was a present from Lord Alfred himself but it remains untrained and wilful. You're to break it so that

Governor Osric may enjoy the gift by riding it despite his advancing years.'

'Where will he take me, sir?' asked Edward, not sure whether he should be pleased or not.

'Does it matter? From what I see of it one stable is as cold and damp as any other!' He hesitated for a moment, looking at the small boy who seemed to almost tremble with fear. 'Lord Osric is Governor of the burh at Wareham,' he added. 'No doubt you'll stay there until he says otherwise. After that God only knows what will become of you.'

Chapter Two

The following morning, all the Garrison Commanders and other nobles who had been summoned to attend Alfred's Council of War assembled in the Great Hall but remained standing in respectful silence as their King entered the chamber. He took his place on the ornate chair which was mounted on a dais so that he was sitting slightly higher than everyone else, one of the few 'vanities of power' which Alfred allowed himself. It was, however, expedient as it also enabled him to see clearly all those who were in attendance and, more importantly, those who were speaking. Once he'd settled, the nobles took their places beside the benches which were lined up in rows, though all remained standing, with the most senior men nearest the front.

The Great Hall was a large building, the walls of which were richly decorated with many fine tapestries, mostly depicting stories from the Bible or recording scenes from the King's great triumph at Edington. It was large enough to accommodate a good many people and Alfred used it to hold court or to hear those pleadings which were serious enough to warrant his personal intervention. It was warmed by a large fire at one end and dimly lit by torches whilst the floors were strewn with rushes. As such, it was a largely functional building but, unusually, it included several smaller chambers to one side which were formed by a partition and which he used to conduct business in private.

Alfred called for a priest to lead them all in prayer and then bless their endeavours. When that was done, the priest left and Alfred signalled for all to be seated and for any attendants and servants to leave as well. With that the guards closed and secured the doors, leaving just two selected warriors from the King's personal guard to remain inside, both stationed immediately behind him. There was also a monk who was allowed to remain so that he could act as scribe to record all that which was debated.

Alfred allowed a few moments for everyone to settle, then called them all to order. 'As your King and Bretwalda of all Wessex, I have summoned you here to discuss matters so grave as to warrant our immediate concern,' said Alfred solemnly. 'It seems that the Vikings are now done with ravaging the lands across the sea and are once more looking for fresh targets here, in my realm of Wessex. They sailed here with over eighty longships, bringing their horses and their war gear with them so we can be in no doubt as to their intent. Now, having wintered here, they've established a camp at Appledore in the Weald of Kent and Jarl Haesten has sent ships into the Thames estuary with the clear objective of setting up another base there. My fear is that they will expect reinforcements to come from those Vikings who have already settled in this land or who might be summoned from the north to join them. Thus they could quickly become a force to be reckoned with so we must again prepare ourselves for war.'

'There!' said Ethelnorth, not troubling to stand and sounding almost triumphant. 'Did I not warn you all those years ago that no good would come of giving land to our enemies! Many of those you call the "settled Danes" will welcome their blood relatives from across the sea or, at the very least, will not do anything to resist them, perhaps even daring to offer aid or support where they can. I knew then what would come of it!'

Alfred waived his point aside. 'Like I say, we must prepare ourselves,' he repeated. 'Above all else we shall need to ensure that their forces cannot properly combine, for it would sorely test our resolve if they do. To that end we must stand ready to drive back those who seek to attack London or Kent – or wherever else they deign to strike.'

'That's but part of the problem,' mused Ethelnorth. 'Before you know it they'll be coming at us from all sides at once! We must stand ready to defend every corner of this realm.'

'Exactly!' agreed Alfred. 'Which is why I've summoned you all here to attend me. As Governors or Garrison Commanders of the burhs, you must all share what resources you have to ensure there are no weak points in our defences. Also, your men must be properly armed and stand ready for when they're needed.'

Another man stood to speak. He was of slight build but known to all as Alston, a warrior with a ruthless reputation. 'Should we not strike first, my Lord?' he suggested. 'We could combine our forces and march forth to meet this bastard Haesten where he stands and thereby overwhelm him. Slay him and the threat is removed at a stroke. Is that not so?'

Alfred acknowledged the point. 'He is but one threat, for there are others who may try their hand as well if they perceive any weakness. Therefore we dare not draw men to join us in any numbers lest that then leaves any part of my realm exposed. I have forces here which can be mobilised to contain the threat from both Jarl Haesten and the warband in Kent. However, whilst I'm doing so, it's essential that you stand ready to defend the remainder of my Kingdom. For that, all the burhs must remain steadfast and be able to support each other. You must also ensure that your own fortifications are fully manned and that your stronghold is properly provisioned at all times. That way you can then withstand an attack long enough for me to reach you with reinforcements if needed. But always remember, the burhs are not just part of our defences. They are also intended as a place of refuge for all who reside nearby – somewhere they can shelter in the event of trouble. To that end, the beacons which herald an invasion or a raid must be properly maintained and tended, for we may yet be tested to the full.'

'What about ships, my Lord?' asked another man. 'I recall you were intent on building more so they could be used to sail out and fight any would-be raiders whilst still at sea. It surely makes good sense to strike whilst they're still weary from having sailed so far and for so long to reach our shores.'

Alfred nodded. 'That remains part of my plan but as yet we don't have near enough of them to tackle a full-scale invasion. Work is already underway to build more, though I grant you progress needs to be quicker. But ships cost money to build and training men to sail them takes them away from securing the fortifications or serving in the fyrd. They also have to continue with their work on the land or we shall all starve next winter.'

'Sire, as I recall you were planning to design ships

21

especially for the purpose,' Governor Osric reminded him.

'I have a design for vessels which will each be fitted with sixty oars so as to be fast enough to intercept any raiders regardless of wind strength or direction. They will also sit higher from the water so we can rain arrows down upon those within the Viking longships. They are not such that they would be suited for a long voyage at sea but, once completed, they should suffice to keep our coastline safe.' With that Alfred allowed time for all to settle. 'Until then, our best defence must rest upon the system of burhs which are, for the most part, complete,' he continued. 'To that end, I would have each of you attend me in turn over the next two days to discuss what more needs to be done at each of them.'

None there objected to that, perhaps seeing it as a chance to be awarded funds for whatever works within their burh remained to be completed.

'Sire,' said another man. 'What of Haesten? Surely whatever threat he poses must be answered?'

Alfred nodded wisely. 'It will be, have no fear of that. As I've said, I have forces ready to march. They will take up a position between the two Viking camps and ensure they remain divided. That should contain them whilst we wait for our chance to drive them off.'

'Will you not simply starve them out, my Lord?' asked another man.

Alfred considered the point. 'No,' he announced. 'They could both be too easily supplied by river and thus it would take too long. We shall bide our time and, when they become frustrated at the delay, they will doubtless risk coming out to ravage what and where they can. When they do, that will be our chance to strike.'

There were various murmurs and whispers among the assembled nobles, none of whom much liked the idea of just waiting with two such significant threats having already established camps.

'The task of defeating both Viking warbands will fall to me,' continued Alfred, sensing their misgivings. 'But I cannot be everywhere at once so your job is to keep your own people secure lest other warbands come seeking to profit from any weakness whilst we are thus distracted. I therefore charge you to remain vigilant.'

None there were entirely at ease with all that which had been said, though knew they'd have the chance to voice any personal concerns when it came to their turn to speak with the King in private.

'Lord Ethelnorth,' announced Alfred. 'As you know, there are those in the west who could not travel here in time to attend this Council. As my most senior Ealdorman and warrior, I know that your defences are already secure and so would have you ensure that all in the west are made fully aware of what has been said today. It's imperative that their defences are similarly well founded.'

Ethelnorth acknowledged the order.

'So far as those assembled here are concerned,' continued Alfred, 'I would now speak with each of you in turn to ascertain what weaknesses need to be addressed. I would start first with the burh at Wareham as it remains one of the largest and most exposed. Also, I have charged Governor Osric who commands there with certain urgent duties which I know require him to return to Wareham in haste.'

With that he rose, as did every man there. Ethelnorth

and Osric then followed him to the small chamber in which he'd spoken with them the night before.

* * * * *

As Alfred and Ethelnorth watched, Osric laid out a plan on the table showing the fortifications at Wareham. They mainly comprised of a stockade of sharpened stakes which was mounted on raised earthworks. The settlement itself was sheltered within those ramparts where it was fully protected and could be easily defended.

'Wareham should be well able to protect our part of the Wessex coastline now that I've finished all the improvements to the fortifications,' Osric informed them. 'However, my concern is that as the land immediately beyond them is mainly marsh and water meadows, many men who make up the fyrd live too far away to be summoned quickly. What we need are ships which are permanently manned and moored, ready to sail out and meet any raiders the moment they're sighted entering the main harbour. It is, as you know, a very large expanse of water which we can use to defeat them or at least delay them long enough for me to muster enough men to offer a credible defence of the settlement itself. That will also allow everyone to reach the safety of the burh in time.'

'That's all very well,' acknowledged Alfred. 'But, as I explained, for now we must work with what we have.'

Osric expected that would be the answer so made no attempt to press the point. Instead, he returned everyone's attention to his plan of the fortifications. 'You'll recall that Wareham has rivers to both the north and the south of the settlement,' he explained. 'The main defences are set between them, with additional ramparts along the northern edge as the river there has several points which might provide a viable crossing.'

Neither Alfred nor Ethelnorth needed any reminder about the settlement at Wareham as it was a place which had once been taken and held by the Vikings. Alfred had laid siege to them at the time but to bring matters to a head, had ended up paying tribute for the Vikings to leave, taking hostages to ensure that they honoured the arrangement. However, this proved to be a ruse as the Vikings then rode off to strike at Exeter instead.

Alfred looked at the plan approvingly. 'This is all to the good,' he observed. 'But you've not protected the southern boundary.'

'There's no need. The river Frome there offers protection enough and I need to leave the quay open for supplies and trade on which the settlement depends. These mostly come upriver from the main harbour.'

Ethelnorth was more interested in numbers. 'How many men can be mustered to serve in the fyrd?' he asked.

'The burh is supported by near 1600 hides, so in theory a force of just over 1500 men can be levied. However, as I've explained, that would take time given the extent of the surrounding marsh which means that many of those at the outlying farmsteads and smaller settlements would struggle to reach us quickly in the event of an all-out attack.'

Ethelnorth did the calculations and shook his head. 'And even if they do reach you in time, at best you would station the men on the ramparts at what? Three paces apart? That won't be near enough!'

'You're assuming the attack is from all sides at once

which, given the terrain, they couldn't possibly manage,' explained Osric.

Ethelnorth still looked far from convinced. 'Even so, you have to ensure that all those serving in the fyrd can be mustered more quickly,' he insisted.

Osric considered the position for a moment then agreed. 'I grant you that time is always of the essence. But I've a permanent guard of fifty men stationed within my Vill, plus there are sixty men who reside within the settlement itself who are all trained and eligible to fight. Together they serve in rotation to keep watch at all the critical points and remain available to provide an immediate defence of the settlement if needed. They can also march out to help see off any raiders who attack any of the outlying farmsteads or smaller settlements.' He then looked at Ethelnorth, desperately hoping the old warrior would be satisfied with that and not spot something he'd overlooked.

'That won't be worth shit if you face a full-blown invasion!' warned Ethelnorth. 'Based on what you've said, that amounts to just over one hundred men to be on hand at any one time. Less if some are away dealing with a raid. You'd therefore be hopelessly outnumbered by even half a dozen Viking ships. They could simply swarm ashore and sack the whole settlement and there'd be nothing you could do to stop them. You have to find a way to muster more men to defend the settlement more quickly!'

'Exactly,' agreed Alfred. 'And the whole point of building the burhs is that they should provide a sanctuary for all. We can't exclude some just because they live too far away.'

Osric could hardly argue with that. 'I've instigated what I can,' he assured them. 'I've organised it so that those who

26

live some distance away form into groups. There are near fifty of these "local fyrds", each comprising about thirty men, half of whom stand ready to fight at any one time. When not on duty, they tend their farmsteads or ply their trade but report to their thane for regular training. Each group also comes into Wareham for at least one week in every year and, whilst so levied, camp within the burh and are obliged to help maintain the fortifications and mend the roads and such like.'

Ethelnorth was still far from impressed. 'How does that help?' he queried. 'I don't doubt their abilities but no man can fight if he isn't there! You'll still be woefully short of men when and where you need them most.' With that he looked again at the plans and tried a different tack. 'How far is the settlement from the main harbour?' he asked.

Osric considered the question carefully. 'If you follow the river Frome it's about two miles to reach the channel which runs through the main harbour. I've set chains in place which can be hauled across the river mouth to impede any ships and there's a watchtower where the two rivers join the harbour. That's permanently manned and there's another set on Haven Point directly overlooking the narrow harbour entrance, plus others positioned on the cliffs from where there's a clear view along the coast in both directions. From these we can follow the progress of any ships which are sighted. In the event of seeing anything untoward, the alarm would be quickly raised, thereby giving us the time needed to muster our defence.'

'That's as well,' observed Ethelnorth. 'A harbour as big as the one at Wareham would provide ideal moorings for an invasion fleet and could thus be a likely target. So how exactly would the alarm be raised?'

27

'By lighting beacons in the usual way,' explained Osric. 'Even the smaller settlements have those which can be lit to summon help or to pass on news of any impending attack. They light one to indicate a raid to which we would respond by sending men to support the local fyrd. If it's a more serious assault or an invasion, two beacons would be lit to summon all to come into Wareham where there's ample space within the fortifications to accommodate everyone, together with their families and essential livestock. We would then have at least 1500 men present. Surely that would be enough to delay any invaders until reinforcements arrive?'

'Even so, it's far from foolproof,' observed Ethelnorth. 'The distance they have to travel remains an issue which needs to be addressed.'

Osric gave a little laugh. 'What do you suggest?' he challenged. 'The distance is what it is and cannot be shortened, nor can the terrain be altered.'

At that point Alfred interceded. 'You can do no more than use the resources you have,' he acknowledged. 'Though if that takes too long then there is cause for concern.'

Ethelnorth realised that Alfred's comment meant that the matter was thereby closed for the time being. 'Perhaps we can look over the defences together when we get to Wareham,' he offered. 'Until then, all I would say is that if Haesten deigns to attack you with his full force, your defences will be sorely tested. And remember, if he breaches them, he could quickly establish a foothold from which he could invade all of Wessex. Thus if your defences fail we are all at risk!'

* * * * *

Ingrid stood before the abbess, not sure why she had been summoned when she still had so much work to do. Even though she was only a lay member of the community of just over twenty-five nuns at the nunnery which was attached to the Minster of the Lady Saint Mary, she was expected to join them in their routine of prayers, thus she had been up since long before dawn. In addition, it fell to her to use her considerable skills to aid the sick, the poor and the injured, all of whom looked to the nunnery for help in that respect.

'Ingrid,' said the abbess. 'Have you thought any more about your future here?'

'Of course, Reverend Mother.'

'Then may I know your decision?'

Having been at the nunnery at Wareham since birth, she was expected to take Holy Orders when she became of age, though knew within her heart that she lacked the commitment to their faith for such a significant step.

'Reverend Mother, I still cannot give you an answer. It's not because I have doubts about my work here. In fact, it's very much to my liking and I feel I have a calling for it.'

'I recall that your mother felt the same, although of course, she was not of our faith. But if you do indeed have a "calling" then should that not move you to devote your life to healing the sick and helping the poor?'

Ingrid hesitated just long enough to show that there was something more she hadn't said.

'What is it that troubles you, my child?' pressed the abbess. 'You know that you can speak to me as you would to God.'

'I'm just not sure that my being here is what God intends for me,' she managed. 'For my heart tells me there's something more I must accomplish first.'

'What? Something more important than serving God?'

'No Reverend Mother, but I feel that if I am to serve Him as I should, I must first learn more about healing and nursing that I may better perform what He requires of me.'

The abbess was silent for a moment. 'Do you not think that He placed you here with us for that very purpose? In so doing, was God not showing you what He wants from you? Besides, it seems to me that you already have a gift for healing far beyond the skills of others and are able to bring much help to ease the suffering of so many. Is that not so?'

'Yes, Reverend Mother. At least, I pray that what I do is of benefit to those who come to us for aid.'

'Then you must soon decide. You cannot reside here unless you are committed to God. You've shown that you have the love and the compassion to be a valued part of this order and would thus be welcomed, but if that is not your intent then you must leave us and seek a life beyond this Holy place.' She hesitated before saying what she somehow knew she would later regret, for she valued all that Ingrid did even as a lay member and desperately wanted her to remain as part of the order. That was particularly so as much of the charity on which the nunnery depended was donated in thanks for the services it rendered to those who were sick, both within the settlement itself and in the Shire beyond. 'One month,' she said sternly. 'One month and I must then have your decision on this.'

* * * * *

Coenred's labours always began at dawn but he dreaded the mornings. He'd woken early enough but had remained abed, tucked up under a ragged blanket on which he'd heaped piles of fresh straw to keep out the cold. With Governor Osric away he thought no one would miss him, though was wary as the Reeve, a man named Ulrich, seemed to have eyes in the back of his head and a nose for sniffing out those who were 'reticent' in setting about their given work.

When at last he did stir himself, he went first to the water trough but decided against washing himself as the air was still too cold. Instead, he returned to the stable and began to attend to his duties there, carefully avoiding the stall at the far end in which the master's black stallion was stabled. He knew little about horses and was so afraid of that particular beast that he kept the stall gate firmly closed and latched at all times. Even so, he couldn't resist prodding the horse with a stick from time to time so that although restrained and confined within its stall, it reared up and snorted angrily. He loved to taunt the animal thus, watching as it tried in vain to kick its way out, straining at its leash and smashing into the walls with its powerful hooves.

Once he'd finished his 'sport', he took the two farm horses from their stalls and led them out into the yard where he set their harnesses ready for whatever work they were needed for that day. As gentle giants, they were much easier for him to handle, though he saw them as little more than beasts of burden which were best controlled with the whip. Having tethered them outside the stable block, he gave them each a nosebag. Normally he would then feed the other two horses which were stabled there as well but one of them was away, the master having chosen to ride it to Winchester.

Some poor wretch there would no doubt have to look after it, which meant he had time to spare, provided nobody was watching.

All this took a little over an hour but when it was done he made his way to the lodge which served as a kitchen. There he was allowed to help himself to a sparse breakfast of dry bread and cheese before being obliged to return to attend to the rest of his labours, most of which involved sweeping out the stables and grooming or tending the horses. Occasionally he was made to help move the livestock owned by the Vill from one field within the settlement to another. That part he enjoyed, for whilst away doing that he was out of sight and pretty much free to idle away what was left of his day, usually playing boyish games or, on warmer days, sleeping under a shady tree.

Better still were the days when he and the Vill's maid, a young girl named Mildred, were alone, for he'd found her to be very free with her favours. Even if the time they were together was brief, they would sometimes arrange to meet later whilst she was about an errand fetching milk or eggs from the Vill farmstead. There were many other buildings serving the Vill which offered privacy enough for what he had in mind, especially when backs were turned or others were busy elsewhere.

Chapter Three

O sric had travelled to Winchester without an escort, joining others who were headed that way rather than drawing men to accompany him from the permanent guard at Wareham. Rather than return alone, he'd accepted Ethelnorth's offer to escort him back there so they could then inspect the defences together. It seemed a sensible arrangement even though it meant a more protracted journey for Ethelnorth who would then go on from there to his Vill in Somerset. Given his age and having ridden hard over the previous days, many thought that the old warrior might have needed first to rest but, in truth, he was ready to leave before anyone else – except perhaps Edward who had risen especially early and had already tended their horses so they were saddled and ready.

'Can you ride, boy?' asked one of Ethelnorth's two guards.

'Aye, my Lord. Well enough,' replied Edward.

'I'm not your Lord,' he snapped. ''Tis better that you learn who you serve from the outset. You do as I say but your allegiance is to Lord Ethelnorth and to Governor Osric and no other, save to the King himself. And for them you would open your veins if they ask you.'

Edward looked a little sheepish but said nothing.

'You're nowt but skin and bone so can hardly weigh much. You can therefore ride Governor Osric's pack mule.

It has little enough to carry so won't complain about the extra burden. But remember, we travel fast across open and unsettled land and thus have no time for a dawdling boy. Just be sure to keep up.'

The pack mule carried their supplies for the journey plus some spare weapons. It was a small, rugged beast but was used to being burdened and well suited to rough terrain. It had no saddle but there were two carrier baskets which were placed either side of its back and secured with a girth strap. Once laden, the baskets left little room for Edward to sit astride the mule but he managed as best he could by leaving his legs dangling in front of them whilst he balanced himself uncomfortably behind.

No sooner had they set off than Edward showed that whilst a well-bred mount was good for fast gallops over level grassland, mules were far better suited for trekking across rough terrain. In truth, all the others soon realised that it was more than just that as, even though untrained, Edward proved himself to be a naturally skilled rider, allowing the mule to pick its own way whilst working with it to find the easiest path. Travelling thus they made good progress and the main party didn't once have to wait for him to catch up.

'As Alfred said, that boy has a way with horses,' observed Ethelnorth.

Osric agreed. 'It seems he's turned my mule into something more than it was born to be,' he said.

After several hours, Ethelnorth ordered the party to stop and rest, choosing a place where a steep bank rose up on either side of a narrow stream. Whilst Edward led all the horses and the mule down to the water to drink, the others took the opportunity to rest and refresh themselves. It was whilst they were doing so that they realised they were not alone. A wretched band of eight thieves had crept towards them, unseen at first but clearly thinking that two old men with just two guards and a stable boy might be an easy target, particularly if taken by surprise – but they were like a dog which takes a rat by the tail, little realising what it has between its teeth!

As soon as he saw them, Ethelnorth stepped forward to meet the rogues as they spread themselves wide, trying to surround his small party. He picked up his shield and slipped free the peace tie on his sword in anticipation of trouble, though stopped short of actually drawing it. Instinctively, his two men joined him, taking up a position on either side of him, spears in hand. Seeing that, Osric drew his sword and went to stand beside one of them whilst Edward remained with the horses, trying to calm them as they seemed unsettled by the sudden arrival of so many strangers.

The rogues looked to be desperate men, dirty and savage from living rough. Ethelnorth guessed that they were probably outcasts or deserters with perhaps even a few Vikings among them left behind after a raid. As such, some would surely have a price on their heads and thus have every reason to fight and no reason not to, particularly if the prize for their treachery was four good horses and a pack mule laden with supplies, not to mention two valuable swords. He let his gaze settle on one of them. 'I know you,' he accused loud enough for all to hear. 'You were with those who sheltered at Athelney were you not? And as I recall you fought well at Edington as well.'

The man looked back at him, then seemed to recognise Lord Ethelnorth and immediately bowed his head in shame.

'My Lord, all at Edington fought well,' he replied boldly. 'And yet there was scant reward for the blood we shed that day.'

'How so?' demanded Ethelnorth. 'All there earned silver and spoils beyond reckoning.'

'Aye, but that was many winters ago. Silver is quickly spent and you can't eat plunder,' said the man. 'I've a family to feed and not the means to do it. Alfred gave lands to the Vikings we fought against and they now fare better than those whose blood was spilt to provident his cause and earn him his so-called triumph.'

Ethelnorth took the point at once. 'So, is that how you come to be with this sorry and sordid band?' he demanded, then turned to his men. 'If this comes to a fight, ensure this man dies well,' he ordered. 'He's earned that right if nothing more.'

The band of would-be robbers seemed unsettled by his confidence. Several eased back a little and Ethelnorth could see they were uneasy, even though not all the fight had gone out of them.

'Old man, are you then Lord Ethelnorth?' called one of them who seemed bolder or was perhaps more desperate than the rest. He was armed with a seax which he had no doubt stolen from somewhere, or possibly found discarded on a battlefield.

'What of it?' demanded the old warrior. 'You need not fear the name, only the man who bears it.'

On hearing who they were up against, all there looked even more unsure of themselves. Only the rogue who had addressed him still seemed inclined to make a fight of it.

'Well, will you try my hand or not?' challenged Ethelnorth, intent on bringing matters to a head.

The robber seemed to find that amusing. 'Be wary old man, you may have once been a great warrior but your time is past and I doubt you'll prove a match for me,' he boasted.

Ethelnorth seemed enraged by that remark. 'Old man or not, I'd as soon die here than rot stinking in my bed! So come any closer and I'll soon show you what I can still manage.' With that he drew his sword. 'And take care, my friend, for if you fall I shall have one of my men flay the skin from your worthless bones!'

The man seemed to lack basic combat skills and instead of keeping his distance, he brazenly sauntered forward seemingly unaware that he was getting much too close. Ethelnorth spotted the error at once and didn't hesitate even for a moment. Instead, he used his shield to smash hard into the robber's shoulder, taking him completely by surprise. The blow was so forceful that the rogue was knocked backwards and fell to the ground, scarce knowing what had hit him. Moments later, Lord Ethelnorth was standing over him with the point of his sword pressed hard against the man's throat.

'We've no quarrel with you, my Lord,' pleaded one of the other men, stepping forward in an attempt to save his friend. 'Many of us fought for our King and have the scars to prove it.'

With that Ethelnorth looked along the line of men confronting him and could see that one had lost an arm below the elbow and that several others bore visible reminders of the wounds they'd suffered. 'Then put up your weapons,' he ordered. 'For old or not, you're none of you a match for me.' Even as he spoke, the sun caught the blade of his sword so that it glimmered brightly.

Almost at once, the robbers began to back off, clearly not prepared to take on such a powerful warrior despite the fact that they still had him outnumbered. It wasn't just Ethelnorth's reputation and obvious skill which deterred them, it was also the fact that they knew that if they slew such an important and well-respected personage, they could expect to be hunted down without mercy. That was more than they'd bargained for. 'We'll go peacefully,' said the one nearest to him. 'But we'll not surrender, my Lord. They'll hang us if we do.'

'And you deserve no less!' said Governor Osric sternly, stepping forward and hoping to calm matters without any blood being spilt.

Lord Ethelnorth said nothing. Instead, he nodded as if acknowledging the wisdom of their decision, then kicked the poor wretch who was still on the ground. 'Get up, you idle fool. And if you make so much as one more move towards me I'll ensure that you delay me no longer than it takes to wipe your blood from my blade.' With that he sheathed his weapon, then turned to Edward. 'Bring food from my baggage,' he said loudly, half turning his head so that Edward would hear him.

Edward did as he was told, fetching a few loaves of bread and some cheese.

'Take what's offered and be gone,' said Ethelnorth. 'You'll get nothing more from me and you've delayed me long enough already. But make sure this fills your children's bellies and not your own.'

One of the men stepped forward, bowing his head as he accepted the gift. With that they all turned and slipped away as quickly and as quietly as they'd come.

'Where were you when you were needed, boy?' demanded one of the guards, looking at Edward.

Edward pointed feebly towards the stream. 'My orders were to mind the horses, sir,' he stammered. 'They needed calming lest they bolt and…'

The guard shook his head, clearly not impressed with the explanation. 'You have a blade in your belt,' he insisted, pointing to a small knife Edward always carried. 'Yet it remains undrawn. When next it comes to a fray your place is here, beside us.'

The knife was a tool of Edward's trade, not a weapon, so it had not even occurred to him to use it as such.

The other guard walked across, then spat at the ground. 'You've no mettle boy, that's the truth of it. If you're the craven coward you've shown yourself to be then may God help you when we reach Wareham, for there you'll find men who'll sniff out that yellow streak in your belly and thrash you to within a hair's breadth of your miserable existence. Now, be about your work for we've wasted too much time here as it is.'

Having given away a goodly part of their rations, the small band had precious little left for themselves. When they'd each eaten their meagre share, the two guards told Edward to fetch the horses so they could continue with their journey.

'We've still a hard ride ahead of us,' one said as he took the reins to his horse and mounted up. 'And there's much danger in these parts so make sure you stay close behind us.'

'The horses are all watered and rested,' said Edward. 'They should now fare well enough.'

'That's what you're here for, boy.'

Edward hesitated before replying. 'Is it, sir?' he said simply. 'For in truth I'm not really sure why I'm here. I wondered last night if there's some special reason for it?'

The guard stared down at him then laughed heartily. 'There's nothing special about you, boy, be assured of that. You're just like the rest of us. The best we can hope for is an easy death. So don't get to thinking there's something more. Just do your job and take each day as it comes. And be grateful whilst you still have food in your belly and blood in your veins.'

* * * * *

On their journey south-west towards Wareham they avoided any of the forests for fear of meeting more robbers or rogues who would be looking out for unwary travellers. Instead, they used an old Roman road but skirted round any of the settlements to avoid being identified as they travelled. In such unsettled times word of their presence would soon reach the wrong ears, for there were many who might think that two such wealthy nobles would be carrying something of significant worth.

Along the way they came across a deserted farmstead where the buildings were nothing more than charred ruins. There was still a lot of debris discarded on the ground but no sign of life or, more importantly, bodies. Ethelnorth dismounted and went to examine the ruins more closely whilst the others remained beside their horses. Edward noticed that the two guards were nervously looking around, perhaps still fearing an attack though he couldn't understand why as the raid was clearly something which had happened many weeks or even months earlier.

'Don't worry, they'll be long gone by now,' called Osric, as if dismissing those concerns. 'This place was sacked weeks ago. It's been picked over a dozen times since then, which is why there's nothing left worth finding.'

Ethelnorth ignored him. With his sword drawn, he continued to explore the ruins, poking about in the ashes and examining anything he could find which had been discarded on the ground. Mostly it was broken pots or items of rain-soaked clothing but one item in particular interested him more than most – a broken spear. Having examined it, he threw it aside and ventured closer to the woods which lined one edge of the stockade. The fence which had once surrounded the main buildings had been breached in several places and, just inside the compound, he found two graves – one of them much smaller than the other but each marked with a crude wooden cross.

'There are two graves yonder,' he said as he returned to join the others.

'Then perhaps that means that enough of them survived to at least bury their dead,' observed Osric.

Ethelnorth merely nodded. 'We should camp here tonight,' he announced as if changing the subject. 'It's already getting dark and there's shelter enough in what's left of these buildings.'

'Was this farmstead then raided by Vikings?' asked Edward who had heard about such things but, having lived most of his life in Alfred's Vill at Winchester, had never seen the results of a Viking raid at first hand.

One of the guards sneered. 'As like as not. Only cowardly bastards such as they would kill for the sake of a few meagre provisions.'

'So if some of the people from here survived where are they now?' he pressed.

'The survivors will have fled to seek sanctuary in the woods or with friends. But most were probably taken.'

'Taken?' queried Edward. 'Where would they be taken?'

'Christ, where have you been all your life! Taken across the water there to be sold as slaves. The women will have been ill used for certain and the men beaten into submission. All will die soon enough having been half starved and worked so hard each day that they can barely stand.'

Edward looked shocked.

'It's the children you should feel sorry for. Some will be raised as Vikings but most will be treated like dirt as menial slaves and worse.'

Edward could think of nothing to say. He wondered how much worse their lives could be than his own. For as a lowly stable boy he was fed on scraps and had been beaten more times than he cared to remember, quite often severely.

'Don't worry,' said the guard. 'Most won't live long enough to endure their torments for long.'

'But what if the raiders return in the night?' asked Edward, clearly worried by all they'd told him.

The man grinned. 'Well, if they do then if I was you I'd run and hide. Failing that, just make sure you don't get taken alive.'

With those thoughts still in his head, Edward removed the saddles from the horses, then rubbed down each of the mounts with handfuls of dry grass, soothing them by talking to them in a low, calm voice. He then fed and watered them and the mule before taking his place on the cold ground with nothing but a thin blanket for warmth. As he tried to sleep he could hear Osric and Lord Ethelnorth talking as they sat beside the fire.

'So, has Alfred done well by you in return for all your loyal service as chief of his personal guard?' asked Ethelnorth.

'Aye, well enough,' said Osric. 'As you know, he appointed me as Governor at Wareham, which is an important role and one which carries a generous stipend, though I'm not the Ealdorman there as Lord Aelfric has that privilege. Alfred also presented me with a fine black stallion to show his gratitude.'

'Ha! A horse you dare not ride!' mocked Ethelnorth, perhaps a little jealous of such a fine gift.

'Be that as it may, I asked for nothing more than to serve him and the Saxon cause as best I could. But I've now put aside my sword and live quietly in my Vill with my family. 'Tis reward enough, for as you and I both know, not everyone gets what they warrant in this world. How many men have we known who didn't live long enough to enjoy their due?'

'Aye, and how many survived and prospered because they dared not risk their own precious skins! As I recall there were many who preferred to let others do their fighting for them! But then I suppose no one ever promised that life would be fair,' he mused.

'So then tell me,' continued Osric. 'Why is Alfred so earnest about seeing Matthew's bastard receive his due?'

Ethelnorth was slow to answer. 'If he is Matthew's bastard. I'm not so easily convinced of it and, besides, there can be no proof. If you ask me it would be better to let the poor boy's soul rest in peace, not spoil his reputation with tales of having fathered a bastard – nor of the other child he is supposed to have sired. Matthew was of a religious

43

persuasion as I recall and as such all that would not sit well upon his conscience.'

Osric seemed to consider that for a moment. 'You could be right but then who are we to say,' he managed at last. 'After all, it was a long time ago and our minds are dimmed with age. All we can do is humour Alfred in this, do his bidding and not question his motives, for the one thing I learned in all the years I served him was that Alfred has wisdom far beyond that of most men.'

* * * * *

They set off again early the next day but it was raining hard, which made for a very uncomfortable journey. They'd been travelling thus for several hours when a group of riders appeared barring the road in front of them. Ethelnorth didn't seem perturbed as he drew up his horse just short of where they waited. One of the riders then moved forward. He was a large, barrel of a man, so big that his poor horse seemed hardly able to carry him. He was swathed in furs and wearing a bright helmet but his sword was sheathed and he was smiling as he raised his hand in greeting. 'My Lord Ethelnorth, you didn't think to send word of your coming?' said the man.

Ethelnorth seemed to find that amusing. 'Lord Aelfric, I saw no need for I'm riding through your lands on specific orders from our King.'

Aelfric considered the response. 'Still it is the custom to send word when accompanied by men bearing arms…'

Ethelnorth waved the point aside. 'Of course. But I saw no need to trouble you, for doubtless you would have felt compelled to offer us sustenance and a bed for the night. Besides, we were hoping to pass unnoticed so as not to be delayed by any who might try to rob us. Already we've been forced to see off one band of rogues with that intent.'

Aelfric looked hurt. 'Not in my Shire, I trust!' he protested. 'The bastards wouldn't dare else I'd have them beaten then skinned alive!'

Ethelnorth smiled, knowing that such bands were everywhere and that few Ealdormen had any realistic chance of bringing them to justice. 'There was a band of about eight but we dealt with them easily enough.'

'I trust that means you put them to the sword and have thereby had done with them?'

'No,' said Ethelnorth. 'Having taught them a lesson I gave them food for their families for there were some good men among them, including some I recognised.'

Aelfric wasn't quite sure what to say at first, then seemed to accept the situation. 'Anyway, you're safe enough now,' he said. 'And no doubt you and my friend Governor Osric will join me at my Vill for the night. It's but a short ride from here.'

'That's very civil of you, Lord Aelfric. And of course, we'd be very glad for some respite from this foul rain and therefore accept your generous offer of hospitality.'

With that they went with the small group to Lord Aelfric's Vill where they were ushered into the main Hall. By then the rain was teeming down and they were all anxious to get under cover. All, that is, except Edward who, though soaked to the skin, insisted on tending to their horses first.

'Put them in the stable and see to them later,' urged Osric.

'My Lord, if it please you, I'll settle them first for we've ridden them hard these past two days and I gather we've yet further to go tomorrow.'

'Do as you will, boy,' said Aelfric, clearly impressed. 'I'll have them set some hot food aside for when you're done.' With that he turned and, having had everyone remove their weapons, led the way inside the large Hall where a table was being set. 'You have a good stable boy,' he said to Ethelnorth. 'Should you ever grow tired of him, I'd readily find a place for him here.'

'He's not mine,' said Ethelnorth. 'He's been sent by Lord Alfred to tame that wilful stallion he gave to Osric.'

Aelfric laughed. 'Ah yes, I hear it's a wild and ill-tempered beast,' he said still smiling as he turned to look at Osric. 'Some gift that is, to give a man a horse he dares not ride!'

Ethelnorth seemed to enjoy the joke. 'Aye, I hear you need your wits about you just to get a saddle on his back, never mind sit astride him!'

Osric said nothing for he knew all too well that most men found his dilemma something of a joke, which only made him more determined to ride the stallion one day if only to prove them all wrong.

Aelfric seemed content to let the matter rest at that. 'So, I assume you were among those who were summoned to Winchester. No doubt Alfred told you of his fears?'

'He did,' agreed Osric. 'It seems that this land will never know a time of peace.'

'As with most of the other Ealdormen, he sent word to me of his concerns but felt inclined to summon only those who are directly responsible for the burhs which he sees as our first and last line of defence.'

'And what are your thoughts?' asked Ethelnorth.

The Ealdorman was slow to answer, as if carefully measuring his words. 'Of course, we have no choice but to defend what's ours,' he managed eventually. 'But I fear these heathen bastards will keep coming until we've killed them all.'

All three men were then silent as they considered what he'd said, though it was a view they'd all heard expressed many times before.

'I think Lord Alfred has the measure of them,' said Ethelnorth at last.

'Aye,' said Aelfric. 'If the fortified burhs hold firm they should offer protection enough, though you wonder what numbers they can withstand. I trust Alfred is satisfied with the defences at Wareham?'

Ethelnorth glanced at Osric before he answered. 'We're intending to inspect them when we get there,' he said guardedly. 'Though I'm sure we'll find that Osric has everything in hand.'

'They'll suffice,' Osric assured them. 'But I welcome Alfred's plans to build bigger and faster ships,' he added, returning to his favourite topic. 'Fortified settlements are defensive but we need to sail out and hit the bastards hard before they come ashore. That's how to beat them. Strike whilst they're still weary from having laboured at their oars and from having been so long at sea.'

'Then let's hope we get them soon,' said Aelfric, then seemed to change tack. 'So, now rest and eat,' he offered, spreading his arms wide. 'And tell me, Lord Ethelnorth, how are things in the west? It seems so long since last you and I met.'

* * * * *

Edward was shown to a small stable where, having removed their saddles, he rubbed down all four horses and the mule then fed them hay and oats from the supplies he found there. Lord Aelfric's horse and those of his escort had stalls of their own and a stable boy to tend them, though he seemed less diligent in his work. At one point he came across to speak with Edward.

'I shouldn't bother with all that,' he said.

'It's what I was taught to do,' explained Edward.

The boy laughed. 'Do no more than you have to,' he said. 'That's my way of doing things.'

Edward ignored him. 'So where do we go to eat?' he asked, changing the subject. 'Lord Aelfric said they would keep some food for me.'

'You can try over there at the kitchen lodge though I doubt you'll get much. After that you sleep in here.'

Having done what he could to settle the horses, Edward hung their rain-soaked saddles and blankets up to dry, then went across to the kitchen. All there were busy but the cook seemed to be expecting him. 'You poor wretch, you look like a half-drowned rat,' she said when she saw him. 'Here, get out them wet things and sit here aside the fire.' With that she helped him strip off his wet clothes, then kindly wrapped a blanket around his puny shoulders for warmth as she hung his clothes up to dry.

'You're shivering,' she said as she gave him a bowl of thin gruel which he drank gratefully, followed by another. He'd never had anyone take such care of him before so thanked her. She seemed pleased at that. 'You can sleep here aside the fire tonight and don't worry, I'll see you're woken early so as you can be about your work before your masters are up and about.'

As Edward settled down to sleep he was aware that others were still working in the kitchen, doubtless preparing food for the new guests. Being all but exhausted and with the warmth of the fire, he was lost to sleep almost before he knew it.

Ironically, having spent a more comfortable night than he was used to, he slept fitfully and therefore rose earlier than was needed. Thus by the time Lord Ethelnorth and his men were up he'd already saddled their horses. Lord Aelfric was impressed. 'So, are the horses set?' he asked, knowing full well that they were.

'Aye, my Lord. Though they're tired so I hope we shall not need to ride them too hard today.'

Aelfric turned to Ethelnorth. 'I can offer you fresh mounts,' he said.

'Thank you, my friend, but we've but a half day's ride from here and shall rest them when we reach Osric's Vill at Wareham.'

'Pity, I had hoped to persuade you to stay longer. We get so few visitors of worth these days, just vagabonds and beggars. But God speed you on your journey.'

With that the small group set off in better spirits all having eaten well and rested. Also, the weather had improved, making the going much easier, as did knowing they had but a short ride ahead of them.

Chapter Four

Although it was a relatively short ride from Aelfric's Vill to Wareham, the journey took longer than expected and it was late afternoon by the time the small party reached the banks of the river Piddle which marked its northern boundary. From there they intended to use the North Bridge to join the road which would then lead them into the heart of the settlement itself.

The bridge was a substantial structure formed from hewn timbers which had been lain side by side and were carried on stone supports. It was easily wide enough for two carts to pass side by side and had been fitted with handrails, plus there was a tall and intricately carved pole which had been erected to one side of it depicting all manner of fiendish beasts. The pole was a remnant from a much earlier settlement on the same site, but a noticeboard had since been attached to it which named Lord Aelfric as Ealdorman of the Shire and, beneath that, Osric and his nephew were cited as Governor of Wareham and Garrison Commander respectively. Beyond the bridge, on the far bank of the river, was a pair of stout gates to which a separate notice was pinned with an inscription in Latin which gave thanks to the glory of God and threatened eternal damnation to any who entered the settlement intent on treachery or violence.

Although the gates were open, Ethelnorth was impressed

to find that all four guards stationed there were attentive and alert. As he and his small party crossed over, he looked down at the river below them and was reassured to note that although not impossible to cross, it was wide and deep enough to deter any would-be invaders – or at least to stall them long enough for a defence to be mustered. From the bridge he could also see some parts of the raised earthworks, all of which were topped off with a high palisade fence. He resolved to inspect those more closely but began to see that the defences were indeed well founded, just as Osric had said.

Wareham was just one of over thirty defensive burhs which together formed the backbone of Alfred's defences against the Vikings, each of them sited close enough to reinforce the one next to it in the event of an attack. However, Wareham was regarded as one of the most important parts of that defensive strategy, being an obvious target for an attack as it could facilitate an invasion of all Wessex by land or via the system of rivers. Indeed, many years earlier it had been taken and occupied by the Vikings for that very purpose. They set up a base in the nunnery there and then ransacked the whole settlement, forcing many people to abandon their homes and flee.

Thus, being strategically important, command of the burh was entrusted to a man with enough military experience to see that the job was done well. For that, Osric was an obvious choice. Not only had he served the Saxon cause well, he'd also been chief of the King's personal guard and remained steadfast as Alfred and what remained of his army sheltered at Athelney after the devastating defeat at Chippenham. Yet, despite having distinguished himself so many times in battle, in the years since he had not fared so well, lacking the administrative skills which were needed to be appointed as an Ealdorman. As he himself admitted, he was better with a sword than a quill.

Having crossed the bridge, the small party followed the road which took them up a steep hill and thence into the occupied part of the settlement itself where the homes and workshops were huddled around a busy crossroads. From there, the road continued all the way down to the banks of the river Frome which marked the southern boundary. Apart from that, most of the area enclosed within the fortifications was given over to open space, some of which was used for grazing livestock but there were also a large number of temporary hovels and tents which were used by those members of the fyrd serving their annual rostered duty, as well as by people visiting the settlement to trade.

Osric's Vill was sited close to the river, opposite the nunnery and, more importantly, adjacent to the quay which was the commercial heart of the entire settlement.

Although a somewhat modest complex of buildings, the Vill was extensive enough to be shared by him and his nephew, Oswald, together with Oswald's wife and their daughter. Its precincts included various outbuildings which were clustered together and which offered several private lodges plus a large kitchen, stores and three barracks that housed the settlement's permanent guard so they were always on hand if needed. The Vill also had its own small farmstead which provided food for those living there, but the only other building of note was a large stable capable of housing as many as half a dozen horses and which had a hay store and a yard attached. Beyond that was a large open pasture which was set aside for the Vill's exclusive use.

As soon as they reached the Vill they all dismounted and Edward took charge of the horses whilst Osric, Lord Ethelnorth and the two guards went inside. Having spent the best part of three days on the road, they were all tired and much in need of refreshment.

* * * * *

As it was getting late, Osric summoned his Reeve, a man named Ulrich who ran all things connected with the Vill and the farmstead, plus he also oversaw all the Governor's other holdings and estates elsewhere within the Shire. Ulrich was a tall, bearded man with long dark hair which was still braided to signify that he'd once been a warrior. He'd retired following a wound which he received during the battle at Edington but which had left his leg stiffened so that he walked with a pronounced limp.

'The boy who is now tending the horses is called Edward,' explained Osric. 'He's to be my new stable boy.'

The appointment of servants and the like was something which Osric would normally have discussed with his Reeve beforehand and he was anxious not to give offence, for Ulrich was a man who had served him well over many years. In fact, he had also been part of Alfred's personal guard and might well have gone on to succeed Osric as chief but for the wound to his leg. As a reward for his loyalty, Osric had found him work knowing that he could be trusted above all others given the service they'd shared.

'Very well, my Lord.'

'He's an unexpected gift from the King,' Osric continued. 'By all accounts he has a way with horses and is to take over all stable duties. I would have you outline these to him but, from all I've seen, he's well suited to the task and my hope is that he can school that wilful stallion of mine.'

At that Ulrich looked surprised and more than a little doubtful. 'If you say so, my Lord.'

'I do. And go easy on him. I don't want him thrashed or beaten without good cause. If discipline is needed you are to bring him direct to me.'

Ulrich nodded. 'And what then of Coenred, my Lord? Is it not his job to attend to the horses? We have but five, so it hardly warrants two boys being given to the task.'

'Coenred can assist with fetching and carrying for the kitchen, there's work enough there to keep him from being idle,' he said, knowing that Ulrich would make the necessary arrangements at once. 'If not, he can help with the livestock at the farmstead.'

* * * * *

Although sorely tired, Edward waited outside with the horses. He was not sure what he was expected to do so tethered them to a post in the small courtyard in front of the stables and set about removing their saddles and grooming them. When he saw this, Ulrich went across to speak with him.

The stables comprised a very large thatched building with rendered walls, open at the front but divided internally to accommodate the horses in separate stalls which were arranged side by side in a row. As such, it was both draughty and damp, but Edward knew that he would be expected to sleep there in order to properly attend to his duties.

'What's required of me, sir?' asked Edward as Ulrich showed him round.

'What the hell do you think is required of you?' said Ulrich impatiently. 'You're to tend the horses, of course. You make your bed here and you take your meals in the kitchen with the other servants. You'll be fed from what's left once the family have eaten their fill.'

None of that surprised Edward so he simply acknowledged what Ulrich had said, realising that for most of the day he would be alone, answering directly to the Reeve who he had already surmised was likely to be a very hard task master.

Ulrich then explained that Governor Osric owned five horses – the small bay which he'd ridden to and from Winchester, two sturdy farm animals which were used for heavy farm work such as pulling a cart and such like, plus a horse belonging to his nephew, Oswald. The fifth was the one which Edward was looking forward to seeing, a magnificent beast which, as he'd been warned, was both untrained and thought to be unrideable.

In addition to the horses, the mule which Edward had ridden from Winchester also belonged to the Vill as did two oxen which were used for the plough and such like and which grazed contentedly in the open pasture. The work horses and the oxen were shared with the various ceorls and tenants who worked lands belonging to Governor Osric and who paid him their dues for that in produce or labour.

Apart from the rats which scurried everywhere, the only other inhabitant of the stables was a large brown dog which was of no discernible breed but had taken up lodgings in one corner and growled when anyone went too close, making Edward immediately afraid of it.

Ulrich laughed when he saw this. 'Aye, you'd be well advised to give that foul-tempered hound as wide a berth as you can manage. He's not above using those fangs to remove a part of your leg if he feels so minded.'

That night, Ethelnorth's horses, which included those of the two guards, were also to be housed in the stable, doubled up in the stalls where necessary so they could all share the shelter, whereas the mule Edward had ridden was simply turned loose in the open pasture.

'Your duties extend to all the horses including those of any guests and you're to mind them all as if they are Lord Osric's own,' ordered Ulrich. 'All are to be groomed daily and the harnesses for the farm horses are to be cleaned and oiled ready for service when needed. You must also keep the stables swept and free from shit.'

'I was told I should also train Lord Osric's stallion,' said Edward, hardly daring to speak. He had already heard the horse kicking and snorting in a separate stall at the far end of the stables, a stall which remained both gated and securely latched.

'Good luck with that,' said Ulrich. 'That horse is as wild as they come.' With that he took Edward to see it for the first time. It was certainly the biggest horse he'd ever looked after and quite unlike those which the Saxons usually rode. It was also one of the most beautiful creatures he'd ever seen, having a glossy jet-black coat and a long flowing mane and tail.

'Well, there he is,' said Ulrich. 'If you're meaning to train the beast then you'd best take care. The first man who tries to sit astride it will likely break every bone in his body!'

Edward had been taught his craft by the horse thane at Alfred's stables in Winchester, a man called Colbert who, although too old to do much heavy work himself, loved horses and always seemed to know what was needed to get the best from them. He taught Edward much before he died, particularly about how to handle horses and how to quieten any which became riled or disturbed. He also tended any which had been hard ridden or abused, even applying some basic remedies for those which were injured. Whilst not as skilled as old Colbert, Edward had learned much from him. Thus when he went to look at the stallion he was wise enough not to enter the stall as it was clear that it was not about to be easily subdued and was certainly capable of lashing out with its hooves even though restrained. It was nonetheless a very fine horse and had been given the name of 'Fleet' because he was thought to be particularly fast of foot.

'Tell me you have broken a horse before?' asked Ulrich, eyeing the small boy with suspicion.

'No, sir.'

'Then God help you!'

In truth, Edward was less frightened of the horse than he was of Ulrich. In fact, he took a shine to the stallion at once. 'What's his purpose here?' he asked. 'For he's surely too finely bred to work in the fields or to pull a cart.'

Ulrich laughed. 'That stallion was a gift to our master from the King himself in recognition of his years of loyal service. A strange gift if you ask me, for the beast is so wild it can be of little use to any man until properly tamed. It's as yet unridden and your job will be to remedy that. You're to train him to the saddle so that our master may one day mount him, for that remains his dearest wish. It's something he claims he'll do before he dies, though many think the one may quickly follow the other. I wouldn't want to be in your place if that were to happen.'

As Edward gazed at the horse it backed away, pawing the ground with its front hoof whilst showing the whites of its eyes and with its ears pinned back. The boy needed no telling what that signalled so left the stallion alone but was already forming a plan as to how he might set about taming it. For whilst he would admit to knowing little about the ways of man, he did understand horses.

* * * * *

Once Edward had settled all the horses which had been ridden from Winchester, he set about making himself a bed of straw in one corner of the stables, with nothing but that and a single flea-ridden blanket to guard against the cold. He'd slept in worse so soon made the best of it, tucking his bed tight against the wall in the large open area next to the stalls for the horses, a place where the saddles, harnesses and other equipment were kept. The mongrel dog slept in the other corner of that same space and kept a wary eye on all that Edward was doing, growling every so often as if grumbling at having to share its home. Having done what he could and dreading the prospect of sleeping so close to the hound, Edward went back to the Vill where he was given a bowl of watery broth and some bread by the cook, a large lady called Ida who seemed to bustle her way around the lodge in which the food for the Vill was prepared. She freely ladled out the broth from a large pot and as Edward ate hungrily, Coenred, the old stable boy, came in and was clearly not best pleased at having been replaced.

'Who are you?' he demanded.

Edward started to answer but was not given a chance to say much before the boy leaned over and spat into Edward's bowl. Edward started to his feet but at that moment Ulrich came into the kitchen, almost as if he was expecting trouble. He was too late to see what had happened but went straight to Coenred and cuffed him round the ear. 'What? Are your new duties so light that you've finished them already? If so, I'll quickly find you more, you idle wretch.'

'No master,' said Coenred.

'Then get about them boy or I'll box your ears so hard you'll not be able to rest your lazy head for a week.'

Despite his impediment, Ulrich was not a man to be questioned so Coenred scurried off. Edward stood up respectfully but was not sure what was expected of him beyond that. 'Thank you for my supper,' he said in the end.

Ida looked up as though surprised. 'Bless me, but you are a well-mannered boy, I must say. I don't think anyone's ever bothered to thank me, not in all the years I've been here.'

Ulrich laughed. 'Manners is one thing, work is another. You just do what you've been brought here for and don't let that lazy sod Coenred bother you none. He's nowt but a bully so you keep yourself well clear of him, do you hear me? Just get on with your duties and stay out of trouble. That's the way we do things here.'

* * * * *

59

'Who does the dog belong to?' asked Edward once Ulrich had left.

Ida looked up at him. 'What dog?' she asked.

'The big brown one which lives in the stables.'

'That flea-ridden hound doesn't belong to no one,' she told him. 'The damn thing's a stray and a blooming nuisance. Why do you ask?'

'I wondered whether I could take some scraps from the kitchen with which to feed it,' said Edward meekly.

'Over my dead body!' snapped Ida. 'Them scraps are all needed to feed the swine. Besides, if you mean to befriend that bad-tempered hound then you'd best be careful, it has a vicious streak, does that one. As like as not it'll bite off any hand what tries to feed it.'

'That's what worries me,' said Edward. 'I have to sleep beside it. I thought that if I could find a way to appease it, it might leave me alone.'

Put like that, Ida felt sorry for the boy. 'It's as well to be wary of it,' she agreed. 'It's bitten several people already for no good cause. What it needs is a good thrashing if you ask me. Three times someone has been sent to put it out of its misery but it seems to know when they're coming and quickly makes itself scarce.'

'I think it could be appeased,' said Edward. 'It will take time but if I showed it that we're friends I'm sure…'

With that she gathered up a bone on which there was precious little meat remaining. 'Here, you can try it with this,' she said giving the bone to Edward. 'But don't blame me if it prefers a piece of you for its supper instead! And don't you tell no one, I'm not supposed to hand out scraps, not to anyone. Lord knows why, the pigs won't eat half of what I send them.'

* * * * *

At first, Coenred had seemed pleased at being told to make his bed in the kitchen as he'd be much warmer there beside the fire than in the stables. Even so, when Ulrich added that he was no longer required to work with the horses, he gave a look that left no one in any doubt but that he felt aggrieved at being removed from his post. The truth was that being left to his own devices for much of the day suited him well. He'd learned how to take liberties with his time, either sleeping or, failing that, playing childish games killing rats or cruelly baiting the dog so as to rile it, just as he did with Fleet. Nothing was said, but when Ulrich reported the day's events to Osric, he mentioned how much Coenred had resented the change.

'I fear we may well come to regret replacing him,' he warned. 'That boy carries a chip on his shoulder as it is. He sees every turn in his life as a slight upon his person, so there'll be trouble soon enough between him and the new stable boy, you mark my words.'

* * * * *

Once all those who worked in the kitchen had left, Coenred settled down beside what remained of the fire and began to see that his new role might have some advantages. Apart from being warmer, once alone he'd managed to steal some more food from what was left in the pantry and which he was certain wouldn't be missed.

He'd barely made himself comfortable when he became

aware of someone else there – he guessed at once who it was.

'It didn't take you long to find me,' he teased as Mildred lay down beside him.

As she put her arm across his chest, he pulled up the blanket to cover them both and began to undo the lacings to the back of her tunic.

'Not here!' she said firmly then slapped his hand.

'What's wrong with here?' he demanded.

'Someone might see.'

'Everyone's abed by now. Besides, what did you come here for if not to…'

'If not to what?'

He grinned and began to toy with the lacing once more. 'I think you know what,' he teased again. 'What you always come to me for.'

She rolled away and got up. 'You're very sure of yourself all of a sudden,' she scolded. 'But perhaps things have changed.'

'All that's changed is that I can tup you more often now that I work here.'

She brushed down her tunic with her hands. 'Don't be so sure of that. Perhaps I'm getting tired of being tupped by the likes of you. Just as I'm also getting tired of waiting.'

'Waiting?' said Coenred. 'Waiting for what?'

'Waiting for you to make something of yourself so we can wed.'

'Who said we're to wed?' asked Coenred sounding surprised.

'Well, some things don't need to be said. Or at least they shouldn't. And there are other matters which might need to be considered as well.'

Coenred had no idea what she was referring to. 'What are you saying?' he demanded.

'I'm saying that not everything is as you might think. You should be looking to better yourself but instead you manage only to get yourself turned from being a stable boy into a skivvy.' Having said her piece, she decided to leave it at that. It was neither the time nor the place to say all that she needed to tell him so instead she turned and stalked away, leaving Coenred none the wiser about what it was she was on about.

Chapter Five

Having slept poorly, when Edward awoke the next morning the first thing he did was to walk along the line of horses to check on each of them in turn. As he did so, the dog followed him at a distance but soon lost interest and returned to gnaw on the bone he'd been given the night before. Relieved and grateful that his ploy seemed to have worked, Edward resolved to try to persuade Ida to let him have a few more scraps from the kitchen whenever she could spare them.

In the meantime, although not easily impressed, Ulrich had noted how before taking to his own bed, Edward had first tended to all the horses and yet was still up and about his duties without being prompted. In fact, he'd begun his morning routine by grooming the two farm horses and then bridled them ready for traces to be attached. The other horses he turned loose into the open pasture so they could eat their fill of fresh grass rather than the feed which was all they'd had whilst travelling from Winchester. That left just the stallion for him to deal with.

When he reached the last stall, Edward could tell at once that Fleet was still unsettled, seeming both anxious and fretful at having been restrained within it by a tether. Edward knew exactly what he needed to do.

He started by ignoring the horse, making no attempt to

touch him or even speak to him. Instead, he started to sweep out the other stalls, whistling contentedly as he did so. When he'd finished, he sat down outside Fleet's stall, leaned back against the gate and waited. Eventually, when curiosity got the better of him, Fleet came forward and put his head over the stall gate, not sure what to make of the new stable boy who it seemed was inclined to pay him no mind whatsoever.

'Easy boy,' said Edward softly, still not making any physical contact. 'No point in you getting roused is there?'

The horse whinnied then shook his head as though responding.

Still Edward waited, allowing the horse time to settle. Then, when he was certain it was calm enough, he got up slowly and offered some feed. At first that was refused but then Edward reached across and removed the halter Fleet was wearing. Almost at once the horse seemed relieved.

'That's better isn't it,' said Edward. 'I know what you want. You want to run free in the pasture like the others, not be cooped up in here.' With that he reached out and gently stroked the horse's forehead which Fleet seemed to like. Next, Edward unlatched the stall gate and opened it. The horse didn't move at first, eyeing the boy suspiciously as he was unused to having the gate to his stall left ajar. Only as Edward stepped aside did the big horse saunter forward but even then he seemed unsure of what he should do. Then, as he looked out at the other horses in the pasture, it was if he realised that he was indeed free, so bolted from the stable and galloped off to join them, frolicking and kicking up his hind legs as he did so.

Edward watched for a moment then heard a voice behind him.

'You stupid little runt!' yelled the voice. 'It takes three good men at least to get that beast back into its stall!'

Edward turned to see Ulrich hobbling towards him. The Reeve said nothing more, instead he struck Edward hard across the shoulders with the stick he used for walking. He then raised the stick as if about to strike him again but held back from doing so when he remembered what Osric had said about not thrashing the boy.

Edward cowered as he waited for the next blow and, even though it never came, was too frightened to move or even speak.

'Do you think we've nothing better to do than go chasing after that wild beast all day! You've not been here but a single night and already you've done more harm than I could speak of. Perhaps you'd like to explain to our master why you've released his prize stallion?'

'Sir, the horse will come back of his own accord,' muttered Edward lamely.

'Oh he will, will he? And how will you manage that? Whistle for it to come home?'

Edward started to reply but Ulrich cut him short. 'Don't be a fool boy. Last time it took us most of the day just to rope him, never mind drag him back bucking and kicking like some fiend from hell! Why do you think we leave him tethered at all times if not to restrain him?'

'Sir, given time he'll return, of that I'm certain,' Edward assured him.

Ulrich shook his head. 'That beast is as wild as you are stupid! That's the last you'll see of him today. Have you even checked that the fences are secure? If he finds even the slightest gap he could be loose and about the settlement before you know it doing God knows how much damage. There may even be places where a horse like that could clear the palisade fence with ease and be running free on the marshes. How the hell would we get him back from there?'

Edward said nothing. It was true that he hadn't checked the fences but they looked to be secure enough, the pasture being bordered on one side by the fortifications and on all the other sides by a hedged fence. Even if Fleet escaped, there was nowhere for him to go, whatever Ulrich said. Certainly no horse would be capable of charging up the steep embankment never mind clearing the fence as well.

'Lord Osric will have you beaten for what you've done. I told you when you arrived here that the horse was a gift from Lord Alfred himself and you've lost him on the very first day!' It was clear Ulrich wanted to say more but he held his tongue. 'I'll deal with you later,' he threatened. 'It's your job to retrieve that beast, so get on with it, do you hear me? And from now on it stays in the stables and remains tethered. That's assuming you ever get him back again!'

Before Edward could answer Ulrich turned and limped off, leaving the boy to set about his tasks.

As he worked, Edward left the stall gate open for Fleet, though he knew the horse wouldn't return until nightfall. He began by putting out feed and water for the other horses then concentrated on making himself as comfortable as he could within the stables, sealing any gaps in the walls with mud to keep out the worst of the draughts, though, with the stables being open at the front, it seemed a futile effort. Thus he started his first day in the stables at Lord Osric's

Vill, doing the best he could yet finding himself in trouble nonetheless.

* * * * *

It was later that morning that Coenred went to the stables clearly intent on causing trouble. 'What the hell do you think you're doing?' he shouted.

Edward looked surprised. 'What do you mean?' he asked.

'Why, wasting good food on that useless hound for a start.'

'I'm trying to appease him so that I might then find something useful for him to do. Anyway, what's it to do with you?'

Coenred picked up a stick and went towards the dog. As soon as it saw him it ran off yelping rather than staying there to be beaten. 'You see! That's the way to treat it,' said Coenred laughing. 'Maybe I should use this to teach you a thing or two as well, for I hear tell that you've already gone and lost Lord Osric's horse. I never managed that, not once in all the time that I was the stable boy.'

'Well, you no longer work here!' protested Edward. 'So clear off.'

'And what will you do if I don't?' challenged Coenred.

Edward was not inclined to back down but neither did he want to get involved in a fight on his very first day. He therefore said nothing.

'Pah! You're yellow!' accused Coenred. 'Just like Lord Ethelnorth's guards said you are.' With that he went across to stand directly in front of Edward and, without any warning whatsoever, punched him hard in the face, striking him in the eye so that he reeled away in pain. Edward recovered quickly enough and was about to strike him back but Coenred gave him no chance to do so. As the coward ran off, Edward knew better than to follow as he was in enough trouble already.

* * * * *

Ethelnorth and his two guards went with Osric's nephew to inspect the fortifications. Governor Osric had intended to join them but having been away for over a week travelling to Winchester and back, he found there was much which needed his attention. The men all went on foot as Ethelnorth was keen to rest the horses given they would shortly have a long way to travel if they were to return to his Vill in Somerset.

'So, you seem well set here,' noted Ethelnorth. 'But I understand that most of your uncle's lands lie well beyond the fortifications.'

Oswald took that as a compliment. 'My Lord, our Vill is supported by two dozen farmsteads which are all beyond the marshes to the north,' he explained. 'Those who reside there are close enough to seek shelter here in the event of trouble. It's the people who live even further afield that I worry about. For some, getting here would take more than a day, particularly if they were driving stock.'

'So how are they protected?'

'Hopefully by being warned in time, my Lord,' said Oswald. 'Though I fear, some would think it better to find somewhere nearer where they could hide in the event of an attack rather than journey all the way here.'

'But surely you rely upon those men to make up the numbers for the fyrd?'

Oswald didn't answer at first. 'Ideally, we would, my Lord,' he admitted at last, knowing that the Ealdorman had touched on the one area of weakness in their defences. 'But we have men enough on hand if we need to see off a raid and can quickly assemble a force to march out from here to support the local fyrd if any of the outlying settlements or farmsteads are attacked.'

'That's not what I asked,' stressed Ethelnorth. 'What I want to know is whether you could manage without those who live further away in the event of a full-scale invasion? After all, it's happened here before!'

'My Lord, even if the fyrd is not at full strength, the fortifications are sound and I'm confident they'd suffice for us to hold out long enough for reinforcements to arrive,' he explained.

Lord Ethelnorth remembered the settlement well enough from when he and Alfred had laid siege to it when it was taken and occupied by the Vikings all those years before. It had proved all but impregnable then and much had been done since to improve the defences still further. As Osric had admitted to Alfred, the only unprotected area was to the south. That was bounded by the river Frome, which was considered defence enough, but it was an area which still seemed to worry Ethelnorth so they went there next to look at the quay, a place which was bustling with trade and commerce. There was no landing stage as such, but many boats had been pulled up on to the muddy bank of the river to be loaded or unloaded and numerous warehouses and sheds had been built to store whatever was brought ashore.

'All here seem to prosper,' observed Ethelnorth. That was certainly true enough, for all who resided in Wareham had fared well on the trade from merchants bringing in goods from elsewhere in Britain and even from across the sea. With that he turned to Oswald. 'How do you cross to that road I can see on the other side of the river?' he asked.

'By ferry, my Lord,' explained Oswald. 'There's a boatman who will carry goods and people across for a fee, though there's little demand for his services.'

'And these boats which have been sailed almost into the heart of the settlement. How do you separate friend from foe?'

'My Lord, all are watched constantly from the time they enter the main harbour or sooner. We have a watchtower on Haven Point at the entrance and they keep a look out for signals from others sited all along the coast. If they so much as suspect anything untoward approaching they have beacons which can be lit to warn us. We then have chains which can be hauled across to deny access to either river. No ship could get anywhere near this far upstream without us being warned.'

Seemingly satisfied with all he'd seen, Ethelnorth next turned his attention to Oswald's own role. 'So, you are the Garrison Commander here?' he asked.

'I am, my Lord,' replied Oswald. 'Though I much value the guidance I receive from my uncle.'

Ethelnorth smiled, knowing how true that was likely to be. 'Your uncle was ever a good man to have at your side in a battle.'

'As I believe were you, my Lord. I've heard many tales of your courage and skill—'

'We can speak of such things later,' said Ethelnorth, not letting him finish. 'For now, let's concentrate on the rest of the defences you have in place.' At that point, all he had seen was exactly as Osric had described to Alfred and he could find no fault with it, apart from the delay in everyone reaching the safety of the burh in time. In particular, he was impressed by the earthworks which, having been topped off with the palisade fence, were high enough to make them all but unassailable. In fact, the outer face of them had been left deliberately steep and, in some places, was almost sheer. 'Your uncle said that you have a permanent guard of fifty men?' he said, recalling what Osric had told him whilst they were at Winchester.

'We do, my Lord,' said Oswald. 'All armed and well trained. There are also sixty members of the fyrd who reside within the settlement itself and who are similarly well disposed. Others are levied regularly to maintain the fortifications, the bridge and the roads.'

'And there is but one bridge as I recall,' said Ethelnorth.

'That's true, my Lord, but a second road enters the settlement via gates to the west and there is a narrow path which leads to the harbour from the east wall. Both are guarded at all times.'

'And I gather that over 1500 men could be mustered in the event of an attempted invasion?'

'That's also true, my Lord,' agreed Oswald. 'Though as I said, some might take longer to reach us than we would like.'

'How then would they be summoned?' Ethelnorth asked.

'There is a warning bell here within the settlement which can be sounded and we have a system of beacons which are set on the high ground and lit to warn of raids both here or at any of the outlying settlements or farmsteads.'

Lord Ethelnorth seemed impressed. 'All that's to the

good, but it requires that you remain vigilant at all times.'

'Yes, my Lord, but there's no need to prompt anyone in Wareham on that account. All are constantly reminded of those dark days when we lived under Viking occupation. Our settlement still bears the scars of the damage that was done and we've not forgotten all the lives which were so cruelly wasted at that time. Hence everyone here knows how important it is to remain watchful and all are more than ready to play their part in defending their homes if needed.'

* * * * *

That evening Edward settled down in the dark stables and tried to sleep, feeling very alone and more than a little frightened. He didn't mind the rats or the cold, nor the noise of the horses as they settled for the night – in fact he found all that to be both comforting and familiar, except that it reminded him of the horses he'd been taking care of at Winchester, all of which he regretted having to leave behind. What worried him was that Fleet had not returned. He knew that the horse was still in the pasture where he seemed content, eating the fresh grass and occasionally setting off on a wild gallop from one end to the other as if exploiting his newfound freedom to the full. Edward's concern was that if Fleet failed to return as Ulrich had predicted, he could expect to be punished. That was something he dreaded for, having taken many beatings in his short life, he'd found that his frail body did not endure them well.

* * * * *

Ethelnorth remained at Osric's Vill for a second night in order to take his rest before completing the journey to his own Vill in Somerset. Once they'd eaten supper together, Osric took him to his own lodge so they could speak in private. Whilst on the journey from Winchester there had been little opportunity for them to talk over all that Alfred had told them without others overhearing and they'd seldom been alone together since arriving at Wareham.

'So, the years have taken their toll on you as they have with me,' said Ethelnorth, recalling their conversation with Alfred.

Osric nodded. 'Aye, getting older doesn't suit me. I still think I can ride and fight as I once did but seem to ache more now than I ever remember doing before. But I recall you were always wont to be a musician, not a warrior. Have you not taken it up again in your later years?'

Ethelnorth held up his hands to show his bent and gnarled fingers. 'These are what I have to show from too many years spent fighting. These fingers are no longer nimble enough to pluck the strings of the lyre, for they refuse to bend as once they did.'

Osric nodded knowingly. 'Age is a cruel mistress, that's for sure.'

'But what of you? I recall Alfred meant for you to undertake some administrative duty when you retired from his guard. Did that not work out as was intended?'

'The role he offered me was a great honour. As you may recall, he originally planned for you and Matthew to set up a standing army in the hope of securing peace. When Matthew died and you returned to oversee matters in the west, it was thought that I might assume that role instead.

The trouble is that I'm not well disposed to administrative matters. Had he lived, I think Matthew would have made a better fist of it than I did.'

'So you were appointed as Governor here instead? That is, in itself, a great honour and a very important role given the settlement's strategic importance.'

'Aye, though as you've seen already, the work of training the fyrd now falls to my nephew since I retired from active service. He's now the Garrison Commander.'

Ethelnorth could see that made sense. 'From all I've seen your nephew seems to know well enough what he's about.'

Osric was slow to answer. 'Of sorts,' he said. 'He's strong and has the skill to be a good warrior but he's also headstrong and overly ambitious for advancement. What's more, he's never fought in a significant battle so remains untested.'

Ethelnorth nodded. 'Yet you've done well enough with the arrangements here. The fortifications look to be strong and well founded.'

'Then do you think they'll suffice?' asked Osric. 'My nephew is concerned that you still have reservations in that respect.'

Ethelnorth chose his words with care. 'I remain worried that unless fully manned your fortifications would not withstand a full-scale attack,' he said simply. 'You might think they will but as you know all too well, Alfred fears that Haesten is already gathering his forces and Wareham is one of the places he might well choose to strike as the harbour here would be the ideal place to shelter his invasion fleet.'

Osric considered that before he answered. 'We'd give a good account of ourselves if he does and could hold out long enough for Alfred to arrive with reinforcements,' he said. 'Any ships would be sighted even before they enter the harbour. After that, given that it's such a large expanse of water, they'd still have to wait on the tide before sailing across it and even then would have to row upstream along the river to reach us. We can delay them even then by using the chains and such like.'

'That depends where they choose to strike,' said Ethelnorth. 'What if they attacked from the north? That would leave many people cut off from reaching you. How would you fare then?'

Osric realised at once what he was saying. 'That would be hard for the Vikings to manage,' he reasoned. 'The only way they could come in behind us like that would be to come ashore somewhere along the coast and march across land. That would take time and, as the terrain is mostly marsh, it would be hard for anything resembling a significant force to traverse, particularly unseen.'

Ethelnorth smiled, for it seemed Osric had indeed covered every option. 'That's to the good,' he announced. 'But the nearest burh is where?' he asked.

'It's at Twynham,' said Osric. 'Little more than a full day's march from here by road.'

'Then you must ensure that they remain vigilant as well and that they watch out for your beacons in case you need them to support you. You should likewise do the same for them,' suggested Ethelnorth. 'As you well know, these Vikings are canny bastards and can sense a weakness in any defence and quickly find a way to exploit it.' With that he changed the subject. 'So tell me, do you believe this stable boy of yours is really Matthew's bastard son?' he asked.

Osric shrugged, for it was a question they'd discussed

before but which neither of them could answer. 'If pressed I would have to answer "yes" for I have only to look at the lad to see the likeness,' he reasoned. 'Is he not the spitting image of his father?'

'It was all a long time ago,' mused Ethelnorth. 'And we are all old men so perhaps our memory is not what it was and we see what we want to see.'

'But Matthew and that girl were close, as you well know. And he did spend that last night with her before he was sent on that fool's errand by Alfred.'

'He spent many nights with her as I recall!' laughed Ethelnorth.

'Yes, but did you know that he'd spoken to Alfred of marriage?'

Ethelnorth nodded. 'In truth, I did, but it would have been quite unthinkable. After all, his was one of the most noble families in all Wessex. Alfred could never have allowed a match like that.'

'Yet it seems he did,' said Osric. 'Or at least that he was minded to do so and even set out the terms on which he would approve. I know only what he told us, but had Matthew not been slain I truly believe he would have been allowed to marry the girl. So the question is, what do we do now?'

'As always we do as our King commands,' said Ethelnorth simply. 'We protect the boy and guide him as best we may until he's strong enough to be told the truth. Then Alfred may restore him or...'

Ethelnorth had no need to finish his point, for they both knew that if his claim was found wanting or if he failed to live up to what was expected of him, Edward would be quietly despatched to some hopeless duty a long way from court. Worse still was the risk of Edward being used to mount a challenge to Alfred's rule, something Ethelnorth had alluded to before. Such a claim might split the Saxon cause asunder which, with the threat of another Viking invasion hanging over them, was something Alfred desperately needed to avoid. The pity of it was that even if used by others, Edward would be held to account for such treachery and would then doubtless end his days at the end of a rope – or even at the hands of a paid assassin so that he quietly disappeared with no one being any the wiser.

'You mentioned Matthew's brother Edmund and his sister Edwina when we spoke with Alfred,' mused Ethelnorth. 'As I recall they were both taken when their parents were slain in a raid prior to the attack on Chippenham.'

'Yes, but both are long gone by now, I shouldn't wonder. Killed or dead from their labours having been sold as slaves,' suggested Osric. 'It's a cruel fate indeed to have ended thus after having been so high born.'

Ethelnorth gave a deep sigh. 'Their father, Lord Edwulf, would turn in his grave to see his line ending thus. His sons all slain and his bloodline come to nothing save for the bastard son of a whore. Mind there was talk of Matthew also having sired a daughter from that pagan wench as well. You told Alfred that she was sent here during her confinement.'

'Aye, that's so,' said Osric. 'As I told him, Matthew's friend Aelred came when the babies were born. He killed Ingar by cutting open her wrist, claiming that as a healer she'd made him promise to do that in order that the babies could both be safely delivered. Unfortunately, having done so he was slain whilst crossing the North Bridge in an attempt to escape justice. His body was left floating in the river.'

'But he was dead?' asked Ethelnorth.

'There can be no doubt about that. I wasn't here at the time otherwise I would have had him apprehended instead and dragged back to be judged by Alfred.'

'And what became of the two children?'

'Like I said, although they shared her womb, Ingar insisted that because they had different fathers they were to be reared apart as she feared one would kill the other. Thus the girl, Ingrid by name, who Ingar claimed was Matthew's daughter, is still here at the nunnery though has not yet taken vows. She is like her mother and is already proving to be a gifted healer. The boy, Coenred, is of a different hue altogether and is as idle as the day is long. He's supposed to be the bastard son of a Viking slaver and I can see how that might be so. He was initially sent away to a monastery but proved too headstrong for the monks to manage so had to be found work at my Vill instead, though he's proved a worthless wretch. I sometimes wonder what I'll do with him.'

'And they have never been told of each other's existence?'

Osric shook his head. 'It was deemed better that way. Though Coenred knows that his father was a Viking, Ingrid has been told only that her mother was a gifted healer. Apart from that they know nothing of each other or indeed that they're related.'

'Then it would seem that Matthew's legacy remains uncertain,' lamented Ethelnorth.

'Worse still,' said Osric. 'His bastard son is reduced to shovelling the horse shit from my stables!'

'His fate may yet improve but, for now, it's for his own good. For Alfred is right, if anyone learns his true identity, he could well fall victim of every fraudster and fortune hunter in the realm.'

Osric got up and poured them both more mead from the pitcher. 'Then I must seek every opportunity to nurture the lad.'

Ethelnorth accepted the beaker. 'Aye, but remember, you're not to favour him, for some might see through that. As your nephew now trains the fyrd, I would let Edward learn how to fight from him, for with all he stands to inherit, that's a skill he'll surely need. And probably a lot sooner than you think.'

Chapter Six

As Reeve, Ulrich prided himself on always being the first to rise so that he could be up and about before anyone else. The first thing he did the next morning was to check to see whether Fleet had indeed returned to the stable as Edward had predicted. As he approached the gate to the pasture he could see no sign of the horse so, certain that the boy could not have recovered the stallion on his own, he assumed it had escaped and was therefore running loose about the settlement. He was about to go over and haul Edward out by the scruff of his neck and then drag him up before Osric but, as he drew closer to the stable, he could see the boy fast asleep in one corner with Fleet waiting patiently in his stall with the gate still wide open. 'Get up you lazy little runt,' he shouted angrily, fearing he'd been duped.

Having found the journey from Winchester tiring and not being used to his new surroundings, Edward had remained abed longer than he'd intended. As soon as he heard Ulrich's voice he roused himself then hurried out, stopping only to glance at Fleet on the way.

'So, try to make a fool of me would you!' accused Ulrich as Edward stumbled into the saddling yard, still rubbing the sleep from his eyes.

Edward was not sure what to say. 'Sir, I'm sorry I…'

'Never mind your excuses. Be about your work, boy. And

tomorrow, just be sure you're up before I am or I'll thrash your miserable hide. As you well know, Lord Ethelnorth and his men leave today and will need their mounts saddled and ready. Also, the farm horses are required to haul out a large tree from the river so must be harnessed and ready. I expect all that to be done within the hour.'

Edward set about his given tasks at once and soon had all the horses out of their stalls. He allowed all the resident ones, including Fleet, to roam free again then attended to those belonging to Lord Ethelnorth and the two guards. As he'd groomed them all the night before he had only to feed them, so, by the time Ethelnorth and his men had breakfasted and emerged from their lodgings, their horses were saddled and ready. He led all three to where they waited outside the Hall.

'Well boy, have they been fed and watered?' demanded Ethelnorth as he prepared to mount up.

'They have, my Lord. And they've rested well,' replied Edward. 'I've also groomed them but I fear your grey will need shooing when you arrive at your Vill. I would have attended to it myself but have not yet found the means to do so here.'

'Why not? The Vill has a forge does it not?' he countered.

'We do,' explained Osric. 'But I doubt the lad has yet had time to find it.'

Ethelnorth said nothing. Instead, he hauled his old bones stiffly into the saddle and took one last look at the ragged and dirty boy with horse shit on his naked feet and straw in his hair. It struck him then that it was a strange quirk of fate whereby such a puny boy might one day be his equal in the realm. With that, having bid farewell to Osric, he and his two guards rode off towards the bridge.

As they watched them ride away, Ulrich scolded Edward again. 'You should have tended to his horse properly,' he chided. 'You can't send a great man such as Lord Ethelnorth on his way with his horse poorly shod! If you needed the forge you should have asked. You have a tongue in your head, do you not?'

Osric raised his hand to settle the matter. 'The boy has done what he could,' he reasoned. 'Now, have you yet thought about how best to train my stallion?'

'I have, my Lord. But first I must win his trust. Already he's calmer but I've yet to show him the saddle or the bridle...'

'Foolish boy,' scolded Ulrich. 'Take the whip to the beast and show him who's master from the outset, that's the way to break a wilful horse!'

Osric waited for Edward to answer, anxious to hear how he'd respond.

'My Lord, Fleet is certainly a strong-willed horse but he'll respond best to kindness, not the whip. That way he'll make a better mount, particularly once he trusts me. The job of then training him to the saddle will also be made much easier.'

'You mean you want to idle away the day like that fool Coenred did before you,' accused Ulrich.

'Oh no my Lord,' protested Edward. 'I've much to do. The stalls must be raked and mucked out and fresh straw lain. Also, the troughs must be filled and...'

'Then get to it boy! Or have you all day to please yourself?'

With that Edward turned to leave but, as he did so, Ulrich noticed that his eye was swollen from where Coenred had punched him. 'How did you come by that?' he demanded.

'Sir, I walked into something in the dark,' said Edward, not wishing to say what had really caused it.

Ulrich caught him by the chin and turned the boy's head so he could inspect the bruise more closely. 'And what exactly did you walk into?' he asked, guessing at once what had really happened.

'It was a door, sir. I wasn't looking where I was going and failed to see it had been left ajar.'

Ulrich nodded as if to acknowledge the pathetic explanation. 'Then perhaps that will teach you to keep your mind on what you're about,' he said. 'Not daydreaming about God knows what.'

* * * * *

Edward had missed breakfast but thought better of asking for any. Instead, he drank a little water scooped from the horses' trough, then bathed his eye. After that he set about sweeping out one of the stalls but was suddenly aware of Osric watching him.

'My Lord…' he stammered, bowing his head meekly. 'I'm sorry, I didn't see you there.'

Osric waved away the apology then noticed Fleet contentedly grazing in the pasture. 'So, did my horse return of its own accord as I gather you predicted it would or do you have some special skill in rounding up stray beasts on your own?' he asked.

'No, my Lord. He knows where he'll be well fed and sheltered so returned willingly enough.'

'And as you said, it would seem that you have indeed managed to calm him. How did you accomplish that so quickly?'

'He's not ill-tempered by nature,' explained Edward. 'It's just that his spirit is hampered by being shut up in a stable all day and he resents being tethered. He yearns to run free which is, after all, what he was born to do.'

'You seem to know your horses, lad.'

'I hope so, my Lord. I find them good company, for I've known little else since I was a child. The stables are a lonely place in which to work so the horses become as friends.'

Osric nodded. 'So what's to be done with such a magnificent beast?'

'My Lord, would it be possible to have a larger stall built for Fleet, one set closer to where I sleep as that would help to build a bond between us?'

'Surely that would mean he's disturbed more often as the other horses come and go from the stables. Will that not mean that he's constantly riled?'

'Perhaps at first, my Lord, but he'd soon get used to it. Unlike men, horses quickly learn to accept that which they cannot change.'

Osric laughed. 'It seems that you know something about men as well as about horses,' he offered.

'Fleet sees himself as Lord of all the horses here. The new stall would let him oversee his "subjects" and thereby help to bolster his pride.'

'I think he's one horse with enough pride already,' mused Osric. 'Let me think on what you've suggested but for now we have much to do within the settlement and I must consider what's needed for the benefit of all before setting about improving the lot of my own horse. So, what do you plan to do next?'

'I need to let him know me before he can be ridden. Then I'll start to train him but have no need to break his spirit to do that, merely to teach him what's expected.'

'And how will you do that?'

'With kindness. And, with your leave my Lord, I would like to ride one of the other horses and let Fleet run free beside us. That way he'll learn the way of things 'twixt a man and a horse.'

'Where did you learn to ride?' asked Osric curiously. 'I recall that on the way here you put us all to shame. You handled the mule so easily it looked as though it was part of you.'

'I was taught by a fine old man who was once horse thane at Lord Alfred's stables in Winchester, my Lord.'

'You mean old Colbert? He was ever a good man to be sure, though near as blind as a bat towards the end of his days. Nonetheless, there was none finer than he when it came to knowing horses so I'll warrant you had a worthy teacher.'

'Indeed I did, my Lord. I've much to thank him for. I've no formal skill but he taught me to watch how a horse moves and to trust it. Left to its own devices it will pick its own way with care. All you have to do is set it on the course you want it to follow, for it'll not stumble unless you ask too much of it.'

Osric acknowledged the sense of that.

'My Lord, will you ride Fleet once I've trained him to the saddle?'

'Hah! Now that, young Edward, remains my dearest wish but there are many who think it's nothing but a foolish whim on my part. They mock me when my back is turned and jest about it even to my face. What I wouldn't give to prove them all wrong and ride such a fine horse one day,' he said wistfully. 'You may not know this but when I was a younger man I had such daring that I would have gladly ridden even the wildest horse but now my nephew forbids it in case I'm thrown, for these old bones would not survive a fall and I fear there would be plenty of those if I took Fleet at even half his pace. Thus I must take my pleasure from seeing others do as I would if I could. Even you perhaps?'

Edward glanced over at the horse which was still in the field but standing not far off. 'My Lord, it would be an honour, but not yet,' he said. 'Soon he may let me, though his spirit is such that he'd probably prefer to be spared the bridle and the saddle at first.'

'Bareback then? You'd need to be a very skilled rider to manage that!'

'I think he'd take good care of me once he's learned we're friends,' said Edward. 'Then, once properly trained, I hope he may yet carry you safely, my Lord, for he's very sure-footed.'

Osric took an immediate liking to the lad so sat down on a rustic stool and motioned for Edward to stand beside him. 'So, you were christened Edward?' he said.

'I was, my Lord. And I hope I shall serve you as best it pleases you.'

'And so you shall, for it pleases me to see someone who has his heart in his work. You've done well in the short time you've been here and I shall remember that. By all means borrow my horse but leave my nephew's in case he has need of it. And ride Fleet when you think the time is right but treat him well.'

'I will, my Lord.'

'Whether I can ever mount him remains to be seen but that would be something. To sit astride him as I would have done in the old days, with a sword in my hand and a shield at my side.'

Edward grinned. 'I've heard it said that you were once a great warrior, my Lord.'

Osric smiled, half remembering the days gone by. 'Not so much a great warrior, but a skilled one perhaps. In my day I was honoured to be chosen as chief of Lord Alfred's personal guard.'

'Then surely, my Lord, with such great courage you will ride Fleet one day.'

As he got up Osric put his hand on Edward's shoulder. 'That would be a good day. One I look forward to, and believe me, as you grow older you'll find there are precious few of those.'

* * * * *

Later that morning, Coenred returned to the kitchen with two pails of water he'd been sent to fetch from the well. He found Mildred there, busily scrubbing the large table on which the food was prepared. 'So this is where you're hiding yourself,' he said, setting both pails down on the floor. 'I thought to see more of you now that I'm to work in the kitchens as well.'

Mildred looked up at him. 'I think you've seen enough of me already,' she teased.

'You can never get too much of a good thing,' he said, grinning as he moved towards her. She was still leaning over the table so he reached out from behind her and fondled her breasts.

Mildred wriggled away, protesting as she did so. 'I've told you, keep your hands to yourself when you're here lest someone should see us. Unlike you, I still have a position here which I mean to keep. Besides, I'm sure you've work to be getting on with.'

Coenred backed off. 'This isn't proper work,' he moaned. 'All I get to do is empty the piss pots and fetch and carry all day.'

Mildred looked at him. 'Well, you only have yourself to blame for that,' she chided. 'Besides, it's not all you get to do.'

He grinned again. 'No, that's true. Sometimes I get to tup this wanton maid when no one's looking.'

'Wanton!' she said, hitting him playfully on the arm. 'Who are you calling wanton?' She then stamped her foot and left the kitchen, though couldn't resist looking back and smiling as she did so.

* * * * *

Suddenly, all hell seemed to have broken out. The bell to summon the fyrd had been sounded and men of all trades began arriving at the Vill from every corner of the settlement, joining those members of the permanent guard who were not on duty elsewhere. Some men carried weapons but most expected to draw arms from the garrison store as they formed up outside Lord Osric's Vill and waited for orders. Edward went across to join them.

'What's happening?' he asked the man nearest him.

The man looked at him then pointed to a column of smoke on the high ground in the distance. 'That's one of the warning beacons. I reckon it's from the settlement at Wool,' he said simply. 'If so, it heralds a raid on a farmstead near there so we're called to attend.'

'Aye,' said the man next to him. 'But it's a waste of time

89

if you ask me. As always, the raiders will be long gone by the time we get there.'

Oswald looked around and decided what numbers he would need. By then most of the fyrd had assembled but he needed to leave a contingent to protect the settlement whilst he and the rest were away dealing with the raid. He therefore selected thirty men to go with him which included twenty members of the permanent guard with the rest being drawn from the resident fyrd, none of whom seemed pleased to have been selected. All the other men were ordered to remain at the settlement with his second in command, a man named Wulfric. He then saw Edward. 'Can you fight, boy?' he demanded.

'No, sir. At least, I never have.'

He hesitated for a moment. 'Then prepare to learn, for we march within the hour and have not a moment to lose. Gather up those supplies over there and be quick about it. You can use the mule to carry them but try to keep up, for we must move fast and can wait for no one.'

Edward quickly tied the carrier baskets to the mule's back and loaded the supplies they would need for the journey, securing them with a rope. They included some food, some battle gear and a few arrows.

As the small force readied themselves to leave, a priest came to bless their endeavours but didn't seem inclined to go with them.

'Surely you'll join us, Father Emmett?' suggested Oswald.

'I would that I could, but I have duties here which I am required to attend to and…'

'Are not your duties to serve the needs of your flock?' he asked. 'If so, then those coming with us are likely to be the ones most in need. So, say what prayers you think may be needed, then join our line, for we must be on our way.'

Father Emmett raised his hand and the assembled men knelt as he recited prayers on their behalf, then blessed them all. That done, he made the sign of the cross and all then rose and prepared to leave.

The men marched quickly, half running and half walking with their shields strapped to their backs, carrying their own weapons and having donned whatever war gear they had. They kept up a pace which Edward struggled to maintain whilst leading the mule which, being of a stubborn disposition, was wont to keep stopping. He gradually fell further and further behind so decided to mount the beast in order to catch up with the main column. Spurring it with his heels, he drove it hard and soon reached the others. He then dismounted but all too quickly fell behind once more. Again he mounted the mule and this time remained astride it until, after marching for several hours with no more than a token rest, they arrived at Wool, a small settlement which, like Wareham, was set beside the river Frome.

It seemed they were expected as a dozen men from the local fyrd came out to greet them. They were all armed and intent on joining the group, leading the way to the south where they said the raid had taken place.

It was almost dark by the time they came to a farmstead which had once comprised several rustic homes and a few workshops and stores, some of which had been reduced to nothing more than charred remains and a few which were still burning. There was debris littered everywhere, items which had clearly been looted and then discarded when found to be of no value or merit. The men searched through the remains and soon found the bodies of two men, a woman and a small boy, all of whom had been brutally butchered. Oswald looked furious as he examined the bodies.

'As always we arrive too late!' he stormed. 'The bastards who did this are long gone from here.'

'Would you have us follow them, sir?' demanded Sigbert who was a carpenter by trade and, although a lot older than some, was an experienced and trusted member of the resident fyrd at Wareham.

Oswald shook his head. 'No, their trail leads towards the coast. They'll have carried their plunder with them and, as like as not, will have loaded it aboard their ships by now and be waiting only on the tide. We'll remain here tonight in case they return but, in the meantime, there's nothing more we can do here except to bury the dead.'

Edward was ordered to join the men who were detailed to lift the bodies into shallow graves which had been hastily dug by others. Apart from a trickle of blood at the corner of his mouth, the young boy seemed to have no obvious wounds. It was as though he had simply fallen asleep and forgotten to keep breathing. Only as they lifted his frail body did they find that he'd been stabbed with a spear which had been driven deep into his back and then withdrawn. He was perhaps seven or eight years of age and all there deeply resented the killing of one so young. The other dead had all been mutilated and probably tortured. Their bloodied remains were mangled and twisted and Edward was horrified by the sight of such carnage. One was a man who had been skewered with a spear, his face grotesquely twisted and his fists clenched in agony as the pain had overcome him. The other man had been beheaded with a battleaxe whilst kneeling, suggesting he had been executed, probably for having resisted too well. It was the woman who seemed to have suffered most, having been stripped near naked and probably raped many times before having her throat cut. Oswald noticed that Edward turned away from the sight of so much slaughter to vomit.

'I'm sorry, sir,' he said, feeling ashamed.

Oswald nodded. 'Not a pretty sight, is it?' he acknowledged. 'Is this the first time you've seen the handiwork of Viking raiders?'

'No sir, we came across a farmstead on the way from Winchester but it was not like this. I mean, the raid had been some months earlier so there were no bodies or—' he stopped himself from saying more. 'Do you think the others who lived here got away?' he asked, wiping his mouth on his sleeve.

Oswald didn't answer but one of the men who overheard the conversation laughed aloud. 'Don't waste your pity, boy. These are the lucky ones,' he roared. 'At least for them the ordeal is over. The rest can look forward to a brutal life of slavery and abuse.'

'Leave him be,' ordered Oswald. 'Let's have the priest offer prayers for these poor souls, then, if we're certain the raiders are done, we'll be gone from here tomorrow, for there's nothing else we can do for them now.'

Chapter Seven

Father Emmett looked relieved that there was to be no actual fighting. Thus, whilst others prepared to make a camp for the night, he set himself to the task of praying for the dead. The men from Wool confirmed that the farmstead had belonged to a man name Leonine and that as far as they knew, at least six more people had lived there with him. They readily recognised and named the two men who had been killed and also the boy, but the woman was not known to any of them, which meant she was probably some sort of servant or perhaps a traveller who had sought shelter for a few nights.

When the prayers were done, the bodies were covered over and being a carpenter, Sigbert fashioned a simple wooden cross to set above each grave. Beyond that there was little more which could be done so the men from Wool returned to their homes, leaving Oswald and the fyrd from Wareham to remain in case the raiders returned, though no one truly thought they would. To make themselves as comfortable for the night as possible, they set about erecting a crude shelter from what could be salvaged from the ruined farmstead, then, having posted guards, the rest of them sat around a fire to eat their meagre supper. One of them, a man named Egbert, started to tell the story of a warrior named Aelwulf, to which they listened eagerly for they all loved a good tale even though it was one most had heard many times before.

'Aelwulf was a great warrior but like all such men, he feared that one day it would be his fate to die in combat. Thus he always prayed earnestly on the night before a battle, spending as much as an hour on his knees entreating God to spare him and allow him to emerge from the fray unscathed. Others said it was wrong to pray thus, for a warrior should expect to die in battle sooner or later so should ask God to give them a quick and glorious death, then hope to be granted a place in Heaven. Aelwulf understood their logic but, whilst he had long ago accepted the risk of being slain, what he wanted was to live to a good age, raise his children and possibly even see his grandchildren before he died. After that he would feel ready to meet his maker.

'However, whenever he survived a battle, he was not quite so earnest in expressing his gratitude to God, often giving little more than a token word of thanks, and even that only after he'd finished stripping what he could from the dead and the dying on the battlefield. Then, one day, his luck gave out and he was counted among the list of those who had fallen in a particularly brutal battle. As he stood in line at St Peter's gate with all the others who had perished that day, he was certain that St Peter would admit him to Heaven, for surely if his prayers had not been answered it was the least he could expect.

'He waited patiently, smug and secure in the certainty of his fate, and watched as others were turned away. Then, when his turn came, he was also quickly disappointed.

'"But I offered prayers for my life to be spared," he reasoned. "Surely if those prayers were left unanswered I should at least be admitted to Heaven?"

'St Peter was not best pleased. "You offered prayers right enough, but that was for your own advantage. Whether you live or die in a battle is a matter for God's will alone, not something for which you can bargain. What you should have done is offered sincere thanks each time you survived a battle and thus showed that you are truly grateful for the blessings He bestowed upon you whilst you were alive."

'"But I died fighting the heathens for the benefit of God's Holy church," he pleaded. "Does that not count for something?"

'St Peter rebuked him at once. "It's true that you followed the cross of Christ into battle, but that was just your excuse to join the fray. What you fought for was glory, blood and plunder, and for the right to brag and boast of your courage to those who fought beside you. That's often the way of it, but has nothing to do with a love for God or His Holy Church."

'Thus it was that despite all his prayers, Aelwulf found no favour in the hereafter.'

As always, the Saxons debated the story late into the night, extracting all the meaning they could from the simple tale and trying to find some reassurance for the way they each lived their own life and for their hopes for salvation.

Father Emmett stood and offered what he felt was the true meaning of the tale. 'We are all of us miserable sinners,' he advised. 'As such we must learn to accept God's will, not seek to mould it with prayer. He is a good and benevolent God who will spare you where He may but, if it is His will that you should die, then die you must. You can expect nothing more and prayer alone will not save you. Therefore before each battle ask only to receive His grace if you should fall and then give grateful thanks if you survive. That's the way to ensure that you can enter the kingdom of Heaven.'

'So, does that mean that all our prayers are wasted?' asked one man.

'Not wasted,' said Father Emmett. 'But most are not properly construed. When you pray you should give thanks for all God's blessings, not ask Him to provide for whatever it is you desire. Trust him and give thanks for His blessings, for He knows what's in your heart but has work enough to do without listening to all your selfish pleas and ramblings.'

Oswald listened to the debate with particular interest. 'Father, are you saying that we should question the reasons for fighting?' he asked pointedly.

Father Emmett said that was certainly so. 'Look to your heart. If that is truly set on the glory of God then you need have no fear for your soul.'

It was one of the other men who then spoke out. 'That's all very well, but most of us are here because we're ordered to be here by our Lords and betters. Forget blood and booty, we would all much prefer to be plying our trade or tending our farms. How else can we expect to feed ourselves and our families?'

'Aye,' said another. 'Or be abed with our wives, not sleeping here in some ruined farmstead.'

'Or someone else's wife!' joked another man.

Father Emmett knew he was on dangerous ground. 'Serving your King and your betters is all part of God's plan, so you can rest easy on that account. What you do here is therefore good for your soul, provided you serve willingly and do so for the love of the Church and your King, not personal glory or riches. That's all that's required of you.'

* * * * *

During the night a woman who it seemed had survived the raid emerged from within the trees where she'd been hiding. She was old and frightened, hardly daring to approach the band of Saxons lest they turned out to be yet more raiders come back to kill or abuse her.

''Tis surely a miracle God spared her,' exclaimed Father Emmett, his hands raised in thanks to God.

Oswald scoffed. 'She was too ugly for them to rape and too old to be a slave. They'd have killed her if they could but she wasn't worth chasing through the trees just for the pleasure of doing that.'

All knew he was right but there was little they could do to calm her. When anyone went near her she drew a small skinning knife and held it out as if to threaten them.

'You keeps your distance!' she screeched. 'Come closer and I'll gut you like a fish. My body is old and frail and is not to be abused by the likes of you!' As she spoke she turned to face each man in turn.

'Come old woman, you've nowt to fear from us,' said one of the guards but, when he moved closer, she jerked the knife towards him and would have stabbed him had he not stepped back in time.

'My child, can't you see that we're trying to help you?' pleaded Father Emmett.

'I know full well the sort of help I can expect from the likes of you! So keep away from me, do you hear?'

'Have some food,' offered Oswald who on hearing the commotion had gone to assist them. 'Or at least come to sleep beside the fire.'

'I want nothing from you! And I'll take no favours from anyone!'

'She's as mad as a march hare,' observed one of the men.

'Aye, well she'll have seen all that happened here,' explained Oswald. 'Most likely all her kin have been slain or taken and it's turned her mind. We'll take her back with us and see if she can be calmed by the womenfolk at Wareham.'

'Pah!' said the man. 'Some chance of that. I'd as soon take a bear by a lead as tackle that old crone whilst she handles that blade with such intent!'

'Well,' reasoned Oswald. 'We can't leave her here.'

With that two members of the permanent guard stepped forward. One drew her attention and, as she thrust the knife towards him, he grasped her skinny wrist and held it firm whilst pushing the blade aside. As he did so, the other man grabbed her from behind. Although they were both strong, she kicked and struggled, writhing and wriggling like an eel as they tried to subdue her. Even then she managed to bite one of them before they were able to contain her. In the end she was disarmed and her hands were tied behind her back. A rope was also looped around her waist so that she could no longer run off and which they proposed to use as a lead when they returned to the garrison the following day, thereby ensuring that she would have no option but to go with them.

* * * * *

The next morning, with no further beacons having been lit, it was assumed that the raiders had not struck again elsewhere nor would they be coming back. The members of the fyrd thus gathered up their belongings and they all returned to Wareham. By the time they arrived back at the Vill Edward was tired but went straight to tend to the horses which, as he'd not had time to round them up before leaving the previous day, had been left roaming free in the pasture all night. They none of them seemed the worse for that so he left them there but filled their troughs with fresh water from the well and put out some feed for them all.

Meanwhile, Oswald went directly to see his uncle at the Vill. He found him settled in a chair at the head of an otherwise vacant table and was invited to be seated as well. Osric then called for mead and for the remains of a joint of cold meat left over from the supper his nephew should have shared the previous night, then waited to hear what he knew would be bad news.

'We were too late as always,' complained Oswald, gnawing at the bone hungrily.

'What more could you do?' reasoned Osric. 'Would you have the men learn to fly in order to reach the raiders in time? What damage was there?'

'A farmstead burned and pillaged. We found two men and a woman dead plus a young boy who was scarce seven or eight years old. All had been butchered as usual.'

'There were no survivors?'

'None that we could find save for an old crone who was too elderly to be worth raping or slaying. We've brought her back with us but her mind is addled. God knows what we're to do with her but I'll send word to those at Wool in case she has kin there.'

'And what of the others who lived there?'

'They were all either taken or fled. And for what? A few pots and whatever reserves of food they had. That's what I never understand, all that wasted blood for so little purpose or profit.'

'It's slaves they're after,' mused Osric. 'The plunder is just like the froth on their ale. Men and women fetch a tidy price from those who would have them, particularly abroad. Did you know any of those who lived there?'

Oswald needed no reminder of what became of those who were taken. 'It belonged to an old farmer called Leonine, though I cannot say I knew him well. Some of the men from Wool seemed to know the others, but not the woman who was killed. So, what's to be done?'

Osric spread his hands. 'I don't know what more we can do,' he said. 'I take it the warning beacons worked well enough?'

'Aye, they did,' said Oswald. 'But as always, they're only effective if we see them in time.'

'Well, at least it's quicker than waiting for a messenger to bring us word.'

'Yes, but remember the smoke is sometimes difficult to spot, especially at night. By the time we do it's often too late as the bastards are gone. Besides, even once we've seen the beacons, it can take several hours to reach the site of the raid as we first have to go to the settlement which raised the alarm so they can direct us to where the attack has actually taken place.'

Both men were silent for a moment as they considered the position.

'How long does it now take you to assemble the fyrd?'

Oswald shrugged. 'That depends. We can summon those who reside within the settlement quickly enough. It takes a short time for them to assemble and be properly armed before we can march out but the real problem is getting them to the site of the raid.'

'What happened this time?' asked Osric.

'This time the raiders must have slipped past the beacons watching the coast but were spotted by the men at Wool. They lit their beacon and because it was nigh on midday by then, we must have seen it almost at once. I selected thirty men from those on duty and they were ready to march within the hour. Most were drawn from the permanent guard and the rest from the resident fyrd. That left the rest of the men to remain in Wareham as a precaution against a strike here whilst we were away.'

'That's as quick a response as could be expected,' acknowledged Osric. 'Yet you say that the raiders were gone even before you reached the farmstead?'

'Exactly. And that's usually the way of it, though there is one thing we could try which might help us to deal with these raids more quickly,' he said tentatively.

'What's that?' asked Osric.

'That stable boy of yours came with us carrying the supplies on the mule. I took him along as I thought he should see for himself what happens in a raid. I gather he's spent most of his life at Winchester so has seen little of what happens here, in the real world.'

'That was a good idea,' admitted Osric. 'He needs to know the way of such things.'

'Well, as we marched out he fell behind soon enough as the mule seemed stubborn, but then easily caught us up by riding it. Why not use horses to get the men to the site of the raid more quickly?'

Osric was not immediately at ease with the suggestion but could see that it might have some merit. 'It's a good thought, but Saxons have always fought on foot. Why change that now?'

'I'm not saying we should, though I hear there are those overseas who now charge a shield wall on horseback...'

'Just let the bastards try that against a Saxon shield wall!' challenged Osric. 'Their horses would be unprotected and therefore make easy targets for our bowmen! More of their men would then be lost in the carnage which followed once there were injured and frightened horses running loose on the battlefield.'

'Perhaps, Uncle. But things change. Horses would mean our men would arrive quicker and be better rested.'

'But they would still be too late to stop the raid. Even with horses, by the time you've seen the beacons and ridden there the raiders would have wrought their destruction and be long gone.'

Oswald considered that. 'Then perhaps we're selecting the wrong target,' he said at last.

'What do you mean?'

'I mean why bother going to the site of the raid if we're always going to arrive too late? What we should do is go to where the raiders have come ashore and then wait there to greet the bastards when they return to their ships. We would not then need to find the site of the raid, but simply follow the coast until we find where they've landed.'

'That's all very well but to equip the whole fyrd with horses would cost far more than we could afford. In time, we might well be able to acquire more but with the threat of invasion I need to spend my coin on stockpiling weapons and supplies.'

'I'm not saying we should equip them all with mounts, at least not at first. What I had in mind was a small force of say a dozen warriors, all perhaps drawn from the permanent

103

guard so they're always on hand. If we kept supplies and their weapons ready at all times, an elite force like that could mount up and set off at once.'

'What? And engage them without the rest of the fyrd in support? They'd all be slaughtered!' warned Osric.

'I don't mean for them to engage the raiders directly, only to hold them up long enough for the rest of the fyrd to get there.'

Osric struggled to his feet and went across to stand beside the fire as he considered what his nephew had said. It was part of a brave new way of doing things which, whilst he found it difficult to accept, was certainly feasible. 'There's merit in this,' he managed. 'How many of the men can ride?'

'That's not the problem, Uncle. Most can manage well enough and we can soon teach those who can't. The question is, how could we get enough horses?'

'Perhaps my new stable boy could help with that,' he suggested.

'What Edward? He's nothing but a boy. What help would he be?'

Osric smiled. 'Because he knows horses,' he explained. 'The lad has a way with them. You've seen how quickly he's earned the trust of my horse, Fleet – something no one before him has ever managed to do. It's as though horses take to him instinctively and he's thus able to get the best from them.'

'There are many wild horses loose on the moors which could be rounded up and trained to the saddle,' suggested Oswald. 'If he knows horses so well perhaps he could help us select and cut out the ones best suited to our needs?'

Osric dismissed the idea at once. 'Maybe. But that would

take time and the men are now busy on the land. If we take them away from that to go chasing wild horses across the moors we'll all starve to death come next winter. Would a dozen warriors be enough to keep the raiders pinned down?'

Oswald shrugged. 'Yes, if they were all expert bowmen they should be able to hold off the crew from a single longship. Any more than that and they'd have to withdraw and wait for the reinforcements.'

Osric knew that such a tactic went against their Saxon creed of always facing their enemy, not shooting arrows at them from behind a rock or a tree. Yet he could well recall how that strategy had worked so well at Combwich where Ubba and his fanatic berserkers had all been slain by a small band of Saxons shooting arrows whilst the Vikings still laboured at the oars of their longships. It had not been what many regarded as a pure Saxon tactic, but that battle was still won against the odds and was spoken of as a great Saxon triumph. 'We have what, four horses here if you ignore Fleet?' he mused. 'Two are sturdy beasts so one could pull a cart with say four men riding on it and the other could carry weapons and supplies. With young Edward's help we could perhaps buy four or five more. That would have to do for now as it's as far as my purse will stretch. As you said, we'd need to select the best warriors who might form this elite squad of yours from the permanent guard or at least from those men normally resident here at the settlement. That way they'll always be on hand to respond as soon as a beacon is lit.'

'That's eleven men including myself, perhaps also taking Edward to drive the cart and to mind the horses once we get there,' suggested Oswald.

'Aye, it could work. But you wouldn't be able to engage the

raiders beyond pinning them down on the beach with arrows, you do realise that?' warned Osric. 'You'd be forced to wait for the remainder of the fyrd to arrive in sufficient numbers before fully engaging them. And if then outnumbered you would be obliged to retreat or our losses could be fearful.'

The last point was lost on Oswald who was already thinking of what could follow if his plan worked. Slaying the Vikings on the beach would bring glory, plunder and the chance for vengeance. It would also do much to enhance his own reputation as a warrior.

Meanwhile, Osric considered the position further. 'Wulfric is your second in command and seems an able warrior. Presumably he would lead the main part of the fyrd if you go with the new squad?'

Oswald agreed. 'But who then would take charge of the forces remaining here at Wareham? We daren't leave it undefended.'

'I will,' said Osric.

'Ah,' teased Oswald. 'But Uncle are you sure you're not too old for that?'

'That's enough of your cheek!' warned Osric. 'I was slaying Vikings long before you were born and there's yet enough fight in me to show you young pups a thing or two, be assured of that.'

Chapter Eight

Having taken pity on Edward, Ida allowed him to take an occasional bone or a few scraps from the kitchen whenever she could spare them, all of which helped him to reach an uneasy peace with the mongrel dog. It still continued to snarl and growl if he ventured too close, but at least it seemed to accept his being there. The reality was that having been regularly beaten or baited by Coenred, the poor creature regarded anyone who approached it as being of similar intent and was thus only doing what it could to protect itself. Realising that, Edward decided that he had to do even more to settle it if they were to share the stables and, with that in mind, whilst the dog was out chasing rats or whatever he set about making a small kennel. He fashioned this from reeds gathered from beside the river, weaving them together like a basket and, when it was done, he placed it in the dog's usual corner of the stable and filled it with fresh straw. He then placed a few scraps of food beside the entrance and waited.

At first the dog seemed both curious yet suspicious of his new home. He sloped towards it, then lay a little way off, panting and watching intently. Only when Edward pretended to busy himself elsewhere did the dog creep forward to sniff the kennel. It then looked around and, once satisfied that all was well, ventured inside and slowly made itself at home.

After that Edward brought more scraps of food or a bone for it to gnaw whenever Ida would let him. It could never be said that he and the dog became friends, in fact it still watched Edward's every move intently, but at least it seemed to accept that he meant it no harm and so tolerated his presence.

Gradually, over the course of the next few days, Edward settled into a routine whereby every morning he went first to Fleet's stall and unlatched the gate. The big horse would whinny then step forward but didn't always try to leave. Instead, he sometimes watched whilst Edward got on with his work. 'This will prove a good day for you,' he said aloud one such morning as if talking to the horse. 'Let me finish mucking out and when I'm done we're going for a gallop, you and me. You'll like that, won't you?'

When all his tasks were completed, Edward saddled Osric's bay mare making sure that Fleet could see what he was doing. He then tried slipping a loose halter over Fleet's neck. The stallion resisted at first, backing off as Edward attempted to get it over his head but, having been tethered before, didn't protest any more than that. Edward then left him standing in the yard without tying him to a post so that he remained free to run off if he wanted to. The stallion shook his head several times as if trying to shake the halter loose but apart from that didn't seem overly perturbed by it, being much more interested in all that was going on.

Once Edward had mounted the bay, he reached down for the halter then led Fleet out and into the pasture. From there he started to trot with Fleet alongside him. They went round the pasture a few times, gradually picking up the pace to a canter and then to a full gallop with Fleet always running beside him. It was clear that the stallion was at nowhere near his full pace but he clearly loved the chance to run. Even as the other horse began to tire, Fleet seemed to have energy to spare and looked as though he could run like that all day.

As they returned to the stables, Edward dismounted, gave both horses some water, then removed the halter from Fleet's neck and began grooming him. 'There, you liked that didn't you?' he said aloud. 'See, the halter's not so bad. We'll do it again tomorrow.'

'What was that all about,' asked a young girl who was standing beside the entrance to the stables. 'Is that all you have to do all day, ride horses round and round a field?'

Edward had noticed the girl at the Vill before but had no idea who she was, except that she was the prettiest girl he'd ever seen. She was about his age but tall and slender with a straight back and long yellow hair that hung in two braids. Her eyes were vivid blue and she spoke with a soft and soothing voice.

'I'm just teaching him not to fear the halter. Next time I slip it on he'll expect something good to follow so won't resist. Then I'll try a saddle, then some reins. Once he's used to all that I hope he'll let me ride him.'

The girl looked surprised. 'Nobody has ever done that before but I've heard it said that you have a way with horses,' she told him.

'Horses do seem to trust me,' managed Edward. 'And Fleet knows now that I mean him no harm.' With that the dog emerged from the stable with its head down and growling, clearly resenting the girl's presence.

'Unlike some creatures I could mention,' said the girl looking at the dog. 'He's a horrid beast.'

Edward laughed. 'He's not so bad when you get to know

him. I grant you that he'll never make a house pet for he's been ill used so often that he no longer trusts anyone. But he growls only to protect his territory.'

The girl didn't look convinced. 'Perhaps, but I wouldn't like to cross him. Still my uncle will be pleased to see what you've achieved with his horse. I'll be sure to tell him.'

'Your uncle?'

'Yes, Lord Osric who is Governor here. He's my father's uncle, so therefore mine as well.'

Edward was not sure what to say or how to address the girl now that he knew who she was. 'So that means your father is…'

'Oswald, yes. He's the Garrison Commander here and also trains the fyrd.'

'I think your uncle would like to ride Fleet himself one day,' managed Edward, desperately trying to think of something to say that might keep the girl from leaving.

'He is a beautiful horse,' she said softly.

'You can stroke him if you like. I'm sure he'd let you.' With that he steadied the horse and soothed him as the girl stepped forward and gingerly stretched out her hand. He showed her how Fleet liked to have his forehead stroked; then she ran her hand down his neck as well, smoothing out his glossy coat as she did so.

'See, by nature he's a very gentle creature,' said Edward as Fleet nuzzled her hand.

'He is,' she said admiringly.

'Do you ride?' asked Edward.

'Of course not!' she snapped, stepping away from the horse. 'It's not considered proper for young ladies such as me to sit astride a horse.'

110

'But you'd like to?'

'That's silly. I'll never get the chance.'

'I could teach you. If your uncle would let me, that is.'

'I think he would,' she said tentatively. 'But my mother would never approve. Nor my father for that matter.' With that she turned and walked away, stopping only to glance back and smile.

Only as she left did Edward realise that he'd not even asked her name.

* * * * *

'Get a move on boy,' shouted Ulrich. ''Tis time for you to see what real work is all about, not rubbing down a few horses and picking up their shit from the stable floor.'

Edward looked confused.

'The fyrd, boy! The fyrd. 'Tis time for the training. You live here now so must do your bit the same as everyone else.'

The training area was a large open space set within the fortifications just to one side of the North Bridge. Many men seemed to have stopped what they were doing and begun making their way there, including all the men who lived within the settlement and made up the resident fyrd plus some other boys of about Edward's age, none of whom he knew except Coenred. All the fyrd were obliged to devote time to training together so that they could be relied upon to fight as a cohesive unit, so Edward did as he was ordered and went at once to join them. Also present was about half of the permanent guard, the other half forming a small contingent to remain on watch whilst the session was underway, supported by those members of the fyrd from the outlying settlements and farmsteads who were in Wareham as part of their rostered duty.

Edward was not sure where he should stand among so many men, for they seemed to have gathered in several distinct groups, each knowing their place. It was Oswald who, when he saw Edward standing alone, called him over.

'Can you draw a bow, boy?' he demanded realising it was his first time at a training session.

Edward shook his head.

Oswald looked him up and down. 'No, you're too puny for that. We'll try you in the shield wall. Join those men over there and do exactly as they say or you'll get hurt for certain, as will others, do you hear me?'

For the training, the men divided into two teams both of which formed up in three lines to simulate a shield wall. Edward was ushered into the first row of his group and given a shield to hold. The man next to him was a broad-shouldered giant known as Aelwyn but he seemed far from happy to see him.

'Tell me you've you done this before, boy?' he bellowed.

Edward shook his head.

'Jesus Christ! They've given me a novice! For God's sake heed me well or you'll get us both hurt. We lock our shields together thus,' he instructed. 'This is only practice so both groups advance on each other to get used to moving as one but our role is sometimes just to stand our ground and try to hold or even push the enemy back. Either way, keep your shield in place at all times and as they slam into us be ready to brace yourself. If this was a real battle, the job of those behind us would be to use their shields to cover us from arrows, javelins and God knows what else the bastards would throw at us.' He looked to see if Edward was listening. 'Then see them men behind us with them long-handled spears?' he continued. 'They'd try to skewer the bastards from between our shields and...' He could see that by then Edward was confused. 'It's a bloody shield wall,' he said sounding frustrated. 'We have to drive the bastards back, hold them off or hack them down if we can. All you have to do is keep your shield raised and locked to mine. And remember, one gap, one sodding gap, is all it takes in a battle for us both to get our bellies split open like ripened fruit.'

When ready, the men from both groups began beating the backs of their shields.

'Close up!' shouted Oswald.

All did as he ordered and men began shouting and calling out as they tried to secure their positions. Edward could already feel the pressure from those behind and leaned back against them to avoid getting squeezed out of line.

'Advance!' ordered Oswald.

Suddenly both units moved forward, closing on each other with their shields raised.

Edward was caught completely out of step. He found himself still pushing back when the rest of the group were moving forward. Needless to say he stumbled and, as he fell, the second and third ranks simply advanced over him.

'Stupid little sod!' said one man, then Edward felt a foot kick hard into his side and another crunch down on his face. The rest tried to avoid stepping on him whilst still moving forward but, when he dared to look up, Edward could scarcely see through the blood which was streaming from his nose and all but covered his face. Even from what little he could see he knew he was in serious trouble, for his whole rank had faltered, the gap created by his falling having destroyed their cohesion. The other group had spotted the gap and driven hard into it, pulling men out where they could and giving them all a beating. At that, the rest of the shield wall broke up as well and all within it were at the mercy of their opponents. Only Aelwyn was still standing defiant as he called others to join him to re-form their rank, but it was all to no avail as most had already fled. It was supposed to be a practice session yet all there knew that Oswald would expect them to behave as if it were real as only then would it serve as a lesson to them all.

When at last it was over, Oswald strode across to where Edward still lay and towered over him. 'What the hell were you trying to do! Five men at least would have died for your stupidity!' Then he remembered that they were going to need the boy for his plans to form an elite squad, so left his rebuke at that and instead just stared down at him.

Edward could think of nothing to say in his defence.

'Give him something else to do,' called one man. 'He's not yet man enough for the shield wall.'

'Give the little sod the banner to carry.'

Oswald nodded. 'Get out of my sight and find someone to dress your wounds.' With that he turned and walked away.

Edward had no idea where he was supposed to go but Sigbert, whom he'd met when they'd attended the raided farmstead, came across to help him. He was one of the most tested men there having been in a battle several times and thus saw it as his job to help the others, particularly those who had little or no experience.

'Are you all right, boy?' he asked kindly, looking at Edward's wounds.

Edward nodded and answered as best he could. He had a few small cuts and several bruises but his nose was bleeding profusely.

'Go to see Ida at the kitchen,' suggested Sigbert. 'She'll see you right.'

Taking his advice, Edward went to find Ida who was busy preparing supper for all who resided at the Vill.

'Lord, what have you gone and done to yourself now?' she said when she saw him. She then stopped what she was doing and washed his face. As his nose was still bleeding, she pinched it tight and made him throw back his head.

'You'll need to wash those clothes,' she insisted. 'Here, put this on.'

Without speaking, Edward took the simple tunic she offered him. It was coarse and not well made but he could see that his own was soiled with mud and covered in quite a lot of blood. As he turned to thank her he was suddenly aware that the young girl he'd met at the stables had joined them. She was laughing at him, which made her long braids seem to dance. 'What have you done to yourself?' she asked.

'I was in the shield wall,' he managed, his words almost lost as he stared at her.

'Then you obviously didn't use your shield very well,' she teased.

Edward shook his head. 'It was my first time and…'

'Obviously,' she said. 'And probably your last I should think.'

'They're going to give me the banner to carry,' he said proudly.

'Are they,' she said.

'Yes it's a great honour, isn't it? To carry the Lord's banner?'

115

Both Ida and the girl seemed to find that amusing.

'What's your name, boy?' asked the girl.

'I'm called Edward,' he managed.

'Well, Edward. I don't know whether it's an honour or not but one thing's for certain, even if it is you'll not live long to enjoy it.'

'What do you mean?'

'I mean that it takes two hands to carry the banner.'

Edward looked even more bemused.

'Two hands means that you can't carry a shield as well,' she explained. 'Nor any weapon other than a seax or a knife with which to defend yourself. Also, every bowman and spearman will target you so that in battle you'll be one of the first to fall, that much is certain. Those who carry the banner into battle don't live long so it's a role they give to the warrior who is least accomplished and therefore the one they can most readily afford to lose.' With that she left without so much as another word. When she'd gone, Ida helped Edward to change into the fresh tunic. As he stripped off the old one she noticed some marks on his back from where he'd been harshly beaten in the past, so much so that he was permanently scarred.

'What's her name?' enquired Edward suddenly realising that he'd not asked the girl direct.

The old woman looked at him. 'God love us boy, what in heaven's name are you thinking? She's not for the likes of you, so don't get any ideas above your station.' So saying she rolled up his old tunic and handed it back to him. 'Here, you can return the one you're wearing when you've washed your own. You can go to the river for that.' As she turned away he had to ask more about the girl.

'What does she do here?'

The woman turned and laughed. 'Do? What does she do? Odelia is no less than the daughter of Oswald, who in turn is the nephew of Governor Osric himself! She doesn't "do" anything except to await a suitable match which with her good looks will almost certainly be a nobleman of some standing. So lower your eyes when you see her – like I said, she's not for the likes of you, you cheeky knave.'

* * * * *

The day had gone badly for Edward, not just because of the injury to his nose which was sore and wouldn't stop bleeding, but also because he had twice been disappointed. First, he'd naively thought that being given the banner to carry would be an honour. Second, meeting Odelia had surely lifted his spirits, yet any aspirations he had in that respect had been cruelly snatched away from him as well. Worse, he had often heard it said that misfortune never comes alone. Thus his heart sank when he returned to the stables to find Coenred and two other boys waiting for him.

He knew Coenred all too well and also recognised the others as having been at the fyrd training session. They'd therefore all witnessed him making a fool of himself so he doubted they'd come to be friends. Whilst waiting, they'd amused themselves catching rats using a long flat piece of wood with a spike driven through one end so that the point of it projected out on the other side. They had a small dog with them which rummaged through the straw, chasing out the rats which the boys took turns in trying to hit with the 'bat'. A good hit sent the rat hurling through the air to land against the stable wall, the impact of which usually resulted in it breaking its back. A better one had the rat impaled on the spike, wriggling and squirming until one of them chose to remove it with his foot and stamp on it.

'Hey!' said Edward as they approached. 'Please keep your dog off my bedding.'

The boys laughed as they watched their dog cock its leg and piss on the straw which Edward used to sleep on. 'So what are you going to do about it?' Coenred demanded.

Edward said nothing. 'I have to sleep there!' he managed at last.

'So what? You probably piss in it yourself, you puny little runt!'

Edward realised that although they were about his age, they were all much bigger than he was. 'Come on, that's not fair,' he protested.

'What's not fair is that I got kicked several times when the shield wall collapsed because of you. Then Oswald made us do the training all over again.'

Edward bowed his head. 'I'm sorry,' he said. 'It was my first time and—'

Coenred didn't let him finish. 'Sorry isn't good enough!' he warned. Then punched Edward hard in the face.

Edward reeled away in agony, blood pouring from his already injured nose once more. As he straightened up, another boy lashed out at him as well. Edward dodged that blow and tried to return it but all three boys then piled in and started hitting him. He was no fighter but had taken beatings before and knew he had to stay on his feet if he was to avoid a brutal kicking. He moved his arms up to cover his already bloodied face but then felt something strike his thigh. Pain seared through his body as he realised with horror that Coenred had struck him with the bat. As they stepped back, Coenred yanked the weapon free and blood spurted from the deep puncture wound it had made in Edward's leg. He collapsed and, as he lay on the ground, the boys viciously kicked him in the belly and the ribs a few times then ran off when they heard someone coming.

Chapter Nine

'So, I gather my stable boy didn't acquit himself with merit?' said Osric speaking to his nephew soon after the training session had ended.

Oswald shrugged. 'He's harmless enough but he has no backbone if you ask me. I grant you that he seems to know a thing or two about horses but he'll never make a warrior. I don't know why you take such an interest in him.'

'I have my reasons,' said Osric, evasively. 'But why do you say he'll never make a warrior?'

'Because he's a clumsy little shit. He got his legs twisted in the practice for the shield wall and went down before they'd taken more than a few steps. The result as you can imagine was carnage.'

Osric knew all too well what happened when a shield wall collapsed, even in a practice session. 'Ida tells me that whilst he wasn't seriously hurt, his nose was bleeding badly.'

Oswald looked at him curiously. 'A dozen men took a beating as well once the others sensed a victory.'

'You shouldn't let them compete like that. They're all on the same side.'

'I train them to kill instinctively. When it's the Vikings they come up against, both you and they will thank me for that.'

Osric considered that for a moment then acknowledged

the truth of it. Whilst harsh, Oswald's training sessions worked well enough. All had seen the proof of that but they always left at least a few men in need of attention, although it was seldom more than a few cuts and bruises. 'I want you to keep an eye on the boy,' he said. 'Don't let him get roughed up too badly.'

'Why? He has to learn like all the others...'

'Just humour me in this. You said yourself that we use every man according to the skill he's best suited to.'

'And what's a puny stable boy good for except to fill a gap in the shield wall?'

'For a start he's the best stable boy I've ever had. More importantly, his skill with horses is something we may need if we're to try your plan of using horses for the fyrd.'

'So, are you minded to give that a try?'

'I'm considering it. It warrants that at least.'

Since coming up with it, Oswald had thought much about his idea of creating a small elite force and was keen for it to become part of a more offensive strategy. He was therefore pleased that his uncle had not dismissed it out of hand. 'So, would you have me keep the boy away from the fyrd on that account?'

'No, as you say, he must learn like all the others. I assume he'll be carrying the banner for the next few sessions?'

Oswald nodded.

'Good. Then I'll take him under my wing and see if I can teach him what's what. I just need you to make sure that he stays out of trouble.'

'It may be a little late for that...'

'What do you mean?'

'Your old stable boy has been boasting how he and

two other lads taught Edward a sharp lesson earlier this evening.'

'What?'

'They were egged on by all the men who got a beating when the shield wall broke down, though I doubt Coenred needed much persuasion. He's made no secret of the fact that he doesn't much like being consigned to the kitchen as he can't get away with much whilst working under Ida's watchful eyes. I suspect they gave your stable boy a sound thrashing.'

* * * * *

It was Sigbert who had first found Edward at the stables nursing his wounds. The boy had stripped off his tunic to bathe all the cuts and bruises, cleansing them as best he could with a rag dipped in the horses' trough then wringing out the bloody cloth on the stable floor.

'I don't like the look of that stab wound to your leg,' said Sigbert, sounding worried. 'Does it pain you much?'

Edward just nodded.

Sigbert was even more concerned when Edward explained what had caused the wound. 'I'll go to fetch Ulrich,' he offered. 'He should know of what's happened here.'

'Please don't,' pleaded Edward, for he'd found that reporting such matters was seldom for the best when it came to dealing with bullies.

'A fight is one thing,' said Sigbert. 'But this is too much and can't go unreported.' With that he made Edward as comfortable as he could, then went to fetch the Reeve. When they returned together Ulrich was hardly able to believe the state that Edward was in.

'What happened here?' he demanded.

When Edward explained, Ulrich realised at once just how serious it was. He ordered him to get up to see if he could still stand but it was immediately obvious that he could only do so with great difficulty. 'If there was any blood from the rats still on that spike, the wound is likely to fester,' he said looking worried. 'Sigbert, go to fetch the girl at the nunnery,' he ordered. 'She'll know how best to treat it. Tell her to come at once. We can't allow wounds like this to go untended, I've seen men die having suffered less.'

As Sigbert went to fetch the girl, Ulrich continued to do what he could. 'Strip off the rest of your clothes,' he ordered. 'Let's have a proper look at what else the little sods have done to you.'

* * * * *

When Ingrid arrived at the stable she found Edward sitting there, near naked and shivering. He was embarrassed that she should find him like that but she dismissed his protests.

'I've tended men often enough before,' she said, scolding him. At Ulrich's insistence she first looked at his leg and frowned when he explained what had caused the wound. She sent Sigbert to fetch fresh water from the well, then set about looking at all the other cuts and bruises as well.

Ingrid was slightly younger than Edward and, although neither of them knew they were related, he seemed at once familiar to her. He, on the other hand, was in too much pain to notice whatever slight resemblance there was, particularly as most of their features were not in any way alike. In fact, quite the opposite given that she had red hair whilst his was fair.

'Do you have a balm to help the wounds to heal?' asked Ulrich.

'For the cuts and bruises yes,' she said. 'It's mixed from wild garlic, onions, wine and salt, all of which have been brewed together in a copper cauldron. It will help them to heal and also serve to soothe them.'

'What about the stab wound to his leg?' he asked.

Ingrid seemed less certain of that and more than a little worried. 'It must be cauterised,' she insisted at last. 'And quickly so before it starts to fester.'

Ulrich nodded his agreement. With that Sigbert took another pail and went to collect coals from the kitchen fire and also a skewer. When he returned, he set the pail down beside Ingrid and placed the skewer in the still glowing coals, gently blowing on them to ensure they remained as hot as possible. Whilst they waited, Ingrid wound one of the cloths she'd been using into a strop and gave it to Edward to set between his teeth.

'This will hurt like hell,' warned Ulrich. 'But believe me, there's no other way.'

Edward looked petrified at the prospect of what would follow. He'd heard about how such wounds were treated and was so ill at ease with the prospect that the colour drained from his face and his whole body trembled.

'Trust me boy, they administered the same treatment to me when I was injured by an arrow during the battle at Edington, but it was done too late. Thus my leg stiffened and I've walked with a limp ever since.'

Edward swallowed hard.

'If you prefer we could leave the wound to fester then hack off your leg to save you?' teased Sigbert, trying to lighten the prospect.

Without waiting for an answer, Ulrich then nodded to Ingrid to indicate that she should proceed as soon as she was ready.

The girl gently soothed Edward's brow and smiled at him. 'It'll be over and done with before you know it,' she told him softly. 'Now, put the strop between your teeth and bite hard against the pain when it comes.'

Edward did as he was told.

Ingrid then had him stretch his leg out straight and turned it slightly whilst Sigbert moved the pail of red-hot coals to where she could reach it more easily and, more importantly, where the boy wouldn't see her take hold of the skewer. Using a rag wrapped around the handle to protect her hand from the heated metal, she grasped the skewer, then deftly pressed the tip directly into the wound.

Ulrich and Sigbert both gripped Edward tightly as he strained against the agony, his eyes screwed tight and his scream barely muted by the strop. It was soon over but not before Edward had passed out and lay limp and wasted on the stable floor.

'I'll apply the balm to all the wounds now,' said Ingrid, looking at the lad. 'Then let him sleep. Have someone tend him for the next few days, applying more of this balm and fresh bandages every day. Also sniff the wound to his leg when you do and if there's any sign of infection, send for me at once.'

* * * * *

Osric and Oswald had barely finished supper when a messenger arrived at the North Bridge on horseback saying

125

that he was carrying word from Lord Alfred and needed to speak with Governor Osric without delay. He was taken to the Vill and told to wait just outside the Hall until Osric and Oswald were ready to receive him. When he was eventually shown through, he found both men seated along one side of a table and was at first not sure whether he should insist on seeing Osric alone and in private.

'You can speak freely,' insisted Osric. 'My nephew here commands the fyrd so needs to know whatever news you bring.'

The Hall was barely lit, having just two flickering torches. He therefore approached closer to the table than might normally be permitted, then dropped to one knee as he held out a small scroll of vellum. Oswald accepted it then passed it to his uncle to read first.

The messenger remained kneeling until Oswald told him to rise, by which time Osric had finished with the document, having used a lighted taper to see it clearly. He passed both to his nephew so he could read the message as well, then spoke to the messenger direct. 'Do you know the content of this?' he asked.

'No, my Lord,' replied the messenger. 'I was ordered to bring it to you in person and not show it to anyone other than those whose name I've been given.'

'Then presumably you've taken it to all the other major settlements along this part of the coast as well?'

'Some, my Lord. There are others I must reach before morning. Word is also being carried by others to those which are further afield.'

Osric nodded then told the guards to leave them. 'Take this man and give him food,' he ordered, then spoke to the messenger direct, passing back the scroll as he did so. 'When you've eaten, you'd best be on your way. Make what haste you can for it's indeed most urgent and must reach all those who would hear it without delay.'

The messenger bowed. 'Will there be a reply, my Lord?' he asked.

'No, there'll be no reply tonight. If I need to, I can send someone from here tomorrow.'

With that the messenger and the guards left.

'So,' said Oswald. 'What the hell do we do now?'

Osric was still considering the implications of the message which reported that a fleet of over one hundred vessels had attacked Exeter. Alfred had marched to relieve the settlement but found the Vikings had retreated back to their ships before he could get there. He now feared they were patrolling the south coast looking for fresh targets. 'Well, they're yet a good way from here,' he said as calmly as he could, though the news clearly worried him.

'That's as may be,' said Oswald. 'But they're still much too close for comfort!'

'Don't worry, Alfred will quickly have the measure of them,' explained Osric. 'Even a hundred ships will find him more than a match if they dare to attack any of the settlements on the coast of Wessex.'

Oswald still looked far from convinced. 'Yes, but this could well be one of the first places they'll try! The harbour here is one of the few places which could accommodate so many ships.'

It was a good point and Osric was pleased to see that his nephew was considering the wider implications of what could well be the start of the full-scale invasion they feared and expected. 'Then we must stand ready to receive them,' he said bluntly. 'Ensure that all are alerted to the risk and that those charged to keep watch on the coast remain vigilant. If the fleet does come this way we'll need all the warning we can get.'

It was Oswald who then spoke. 'This threat couldn't come at a worse time,' he mused. 'Many men are still busy on the land and we dare not distract them from that.'

'Nor shall we,' said Osric. 'Our fortifications should suffice. Most likely the first thing that will happen is that a few ships will break away from the main fleet looking to profit for themselves ahead of the others.'

Oswald still looked unconvinced. 'That we could handle well enough. But what if the whole fleet comes straight to attack us instead? We can't possibly defend this settlement against a hundred ships as that could mean as many as 4000 or even 5000 men!'

'We won't have to,' Osric assured him. 'At least, not unaided, for Alfred will keep track of them and come with his army to reinforce us if they do.'

Despite Osric's calm reassurance, it seemed that his nephew still had doubts. 'Uncle, that's all very well but Alfred is already fighting on several fronts, not only here but also in both London and Kent. He can only spread his men so thin before he becomes outnumbered. And if other Viking warlords smell even the smallest chance of success, they'll flock to join this fleet – or perhaps select other targets of their own.'

'Which is why we must all play our part,' said Osric. 'Just make sure that everyone is fully prepared and remains vigilant.'

'Much good will that do us! We've been fighting these heathen bastards for as long as I can remember and still they keep coming – only now it's in even greater numbers than before!'

Osric rose as if to leave. 'Be that as it may, we have to ensure we're ready, for this may herald that war will soon begin again in earnest. And if that's the case, you can be sure of one thing – the worst is yet to come.'

* * * * *

It was just after the messenger had left that Ulrich came to give Osric his daily report. When he told his master about all that which had happened to Edward, the Governor was furious.

'What! Why did you not tell me sooner?'

'My Lord, you had so much to contend with…'

'But this is more serious than I was led to believe! Will he mend?'

Ulrich hesitated for a moment. 'It's hard to say, my Lord. I had the girl Ingrid from the nunnery attend him. She cauterised the puncture in his leg, then applied balm to that and to all his other wounds. The boy will be stiff and bruised beyond reckoning but I think he'll recover in time, though whether he'll ever walk properly again remains to be seen.'

'Tell me, did the boy say anything when he first saw Ingrid?'

'Say anything, my Lord? What should he have said?'

Given that Ingrid and Edward reputedly shared the same father, Osric was interested to know whether they'd recognised each other in any way, though of course Ulrich knew nothing of that.

'She's a very striking girl if that's what you mean,' mused Ulrich. 'With that red hair many men look twice at her but I think young Edward was in too much pain to notice her in that way.'

Osric smiled and let that aspect of the matter drop. 'How many were responsible for setting about him?' he asked, changing the subject.

'Coenred was the main culprit but there were two others with him as well, not to mention those who encouraged them. I'll see that they're all punished, my Lord.'

'Do that. Start by making an example of Coenred, for he deserves to be flogged for what he's done. Let me know when you ascertain who else was involved and we'll decide how best to punish them as well.'

Ulrich acknowledged the order.

'I'll go to see Edward tomorrow and look at the wound myself. I'll also ensure that the dressing is attended to. Hopefully he'll still be able to carry out his duties once it's healed.'

'Aye,' said Ulrich. 'Which is more than that wretch Coenred will be able to manage once I've done with him.'

Chapter Ten

Oswald arranged for a proclamation to be prepared warning that a large fleet of Viking ships could soon be attacking settlements all along the coast of Wessex. It urged everyone to remain vigilant at all times and was signed by his uncle as Governor and then pinned up at several places throughout the settlement.

As few people could read, those who could were told to ensure that everyone knew exactly what the proclamation said. Needless to say, word then spread quickly enough given that Wareham had once been taken and ransacked by a ruthless Viking force, albeit some fifteen years earlier.

That done, Oswald's next concern was to send word to all the outlying settlements and farmsteads and to notify the men who were stationed at the various watchtowers along the coast. All were ordered to remain alert and to replenish the warning beacons with fresh firewood and ensure they were properly maintained. Whilst he hoped all that had been done as a matter of course, he wanted to be absolutely certain that the defences were all in good order. To that end, he also ordered men within Wareham to carefully check the perimeter earthworks and fences and to ensure that the stores included adequate provisions to withstand a siege. Beyond that, there was not much else he could do as their fate then rested in the hands of God.

* * * * *

At just after midday, Coenred stood in the training area with his back to the whipping post, stripped to the waist and with his hands tied in front of him. He was trembling as Oswald recited the charges which had been levied against him.

'You have caused bodily harm to another,' he said sternly. 'There were others both present at the time who are guilty of aiding you in this crime, but you are the main offender. I am appalled that it took three of you to beat a stable boy almost senseless but even for that you would have received nothing more than a stern warning. However, to set about an unarmed boy with a weapon is not within our creed. The sentence for that alone is ten lashes unless you can give good cause for your actions.'

Coenred shook his head. He had been beaten before but never whipped. Yet he'd seen what happened to those who had and was terrified, not just of the cruel lashes themselves, but also of the pain he would suffer as the weal marks left on his back took their time to heal. He knew there would be no mercy; he would be expected to endure the pain and then carry on his duties without complaint, though as like as not would find it difficult to even straighten his back for the next week, never mind work. 'It wasn't just me!' he pleaded, hoping for a last-minute reprieve. 'You said yourself there were others who had a hand in this!'

'Take your punishment boy and learn from it,' ordered Oswald. It had fallen to him to oversee the flogging on his uncle's behalf, Osric having declined to attend in person on the basis that even though he'd ordered it, he'd seen enough whippings and had no wish to see yet more. Likewise, many others who had served in the fyrd found better things to do with their time than watch.

Coenred shook his head, tears running down his cheeks. He looked at the five Saxons who had been ordered to witness the brutal punishment, all of whom were thought to be among those who had encouraged him to beat up Edward as revenge for what had happened when the shield wall collapsed, though none of them seemed inclined to admit as much in the boy's defence. Osric was therefore determined to make a point by forcing them to watch what was meted out to the wretch. Ideally, he would have punished them as well but was anxious not to do anything to diminish morale given what they'd learned from Lord Alfred's message the previous evening.

'Proceed!' ordered Oswald. Two of the guards stepped forward, forced a strop between Coenred's teeth, then untied his bonds and turned him to face the whipping post. His hands were then retied to a cross bar so that he could do nothing to avoid the whip. As he waited for the cruel punishment to begin, Coenred felt the warm trickle of urine run down his legs. Realising that he'd pissed himself with fear, he crossed his legs then looked back at Oswald pitifully. One of the men who was there to witness the flogging glanced down at the damp patch on the ground and sneered. Then, at Oswald's insistence, another of the guards stepped forward brandishing the whip.

The first lash bit deep into Coenred's back. He tried to cry out but his voice was muted by the strop. The second and third brought tears to his eyes but after that he felt nothing, for he'd collapsed and was held in place only by the fact that his hands were still tied to the crossbar. The men either side of him knew better than to let him hang there limply like that so did what they could to lift him up and support him until the punishment was over.

* * * * *

Several of the women from the settlement tried to comfort the old crone who had survived the raid on Leonine's farmstead but none had managed to do more than arouse her anger. They took her small gifts of food but it seemed that her rage was so deep set that she hardly saw those who were trying to help her, mistaking them in her mind for the Viking raiders who had doubtless butchered or taken her kin. Thus, although still constrained by ropes for her own protection, she ranted and raged at everyone who dared to get too close.

'We should untie her,' advised Osric when he went to visit her that afternoon. 'She feels she's a captive here and that makes her ravings worse.'

Ulrich thought he was joking. 'Shall we give her back her knife as well, my Lord? She can then more easily murder us all if that's what she intends…'

Osric was not amused. He'd taken pity on the woman as it seemed that no one from the settlement at Wool was prepared to recognise her as kin. 'She's of Saxon blood,' he announced loud enough for all to hear. 'And there are enough people intent on enslaving us, so we should not do as much to one of our own. Release her beyond the fortifications. There she may perish or come to her senses and return calmed and hopefully more settled. Either way it's kinder than keeping her here bound and frightened like a tethered beast.'

Ulrich thought it was madness but did as he was ordered. Before releasing her Osric spoke to the woman direct. 'Old woman, you are ever welcome here. Go where you will but return if you wish. Food and drink shall be left for you daily on the bridge across the river yonder. Fare you well and may God be with you.'

As soon as her bonds were released she ran off across the bridge and then into the marshes, cackling like an old witch as she went. Most thought never to see her again.

* * * * *

Having arranged for the old woman to be set free, Osric went next to visit Edward taking his great-niece, Odelia, with him. As they approached the stable they were aware that Fleet was standing just inside it, almost as though he was keeping guard over Edward who was lying on his straw bed under a blanket, still nursing his wounds. When Edward saw who it was he reached up and let Fleet nuzzle his hand as if reassuring the horse that these were friends who meant him no harm. To Osric's surprise, the horse backed off a little but remained nearby as if still intent on protecting the boy, just in case.

It was clear that Edward was in a great deal of pain. He told them that all his other wounds were marked by heavy bruising and they could see for themselves that whilst his nose was not actually broken, it still looked extremely red and sore.

'What about your head,' asked Osric, surprised to find the boy in reasonable humour. 'Does that pain you as well?'

'In truth, it does a bit, my Lord,' replied Edward who,

with Odelia there, was anxious to show that he could endure his pain without undue complaint.

'Then I'll send word to Ingrid. She has a potion she makes from the bark of the willow which may help with that. I'll have her send some for you to imbibe.'

'Thank you, my Lord.'

'Now, what about the wound to your leg?' asked Osric. 'That's the one which most concerns me.'

Because of the dressing Ingrid had applied, Edward was not wearing leggings so was able to unwind the bandaging to show them that it was both raw and swollen, so much so that he could scarce stand unaided.

'Odelia will come each day with the maid from the Vill and have her change that dressing and apply more balm,' offered Osric. 'But you must rest for several more days to give the wound every chance to heal.'

'But the horses will still need feeding and…'

'The horses will be fine,' Osric assured him. 'I'll have Coenred resume his duties until you're well again.'

'If it please you, my Lord, let me continue to mind them. I'll rest when I can and do only what's needed, but I want them to trust me, particularly Fleet.'

'Fleet seems to have taken to you,' mused Osric. 'I see that you now leave him free to roam in the pasture at will.'

'Yes, my Lord. He prefers that. He needs fresh water each day but otherwise can look out for himself. It's the other horses and the mule I worry about. And also the dog.'

Osric thought for a moment. Secretly he was impressed with how committed the boy was but he knew that the lad needed to rest. He also realised that Edward was anxious not to have to confront Coenred again. 'Very well,' he agreed. 'Odelia will keep me advised of how you fare and I'll have Sigbert come by to do what's needed until you're well enough to manage for yourself.' With that he looked at the dog. 'Though I'm not sure he'll be keen to do anything with that vicious hound. Every man in the settlement is afraid of it!'

'He's not so bad once he gets to know you. He asks nothing more than a few scraps from the kitchen and to be left alone. Besides, Sigbert doesn't have to go to near him. He can just toss the food on to the ground beside the kennel and he'll find it soon enough for himself.'

'It seems you have a way with all animals, not just horses,' observed Osric.

'They all respond to kindness, my Lord. Not like people who it seems to me thrive only on hate and cruelty.'

* * * * *

'Well, at least that bastard Coenred was properly punished,' said Sigbert when, at Osric's request, he went to help Edward and could see how much pain the boy was in. 'You can take some comfort from that. So what would you have me do?'

'Thank you,' said Edward. 'If you could turn out the horses each morning and provide feed and fresh water for them they'll manage well enough, though they'll need to be brought in again at night.'

Sigbert nodded though in fact he had little experience of caring for horses.

'Ideally, they'd be groomed but that can wait. Hopefully I'll be well enough to do that myself within a few days. The stables will have to be mucked out and if the farm horses are needed they'll have to have their harnesses attached and...'

Sigbert raised his hand. 'I'm sure we'll manage if you show me what's needed day by day. Lord Osric has promised to pay me or at least regard the time I spend here as part of my dues so I'll be happy to assist where I can.'

They did indeed manage well enough. Edward found that with Sigbert's help the horses were looked after even though it was, by his reckoning, not quite all that was needed. However, he looked forward to Sigbert coming each day, though not as much as he did the visits from Odelia, even though she never once came unless accompanied by Mildred, the maid from the Vill.

* * * * *

It was several days before Edward could stand properly and even then he could only walk if he avoided bending his leg so that he limped along like a cripple, relying on support from a stick which Sigbert had fashioned for him.

In the meantime, Odelia and Mildred had been visiting each evening so that the maid could sniff the wound for signs of any infection and renew the bandage after applying more of Ingrid's balm. On one such visit they found Fleet standing over the boy and were not sure whether it was safe for them to enter the stable.

'Don't worry,' said Edward. 'He'll not harm you. He likes to make sure that I'm safe, that's all.'

It was almost as if Fleet could understand what was said for with that he withdrew and trotted out into the field to graze, leaving Edward to Mildred's ministrations. Odelia always insisted on accompanying the maid who seemed to find it strange that such a noble young lady should show concern for a common stable boy.

'He's my uncle's stable boy,' explained Odelia. 'And he has need of him. Thus he's charged me to see that all his wounds are treated daily.'

It was doubtful that the maid believed this was the real reason and she said as much to others so that rumours soon began to circulate. Whilst she'd probably not instigated them herself, there was no doubt that she was at least in part to blame for the way they spread. The rumours became so prevalent that Oswald challenged his uncle on the matter.

'My daughter's reputation is becoming tainted,' he accused. 'You're using her to tend your stable boy and tongues are wagging.'

'Idle gossip,' snapped Osric, dismissing the charge. 'It's your maid who actually tends him so what harm can there be in that?'

'That's as maybe,' said Oswald. 'But there's no smoke without fire. And the cook tells me the boy has aspirations of his own in that respect. You must put a stop to this before it's too late. Or would you have my daughter be obliged to marry a humble stable boy?'

Knowing of Edward's true lineage and bloodline, Osric laughed at the prospect but could reveal nothing of what he knew to his nephew.

'Why do you find that so funny?' demanded Oswald angrily.

'I'm sorry,' explained Osric. 'It's just that there are things you cannot know. Secrets shared only by a few who are bound by oath to keep them. All I will say is that whilst Matthew is, as you say, a humble stable boy, he's also an honest lad who knows his place. But there is more to him than that.'

'Matthew?' queried Oswald. 'Who the hell is Matthew? We're talking about Edward, your stable boy.'

Osric suddenly realised his mistake and raised his hand in apology. 'I'm sorry, my mind was elsewhere. I was thinking of someone else, someone I used to know of whom the boy reminds me.'

'Then you had best call your mind to the matters in hand – and in particular to the reputation of my daughter.'

'You're right. He can fend for himself now anyway. He's much improved and I gather the risk of infection has passed. I'll have him report to Ida in the kitchen if he needs anything more by way of treatment.'

'That's a lot of trouble for a stable boy,' observed Oswald.

'He's the best stable boy we've ever had. And diligent too. Thus he warrants the trouble it takes to see him well again. Besides, we'll need him to help implement your plan for the fyrd to use horses which, given Alfred's message, may be required much sooner than we think.'

* * * * *

That evening Mildred looked at Coenred's wounds and pouted. 'They've spoilt your beautiful skin,' she said sadly, then ran her hand through his hair. She was clearly as playful and wanton as usual, but Coenred was in far too much pain to respond.

'Will the wounds leave a scar?' he asked.

She examined the livid weals which still striped his back. 'I fear they will. The whip has cut deep into the flesh so will

140

surely leave its mark in several places,' she told him. 'Here, let me tend them again.' So saying, she took a cloth, dipped it into the bowl of fresh salted water and gently bathed each wound in turn. He winced even at her light touch as the salt seemed to bite into those parts of the wounds which were still raw and open.

'That bastard Edward will pay for this, you mark my words!' he swore aloud.

Mildred scoffed. 'So far all you've done is favour him. My mistress always comes whenever I go to attend him and I swear that if I wasn't there…'

'Don't worry, he'll pay for the wrongs he's done to me!' stressed Coenred. 'I already owe him for getting me assigned to the kitchen where I spend all day fetching and carrying piss pots and pig swill. And now I owe him for these stripes on my back as well but I will get even, I swear it!'

'You've gained as well,' suggested Mildred modestly.

At first he was not sure what she meant.

'Through working here you've been able to enjoy my favours more often. Surely that's compensation enough?'

Coenred grinned, then turned to face her. He put his hands on her breasts and fondled them freely, though made no attempt to go further. 'Then you'd best tend me well. For I can scarce bend my back at present, never mind tup you as you would like.'

Mildred giggled. 'And who says I want to be tupped by the likes of you?'

'Well, if you don't, it comes as a surprise to me, for I've not once heard you complain.'

'Well, there is a way whereby you could tup me whenever it pleases you.'

'You mean if we were to wed?'

She laughed. 'And why would that not suit you?'

Coenred was suddenly in no mood to continue what they were doing and was certainly anxious to avoid answering that particular question. Instead, he picked up his tunic and, despite the pain, pulled it on over his head and then made his excuses and left.

* * * * *

'So how does Fleet's training go?' asked Osric when he next went to the stables.

Edward whistled for Fleet to come and Osric was impressed to see the horse pick up his ears, then, when Edward whistled again, trot over to join them in the stable.

'As you can see, he fares well, my Lord. Whilst recovering and doing only light duties I've used the time to work with him. He now wears the halter without complaint and is becoming used to it, for he likes what follows.'

'Which is what, exactly?'

'He gets to run beside me whilst I ride your other horse, though always with the halter. He loves to run and to race, the problem is not letting him get too far ahead for he can outpace any other horse with ease.'

'Good. But are you up to riding?'

'In truth, I find it much easier than walking, my Lord. Though I dare not let either horse get out of hand lest I should fall.'

'So, when will you try Fleet with a saddle?'

'Soon, my Lord. But I must first get him used to carrying the weight of a man on his back.'

'Excellent.' With that Osric sat down on a stool from where he could watch Edward work. 'Come and sit here,' he said after a short while, pointing to another stool. 'I would have you tell me more about yourself.'

Edward stopped working and looked down at his feet, not sure what to say as he felt awkward at the prospect of sitting beside his master.

'So, you are the son of Emelda?' asked Osric.

Edward nodded.

'You should not be ashamed of that,' said Osric. 'Or perhaps you're inclined not to speak of it because men tell you she was a whore, am I right?'

Again Edward nodded.

'Then you should know that your mother was not a whore by choice or by nature,' Osric assured him.

'You knew her?' asked Edward.

'Aye, but not in the sense that most men might claim to know a woman in her position. She was commanded to become a whore by Lord Alfred because her father was a traitor. Someone was needed to quell the base desires of the men who sheltered with us in the dark days at Athelney and she was the only option we had. As I say, it was not in her nature and many of us regretted what was required of her.'

'Then did you know my father?'

He knew he had to be careful how he answered that particular question. 'Perhaps. But it's not for me to say. If it was who I think it was, then he was surely a good man and a very brave warrior. But all the men at Athelney were worthy, so you can be proud of whoever's blood you have in your veins. That's all I can say for now.'

Edward smiled, gratified to hear someone say something

good about his bloodline for a change. 'So either way my father was probably a warrior!' he exclaimed, clearly delighted at the prospect. 'If that's so, then 'tis a pity I can't emulate him,' he said.

'Perhaps you can,' suggested Osric. 'I can teach you the basics of combat, though not with the sword, for my skills are not as once they were. However, there are things you can learn which may help you to defend yourself if you are attacked again.'

Edward looked up at him, not sure what to say. 'Thank you, my Lord. You're very good to me and yet I don't really know why,' he managed.

'Good stable boys are hard to find,' he lied, hoping the lad would be satisfied with that, but he could see the doubt in Edward's eyes. 'If your father was who I think he was then he once did me a great turn, for which I owe him my thanks.' With that he held up his hand to stop any further questions. 'Don't press me on this, for I'll say no more. Suffice to say that I value your service and also have a plan with which you can help me, so to teach you what I know is the least I can do. Now, how's that leg?'

Edward got to his feet but still limped as he took a few steps.

'Does it still pain you?'

'A little, my Lord. It seems stiff and awkward but, as I said, I can ride and manage my duties well enough if that's what you're asking…'

'No, I can see that plain enough. Let me look at it again.'

With that Edward stripped off his leggings so that Osric could examine the wound itself. It seemed to be healing well enough, a scab having formed, but the skin around it was still puckered from where the heated skewer had been used. 'And what of all your other wounds?' he asked.

'They also seem to be healing well, my Lord,' said Edward.

'Yet you still walk with a limp?' observed Osric.

'It is only very slight,' said Edward. 'Some days I hardly notice it at all.'

'We'll give you time to fully heal but next week you have a journey to make.'

'A journey, my Lord?'

'Yes, to buy horses. I plan for you to go with Ulrich to Our Lady's Day Fair at Wimborne. I shall need you to advise on which are best suited to our needs.'

Edward looked excited.

'But first I need to teach you how to defend yourself. We can start your training now, even if your leg still pains you, for a warrior must often fight on despite his wounds.' With that he passed Edward a staff. 'Although a plain and simple weapon, this has been cut from seasoned oak and is as strong as iron. Hold it and feel the weight of it.'

Edward did as he was told.

'Now, drop low and, as you do so, strike out at that sack of feed over there as hard as you can.'

Again Edward did so, but the stroke made little impression.

'You must learn to put all your weight behind each stroke,' advised Osric. 'But practise keeping your balance, for if you stumble your opponent will have you at his mercy. Also, listen to this and heed it well for it's a secret few but the very best warriors ever truly understand. In battle, each fight lasts but a few strokes. If it goes on longer you'll tire yourself and even if you then prevail, your next opponent will find you an easy kill. You must therefore seek to win the contest as quickly as you can. So, wait for the chance to strike and don't waste your efforts. Then strike and prevail. Two moves. One to take away his guard, the second to fell him quickly and cleanly. A third stroke will then ensure that he stays down – whether dead or just wounded, it matters not. Finish it as you will and move on.'

Edward tried wielding the staff but without much success so Osric took the broom used for sweeping the stable and demonstrated. His first blow knocked Edward's staff aside, the second came down hard from above, stopping just short of his head. Edward tried his hand again but Osric drove one end of his staff into his chest, then, as the boy stumbled backwards, delivered a blow which, had he not stopped it in time, would have struck the side of his neck.

'Remember, the staff is three weapons in one. You can use the length of it to block your opponent's blow. You can wield it to smite him from above or from the side or you can drive the end of it into any part of his body left exposed. If delivered hard enough, a blow to his face, his belly or his ribs will all fell him and leave him wasted. As a last resort, a good root with it between his legs will surely stop him and cause him to lean forward so you can then smite him across the back of his neck.'

Osric could see that Edward had done enough to start with. 'Practise that every day until you master the art of putting all your weight and power into each stroke. You should be able to split that sack of feed wide open with a single blow. If your arms tire, help them to get stronger by lifting the weight of the sack and carrying it back and forth as many times as you can each day.'

146

Edward liked the idea of learning how to defend himself and offered the staff back to Osric, meaning to find one for himself.

'No, I want you to keep it as it's stronger than anything you can fashion for yourself. But you must practise with it, Edward. Practise with it until you can do no more, then practise again despite the pain.

Chapter Eleven

I t was a few days later that the body of the old woman who had survived the raid at Leonine's farmstead was found floating in the river. It was assumed that she'd drowned herself but those words were not actually spoken, as to take one's own life was regarded as a sin for which there could be no redemption. Father Emmett was therefore reluctant to give her a Christian burial in the grounds of the Minster.

'If we inter her on consecrated ground, I fear that her damaged soul may taint those of the other good Christians who are buried there,' he warned when the matter was raised.

Osric was not prepared to accept that. 'Who are we to judge her?' he argued. 'We can't be certain that she took her own life. After all, she was both old and frail, so for all we know she may have simply slipped and fallen into the river. Besides, if her mind was turned by all she'd seen and endured, then surely God would not begrudge her the comfort she would find in Heaven?'

Father Emmett reluctantly agreed but as she'd only been at the settlement for such a short time there were few to mourn her passing and none who had even learned her name. Hence her burial was witnessed by just those who had tried to help her and by Osric as part of his duties as Governor.

* * * * *

Despite the threat of invasion being on everyone's mind, life within the settlement went on regardless, although all dreaded any news of the Viking fleet being sighted. For his part, Edward continued to practise with the staff just as Osric had shown him, paying particular mind to putting as much force into each blow as he could manage. To this end, he worked hard to improve his strength and soon found that he could wield the staff more easily and to much better effect, even managing to split sacks with ease.

During that time he also took every opportunity to continue training Fleet to be ridden, knowing that it would take time and patience if he was to avoid breaking the horse's spirit. Old Colbert had once explained to him how it was done, stressing that it depended on first winning the horse's trust, something which Edward was certain he'd already achieved.

The next part of his plan began as soon as he was able to stand unaided. He started by tethering Fleet to a post and, having soothed him, climbed up on to a stool, then laid himself gently over the horse's back so that he became used to the weight of a rider. At first, Fleet reacted by shying away but, apart from that, it didn't seem to distress him unduly so Edward repeated the process several times, remaining there for longer each time. He always followed this by praising the horse and offering a handful of oats or an apple as a reward.

That accomplished, Edward shortened the tether, then produced a saddle blanket which he first allowed Fleet to sniff before placing it gently over his back. Although initially unsure about it, Fleet quickly accepted the blanket without complaint so Edward then laid himself across it as well, then swung his leg over so as to sit properly astride the horse for the very first time. Sensing the change and not much liking it, Fleet tried to back away from the post but soon realised that with the shorter tether any refusal was pointless. Edward repeated the exercise several times, gradually lengthening the tether until eventually he didn't need to use it at all. At first, Fleet didn't seem to realise that he was no longer restrained but, when he did, he bolted out into the pasture and settled into a fast and almost frantic gallop. With no bridle, Edward clung to the stallion's mane for all he was worth, particularly when Fleet seemed to remember he was there and so bucked and even kicked out his back legs in an attempt to dislodge him. Yet the horse's protests were quite half-hearted as all he really wanted to do was run, even if it meant taking Edward with him.

Within a few days it was as though he had fully accepted the position and actually seemed to enjoy it. It was as they continued to work together in this way that Edward found out just how fast the horse could run. As the ground simply flew beneath them he realised that never before had he known a horse to be so aptly named.

The hardest part was getting Fleet used to a bridle. He started by placing it over the horse's head then gently persuading Fleet to accept the bit. It took many attempts with the horse always trying to spit it out but, with patience and encouragement, he persevered until Fleet accepted it. He then left it there whilst they raced around the pasture but at that stage made no attempt to use the reins in order to control the horse. He saw no danger in that given the confines of the pasture so simply let Fleet have his head whilst he held on as best he could. Gradually, he taught him how to respond to his signals by anticipating the horse's moves and pulling on the reins accordingly so that Fleet quickly learned what each movement meant. At first he was not sure whether Fleet would understand his signal to stop, but the horse did so instinctively. After that Fleet quickly learned all that was being asked of him.

After each session Edward dismounted, then praised the horse as usual, knowing that the bond between them had allowed him to train the stallion more easily, but he also knew that he still needed to school Fleet so that others could ride him as well. That meant getting him used to the saddle.

To do that, Edward let Fleet watch as he first saddled Osric's mare so that he would see that she was not perturbed by having one placed on her back. Then one morning he put a saddle on Fleet's back as well, having first let him sniff it before securing the girth strap. He left it there as he mounted the mare and let Fleet run freely beside them as they went for their customary gallop. Fleet clearly didn't like the saddle but tolerated it well enough, seeming to ignore it rather than miss out on their run. Then, once he seemed used to it, Edward didn't get the mare from the stable as usual; he simply led Fleet from his stall, tethered him to a post, fitted his bridle and threw first the blanket and then the saddle on to his back. Then, without making any fuss whatsoever, he simply mounted the horse, pulled a little harder on the reins than normal and guided him to the open pasture.

* * * * *

During this time Osric visited Edward on several occasions under the pretext of concern for his horse's progress, which he could see was going well. He marvelled at the way the boy had gradually persuaded Fleet to trust him and could see he was right, the horse would be better schooled by kindness and coaxing rather than force.

On each visit it became their habit to spar with the staffs for a short while and Edward soon found that his skill improved, but the real difference was in his confidence, which was reflected in his ability to surprise Osric with some deft and clever moves.

'The art of a warrior is to see any weakness in your opponent,' explained Osric after a particularly arduous session during which Edward had fought well and given a good account of himself. 'The signs to look for are not hard to spot but can make all the difference when it comes to combat.'

Edward looked puzzled.

'A warrior who is fresh and confident will hold himself erect. If he's tired his shoulders will stoop and his weapon will look heavy in his hand. Look for those signs and for any wound or weakness. A man will always favour one limb if the other is injured, which is why you must try to hide any pain you feel from that wound to your leg. It will be spotted quickly enough by any seasoned warrior and could thereby be your downfall. If you see such signs in an opponent you have two options. Either exploit it and prevail as quickly as you can, which, as I've told you before, is what you must try to do in a battle because you need to preserve your own strength to fight on.'

'And the other?' asked Edward.

'The other applies if your opponent is weary, for then you can tire him further and, when he looks as though he's all but done, either kill him or spare him as you see fit.'

Edward could see there was cold logic in all Osric had

told him. 'But, my Lord, what if I can see no weakness and he holds himself strong and ready?' he asked.

Osric smiled. 'Then stare directly into his eyes. The man who then looks away is not to be feared, but if he returns your gaze and holds it, you're confronting a true warrior and will need all the skills I've taught you and more. In that case strike fast and prevail as quickly as you can, bring him down and then finish it. In contests such as that there can be no room for mercy.'

With that Osric looked tired so they settled on the stools where they could talk further. 'You must come to know your weapons,' he explained. 'Swords are only for those noble or rich enough to afford them but they carry a value far greater than their worth in silver. The reputation of the warrior who wields it is a significant part of its provenance as is that of those whose blood has soiled its blade. In terms of other weapons, most men carry what they can find or that which they use for hunting. Thus a spear is most common, for a good man can easily fashion one for himself.'

'What about an axe?' asked Edward.

'Ah, now that's a truly fearful weapon to come up against. The daneaxe is the most terrifying of all, for it can be used to haul a shield aside or split a man's skull even if he's wearing a helmet. Hence the Vikings often favour it as it strikes terror in the heart of any foe even before the fight begins. But hear me on this, whilst deadly in attack, it takes two hands to wield one effectively and it's much more limited in defence, particularly if it becomes embedded in a shield, for that leaves the one who wields it exposed as they struggle to prise it free.'

Edward listened intently, surprised at how much he needed to learn and master.

'This is a weapon I favour,' continued Osric producing a seax from a leather sheath he wore at his side and offering it to Edward to hold. 'I used to carry something quite like it but with the sheath strapped to my back.'

'Is it a short-bladed sword or a long-bladed knife?' asked Edward, having never before held one.

Osric laughed. 'It's both. We use it for battle at close quarters, particularly in the shield wall where it can be wielded where there's little room for a longer blade. It can be thrust out to strike between the shields of those pressed up hard against us so that they fall and thereby open up their own defences. You'll recall from your own experience what happens when a shield wall is breached.'

Edward needed no reminder of that. He felt the weight of the weapon and even from what little he'd seen of fighting in a shield wall could well imagine the damage the blade would do at such close quarters.

'We'll work with all these weapons in time,' said Osric. 'But for now, do you have any questions?'

'There is one other thing, my Lord, but it has nothing to do with combat.'

'What is it?'

'Your great-niece Odelia no longer comes to visit,' he said, knowing that in asking about her he was trespassing on that which he was allowed to mention given their respective ranks.

Osric tried not to look too surprised. 'And why should she? She served you well enough but it's not her place to attend a lowly stable boy!'

Edward knew that Osric was not angry but said no more, preferring to accept what he knew to be true. Nonetheless,

Osric was left in no doubt but that the boy wanted to see her again.

'Anyway, there's no time for you to dwell on matters of the heart, you cheeky knave. You've a journey to make tomorrow.'

'A journey? Where to, my Lord?' asked Edward.

'To Our Lady's Day Fair at Wimborne, there to buy some horses. I need at least five good mounts.'

Edward looked surprised. 'Five horses! What for, my Lord?'

Osric hesitated before replying. 'We have a plan to use them to get some members of the fyrd more quickly to where they're needed,' he explained. 'So we're looking for fast steeds like Fleet.'

Edward shook his head. 'Fleet is a superb horse, my Lord, but you'll not find another like him in the whole of Wessex. His bloodline includes stock which comes from lands far away from here where such creatures are much prized for their stamina and speed. But why would you buy such fine animals anyway? You'd be better securing sure-footed ponies which can cope more readily with rough terrain, even when carrying a heavy load such as a man plus his weapons and supplies.'

Osric was impressed with Edward's logic and said so. 'You're right. And not only will they be cheaper but the men will be more used to such mounts,' he noted.

'And why buy them, my Lord?' added Edward. 'There are many which roam the moors freely, could we not simply round them up?'

'That would take time, not only to catch them but also to train them. All the men are busy at this time of year and, with the threat of an imminent invasion hanging over us, we need to keep them here to defend the settlement, not go chasing about on the moors looking for horses. Perhaps in the winter we can think of getting more that way. Would you know how to round them up if we do?'

Edward nodded. 'I've heard it said that you form a pen and drive the horses to it, then close the entrance behind them. You then simply cut out the ones you want, rope them and lead them away.'

'That all sounds simple enough but what about then training them?'

Edward thought about that carefully before replying. 'I've never trained one to the saddle, my Lord,' he admitted. 'Whilst they wouldn't be as spirited as Fleet, training a horse which is not used to people is likely to be a much harder task.'

'Well, we can worry about that when the time comes. For now we have precious little time to spare. Horses are traded at the fair in Wimborne. I therefore need you and Ulrich to go there to buy what we need and thereby get our plan underway as soon as possible.'

'Will you be coming with us, my Lord?'

Osric shook his head. 'No, I have other duties which will keep me here. But I will send another man to help you. Do you think you can manage to find what's needed?'

'I'll do my best, my Lord.'

Osric placed his hand on the boy's shoulder. 'I'm sure you will. And I have great faith in you for you've shown you have a wise head on those young shoulders. I was minded to reward you for all your good work in training my horse but, on reflection, I fear that if I do your head will soon grow too big so I think I'll just box your ears instead.'

* * * * *

As the men gathered that evening for the next training session of the fyrd, Oswald outlined his plan to use the horses. Most thought it was a good idea, though several were worried about how they would learn to ride.

'Edward will go with Ulrich to buy the horses which, with those we have already, will make nine at our disposal if you include the farm horses, plus, of course, we have the mule but that's too stubborn for us to rely on. We'll need more in due course but for now that's all we can manage. They'll be stabled here so that Edward can look after them and ensure they're always ready when needed. Eventually we'll all ride to meet the raiders but for now I shall pick ten men who, with myself as commander, will form an elite force to strike as soon as the raiders are sighted. Our task will be to find where they've moored their ships, then wait there until they return, at which point we'll keep them pinned down with arrows long enough for the rest of the fyrd to arrive and support us. After that we'll slay the bastards, recover whatever plunder they've stolen and free any Saxons who've been taken for slaves.'

All seemed to like the idea, for most had suffered at the hands of raiders in one way or another but had seldom had the opportunity to strike back.

'Once we have enough horses, all members of this new elite squad will ride but, until then, those without mounts will travel with Edward by cart to where they're needed, carrying our weapons and supplies as well. Edward will then remain with us to look after the horses whilst we wait for the raiders to return to their ships. That way, if we find we've taken on too much and need to retreat, we'll have the horses on hand to ensure we can do so.'

All seemed to accept that, so Oswald outlined his plan for a competition to decide who among them would form the elite squad. 'Our task will be to pin the Vikings down on the beach with arrows so we shall need good bowmen. Therefore you each have a chance to practise, then we shall set a target and those who lodge an arrow closest to it shall be picked. As I say, it's the main skill we shall need so let's see who among you are the best marksmen.'

After a few trial shots the men assembled ready to try their hand. Oswald set up a straw buttress to which he pinned a small square of cloth marked with an X in the centre. The men lined up and each took their shot in turn. The one whose arrow landed furthest from the mark or any who missed the target altogether then dropped out and the remainder took three steps back, then tried again. Eventually just ten men remained but, as everyone was enjoying the competition with numerous ribald jibes and comments being exchanged, he let them carry on until just one man emerged as the winner. Few were surprised that it turned out to be Sigbert, who was not only one of the most experienced warriors in the fyrd but also known to be a good hunter. He was given a small coin as a reward for his skill and offered the privilege of going with Ulrich and Edward to buy the horses.

* * * * *

As Edward watched the contest, Ulrich came across to stand beside him. 'Impressed?' he asked.

'They seem more than able,' said Edward, surprised at how skilled they were yet not sure what he was expected to say.

'Most use a bow for hunting, so have had much practice,' explained Ulrich, seeming almost envious of those who were to join the squad, perhaps recalling his own days as a warrior and wishing he could take his place among them. 'But it's all very well shooting at targets or game, confronting a warrior who is coming at you intent on hacking you to bits with a daneaxe is quite another. It's then that a warrior needs to know what he's about.'

'Lord Osric has told me much about what to do when facing another man in combat,' said Edward.

Ulrich looked at the boy, surprised that Lord Osric should have said anything to him about fighting – for it seemed strange that he'd even spoken to the boy at all.

'He showed me how I might defend myself if set upon again,' explained Edward.

'Well, then you'd do well to listen to Lord Osric on such matters, for few are as able as him in that respect. Not only that, but he's fought in and survived more battles than most men can count.'

Edward nodded to acknowledge the point. 'I believe he was once chief of the King's personal guard?'

'That's true. I was proud to serve under his command at that time and never once saw him falter. The years have not been kind to him but he's a man most warriors still respect and will gladly follow. If he gives you any advice about fighting then you'd do well to heed it. For if you're to go with this so called "elite squad" even just to mind the horses you can be sure of one thing, sooner or later you're going to find yourself in a battle.'

Chapter Twelve

For the journey to Wimborne, they planned to follow known tracks or drovers' trails where they would be relatively safe, although the prospect of meeting armed robbers could never be discounted. They would travel by cart so as to be able to purchase saddles and bridles as well as a host of other items Ulrich had been instructed to buy, the money for which he carried in a purse secured to his belt. It was mostly coin but he also had a small quantity of silver from which pieces could be hacked off and weighed to cover the purchase of the horses or some of the more costly equipment. All told, it was more than most men would feel safe carrying whilst travelling, hence both he and Sigbert were armed. Sigbert was wearing the leather jerkin which he normally donned for the training sessions with the fyrd and had placed a spear and his bow in the cart where he could quickly reach them if needed. Ulrich was similarly attired in his own war gear but also carried a seax which was tucked into his belt where it could be plainly seen by all.

'The war gear and weapons are just a precaution,' explained Sigbert when he could see that Edward looked worried at the prospect of there being any trouble. 'After all, 'tis better to be safe than sorry.'

As always, they started out early as it would take at least four hours for them to complete the journey there and as long again for them to return. On the way, Ulrich explained how he intended to agree a price for the horses. 'You are to carefully look each one over then let me know what you think,' he instructed Edward. 'I shall then ask the owner for his best price and negotiate from there. If I look towards you during the haggling you are to shake your head as that will make the seller think that we're inclined to walk away. If he calls our bluff we can always return to him later, but most will be anxious to avoid losing the chance of a ready sale. Also, be sure to reject some horses to make it clear that we are not about to buy any old nag,' he added.

Edward understood at once and was looking forward to it. Sigbert on the other hand complained that his time would have been better spent at his trade. 'I wish now that my aim had not been quite so good,' he moaned. 'I look forward to serving in the new squad but someone else could have wasted their time on this fool's errand.'

Ulrich laughed. 'You'll have your part to play right enough,' he said. 'I have a bag of coin and silver here which many men might see as an easy target. And trust me, the fair attracts as many rogues as it does honest traders.'

Although not as big as Winchester or Chippenham where Alfred's royal Vills attracted a constant stream of merchants and petitioners, Wimborne was still a bustling and busy settlement, particularly on the day of the fair. The noise of so many people arguing and bartering was distracting as they each called out to draw attention to what they had to offer. Some wandered from place to place whilst others set up stalls or carts loaded with the goods and produce they hoped to sell. There were also men offering fresh baked bread, meat pies, cheeses or mead, all of whom seemed to be doing a lively trade.

Ulrich drew their cart up beside one of the pens containing livestock and let it be known that he was there to buy horses and was prepared to pay a fair price. As word of that spread, the horse traders soon came to seek him out. Most of them found it strange that it was left to a stable boy to assess the mounts though none mentioned it, thinking it might be easy to dupe him. They soon realised their mistake.

One horse in particular was a chestnut mare with a fine flowing mane.

'You'll agree that she's in fine fettle,' said the man who seemed overly keen to sell the horse, even as Edward examined her.

Edward stepped back. 'Indeed she is,' he said having checked her teeth. He then looked first at Ulrich then at the seller, both of whom waited expectantly. 'And must have been well treated to have lived so long!'

As Ulrich and Sigbert burst out laughing, the seller grabbed the horse's tether and stormed off, muttering something under his breath about the boy knowing nothing about horses and wouldn't recognise a good one even if he saw it.

Ulrich looked at Edward approvingly but said nothing.

'Sir, that horse was well beyond her prime,' said Edward as if to explain himself. 'She would have made a docile mount for a lady or a child but would tire too easily for what you have in mind.' Neither Ulrich nor Sigbert were of a mind to disagree.

Another horse brought before them was clearly in foal, though the owner said nothing of this. Edward pretended not to notice as he went through the motions of looking the animal over. When he'd done, he announced that the horse would be an excellent bargain. 'Not least because with this fine animal you'll soon get two for the price of one – though I doubt she'll be of much service until she's dropped the foal.'

As they rejected the horse, Ulrich realised that the boy did indeed know horses and had a keen eye. He watched as Edward vetted each animal carefully, looking at their teeth, running his hand down each leg and then watching them walk to ensure they weren't lame. He also rode any which seemed to suit their purpose, thereby gauging their temperament. He rejected many if only to show that he was not about to buy anything other than serviceable mounts and only when he approved a particular horse did Ulrich begin to negotiate a price. There was one particular horse which Edward took an immediate shine to: a piebald mare aptly named as Knave. He'd first noticed her when her owner was showing her to various possible buyers, all of whom also liked the look of the horse but quickly changed their minds when they realised that she had a vicious and uncertain temperament. In fact, the horse became something of a spectacle as several men sought to subdue her, all of them without success. The first to try was bitten when he grabbed her reins and tried to force open her mouth to inspect her teeth whereas the next one caused her to rear up when he went towards her wielding a stick. The last man to try resorted to shouting at the frightened horse but he nearly got caught when she turned away from him and kicked out with her rear hooves. Both Ulrich and Sigbert looked surprised when despite having seen all that, Edward went over to the horse to look at her more closely.

'May I examine her?' he asked calmly.

The horse's owner scoffed. 'Why, do you think you can do any better?'

'Perhaps,' said Edward, then offered the horse a handful of oats. 'Easy girl,' he whispered, letting her nuzzle his palm. 'No need to get riled. We're going to be friends you and I.' With that he reached up and stroked the mare's neck.

'Well, I've never seen anyone manage that,' admitted the owner. 'Not in all the time I've had her.'

'I'd like to ride her if I may,' suggested Edward.

'Phew! Good luck with that if you've got the balls,' said the owner. 'But I warn you, if roused she can be a real handful, can this one.'

Edward reached up and gently stroked the horse's forehead. Once she was used to that, he laid his hand firmly on her back and kept it there as he eased his way round to stand to one side of her, then waited thereby giving her enough time to settle. When he was sure she was ready, he lifted himself into the saddle and, once astride the mare, leaned forward and whispered something in her ear. Gradually, he coaxed her to walk up and down a few times, then dismounted before praising and petting her some more. To everyone's surprise she then even let him check her over without complaint.

'She'll do,' announced Edward when he'd finished. 'But only if the price is right. It'll take a lot of work to school her properly.'

The man looked surprised and then quickly named his price, but it was much too high.

'You'll not sell her to anyone else today as all here will have seen what she's like,' warned Ulrich. 'If my stable boy says he can manage her that's good enough for me, but I'm not keen to take on a troublesome horse. At least, not at that price.'

The man reluctantly lowered his figure slightly, but even then Ulrich was far from satisfied. 'I'll pay half that, but only if you throw in the bridle and the saddle as well.'

The man looked shocked and protested but Ulrich was having none of it. 'Take it or leave it,' he said. 'This boy is probably the only one in Wimborne who can handle this mare. And certainly the only one fool enough to try!'

The owner looked dismayed but realised he didn't have much choice so accepted the offer. Once he'd gone, Ulrich asked Edward how he'd managed her.

'I simply approached her calmly and openly from where she could see me, not creeping up at her from the side or from behind,' said the boy, stroking Knave and feeling particularly pleased with the purchase. 'The others sought to beat or bully her into submission, something which I'll wager she's become well used to over the years. Thus when that man approached her holding a stick and the other one grabbed her reins, it served only to make the poor beast defensive. Horses need to know who's master, but showing kindness settles them far quicker than a whip.'

By early afternoon they'd secured all they needed in terms of both horses and equipment but, before leaving the fair, Ulrich bought some hot food for them all. 'Don't worry,' he said. 'We can afford this from what we have left over, especially as that last horse cost so much less than the others, thanks to young Edward here.'

Having supped well, they began to make their way back to Wareham. Ulrich rode in the cart which was, by then, fully laden with all the gear they'd purchased, so Edward suggested that he and Sigbert should walk behind, each with a string of horses in hand. Travelling thus, the group had not gone far when they encountered a band of men who appeared from within the trees which lined the road at that point. Edward and his two companions were alarmed, particularly when they realised that the road was blocked both ahead of them and behind. They knew at once that the rogues were intent on stealing the horses and whatever Ulrich had left in his purse.

'What do you want with us?' demanded Ulrich.

'Your horses and your purse!' said one of the rogues, a big man with long black hair which was tied back with a silver ring. He looked to be an unpleasant fellow, his clothes and face dirty and his chin unshaven for many days. To everyone's surprise, it was Edward who responded.

'The horses are in my charge,' he said defiantly, passing the reins of those he was leading to Sigbert. 'If you steal them I shall be required to make good the loss.'

'Then my heart bleeds for you boy,' he said, then stepped forward as if intending to examine the beasts more closely.

'It's not just your heart that will bleed if you come any closer,' mocked Edward bravely. 'Or perhaps you've enough men hidden in the trees to make a fair fight of it?'

The thief looked surprised. 'What's the matter boy, can't you count? We have six men. That's two to one and all of us are armed. I fancy we'll not need better odds than that.'

Taking his staff from the cart, Edward just smiled, trying to remember at least some of what Osric had taught him. '*Strike and prevail,*' he whispered to himself by way of a reminder. He also remembered to look his opponent in the eye and noticed that when he did so, the man almost immediately looked away. He knew then exactly what he had to do. Although the man was armed with a seax which looked old and pitted, it was doubtless still sharp enough to cause a serious wound. So, as he edged towards Edward and raised his weapon, the boy didn't hesitate even for a moment. His staff came up and struck the man hard between the legs. The rogue groaned, then dropped to his knees, dazed and in obvious pain. Edward raised the staff again and prepared to finish him with a blow to the back of his head but held back from doing so when he realised the man was already beaten.

'So, would anyone else care to feel the weight of my staff?' he challenged. 'Or are we agreed that the horses are mine?'

Not one of the robbers seemed inclined to argue, particularly when Edward looked back to see that Ulrich had jumped down from the cart by then and that both he and Sigbert had their weapons in hand, ready to make a fight of it.

The robbers clearly thought better of taking on a group of three armed men of which even the youngest was clearly a skilled fighter, so slowly backed away. As they did so, Sigbert went across and put his hand on Edward's shoulder. 'Well, that was a turn-up, that's for sure,' he said admiringly. 'Where the hell did you learn to fight like that?'

Edward just grinned, knowing better than to mention that he'd been taking lessons from none other than Governor Osric himself.

* * * * *

The rest of their journey passed without incident but, once back at the Vill, word quickly spread about how Edward had so bravely taken on the leader of a gang of robbers and despatched him with a single blow.

'The boy used his staff to hit him where it hurts,' said Sigbert, laughing as he recounted the story to the men who were gathering to inspect the new horses even though it was dark by then. 'The poor bastard went down hard and barely had the strength to stand after that, never mind carry on fighting!'

'Tripped over his feet more likely,' said one of the men.

'Yes, that's something the lad could teach him, for he knows how to lose his footing right enough,' teased another.

But the banter was so good natured that Edward took no offence when he overheard what was said. It seemed that everyone was even more impressed with his ability to select the horses, particularly when Sigbert recounted how Edward had seen through the man who was wont to sell them an old nag and also the one who had forgotten to mention that his mare was in foal. The Saxons loved that sort of humour and began to form a more kindly opinion of the boy.

In the meantime, Edward started settling the horses into their new surroundings. Feeding and grooming them all would mean that he would have to work late into the evenings from then on but he made no complaint as it was work he enjoyed. Until an additional shelter could be constructed there was not enough room in the stable for them all so he decided they would have to be left to graze freely in the pasture, even overnight. That meant that when they were needed he would have to hurriedly round them up, work for which Fleet was much too finely bred. He therefore selected Knave for that job and decided that she would also be kept in the stable so she would be on hand when needed and where he could begin to calm her, advising everyone not to even attempt to ride her until he'd done so. 'She's aptly named,' he warned. 'For she seems less inclined to do as she's told by me or by anyone else for that matter. She can also be quite vicious – there were men at the fair who can testify to that!' Having sorted out all that, Edward showed all the horses to Fleet one by one as if introducing them and seeking his approval for the new arrivals.

* * * * *

Even though most of those selected to form part of the elite squad could ride well enough, Oswald decided that they should all undergo some further training as they were only used to sturdy farm animals. Therefore improving their riding ability was to become part of the fyrd's training sessions and an additional one was called for the following afternoon for that very purpose. He decided it would also encompass other training as well given the threat of a possible invasion still loomed large in all their thoughts.

Whilst attending, Coenred started beating one of the horses which he'd been told to fetch for one of the men to ride. It had stubbornly refused to move and the more he beat it the more steadfast it became. When Edward saw him, he quickly dismounted from Knave, took up his staff and went to confront the bully.

Coenred was using a birch twig to brutally whip the horse whilst it was still tethered, striking it so that it whinnied and tried to back away in terror and pain.

'Leave it alone!' challenged Edward.

It was the excuse Coenred had been waiting for. He

turned to face Edward, still swishing the improvised whip viciously from side to side. 'Then perhaps you'd like to take its place?' he said, grinning.

To his surprise, Edward made no attempt to back off. Instead, he stood his ground and seemed more than prepared to make a fight of it. 'It's not like you to take on even a defenceless horse without your bully boys at your side,' he sneered. He recalled what Osric had taught him about looking for his opponent's weakness but already knew exactly where that was, for Coenred had complained often and loudly about how the weals on his back still pained him and refused to heal. The only problem was that he would need to get in close if he was to exploit that weakness without getting caught by the whip. He realised that in doing so he would probably suffer at least one lash but, if he could endure that, he knew he'd have the bully at his mercy.

As the men gathered round sensing a fight, Edward simply smiled, then half turned as if to step away. As he did so, Coenred raised the whip intending to strike him whilst his back was turned, but Edward gave him no chance to do so. Instead, he sprung towards the coward, taking him completely by surprise. In fact, if anything he got too close as he jabbed the end of his staff hard into Coenred's belly. As the bully groaned and leaned forward to absorb the blow, Edward stepped back and struck him again, this time using the staff to swipe him hard across his arched back thereby opening up the wounds from when the boy had been flogged. Coenred screamed like a startled pig, then fell to the floor in agony. There was no need for a final blow, for Coenred was beaten and in far too much pain to retaliate, but Edward's anger was roused. He picked up the whip and gave the fallen coward five hard lashes, one for each of those he'd seen him inflict on the poor horse. Unlike when he'd fought the robber on the way back from Wimborne, this time he seemed to lose control so that Sigbert had to step in to restrain him.

'He's had enough,' he said softly. 'You've had your revenge so let him alone lest you become as guilty as he is.'

Edward nodded, realising he was right, then threw the whip to the ground. He looked at Coenred, whose back was livid with stripes from where the blood from his wounds was soaking through his tunic. Having never before given anyone such a brutal thrashing, Edward felt a surge of remorse and turned as if to explain himself, tears running down his cheeks. It was only then that he realised everyone had witnessed his revenge and now stood in stunned silence knowing that the rumours of his new-found skill were indeed true.

Oswald made no attempt to intervene in what was, after all, a fair fight. He simply hurried everyone back to the training area leaving Edward to attend to the still terrified horse. He calmed it, then led it to where it could graze and get fresh water before rejoining the training session. When he got there, the riding practice was over and the banner lay on the ground as the men formed up for shield wall training. Edward assumed he was expected to carry it but, as he bent to pick it up, Oswald called out to him.

'Leave it, Edward. We'll find a place for you in the shield wall. Coenred can carry the banner from now on, assuming he still has strength enough to lift it.'

Coenred, who was struggling just to keep himself upright, could hardly believe his ears. 'But I'm...'

'There's no place for the likes of you here,' said Oswald bitterly. 'Go and get your wounds seen to and don't bother coming back until you can fight like a man.' With that he turned to Edward. 'Now, let's find a place for you to stand.'

All had been impressed by what they'd seen during his fight with Coenred and were thus more than happy for him to take a place beside them. Sigbert, who had come to like the stable boy, promptly called out for Edward to join him but, in the end, Oswald sent him to stand beside Aelwyn as he had done the time before, even though that session had not ended well for the boy. Aelwyn was the blacksmith and, because of his stature, always stood in the centre of the front row, a position reserved for the strongest warrior. 'This time, do as he says and you'll not go far wrong,' advised Oswald quietly. 'He knows the way of things and will teach you well.' What he didn't say was that if the shield wall did collapse again, Edward would be quite safe standing next to Aelwyn as few men would dare to venture anywhere near the giant in the ensuing scuffle, never mind take him on!

Once again, Aelwyn showed Edward how to hold the shield and lock it into place by overlapping his with those on either side of him. 'Do you remember what I told you last time?' he asked.

Edward said that he did.

'Good, then this time try to keep on your feet as we advance. As we and the other group come together you must brace yourself for the impact. In a real battle, spears and swords would be thrust towards us in the hope of getting the blades into any gaps. All manner of throwing spears, arrows, javelins and even stones would also rain down upon us and men would try to hack your legs from under you to open up our defences. Thus we must keep our shields raised and locked together at all times.'

With that the men started beating the backs of their shields. The rhythm was enough to help them all keep in step but Edward could see little ahead of him as they advanced. Then, as the two lines locked together, the pressure was such that it seemed to suck the very breath from his body. The noise of shouting was incredible and the stench of sweat, piss and wind almost overpowering as both sides used all their strength to try to force their opponents back. They were only using wooden weapons or blunted spears but there was danger just the same, and every man was keen to ensure that his team won. Then, all of a sudden, the other side gave way.

'Stay locked!!' screamed Aelwyn. 'We don't break until ordered to do so!'

Thus, still keeping their positions, they marched over their fallen opponents. As they did so, many men gave those on the ground a sly kick or a prod but, once they were beyond them, victory was theirs. When the word came they broke rank and charged back to complete their triumph.

After the training session Edward thanked Aelwyn.

'You've still much to learn, lad. But you did well enough this time,' the blacksmith assured him. 'It takes practice and we can afford no weak links in a shield wall. But then you know all about that already...' he teased, recalling Edward's first attempt at serving in one.

As the men took a break from the training, Edward went to look for Coenred to ensure that he'd not gone back to take revenge on the poor horse, knowing that such a cowardly act was not beyond him. The bully was nowhere to be found but he was grateful for a chance to check on the horse again. It seemed to have suffered no serious harm beyond becoming nervous and inclined to shy away from anyone who approached it, particularly if they were carrying anything which resembled a stick. Edward did his best to soothe it by gently stroking it and feeding it from his hand. However, even once settled, he judged it unfit to be ridden for the rest of that day.

He didn't mention being unable to find Coenred when he returned to the training session, presuming that he'd gone to have his wounds tended. Instead, he went to stand beside Sigbert and Aelwyn ready for the next phase of training.

As well as their practice in the shield wall, all the men were given the chance to hone their skills with their weapon of choice and, if so minded, also to try their hand with other weapons to see if there was one which suited them better. Few could afford a sword but most had an axe or a spear which were both deadly in close combat. Having mastered the staff to a reasonable standard, Edward was given an axe to try. He seemed to manage well enough but found the weight of it was beyond him so would need a lot more practice if he was to survive his first battle which, with the prospect of the Viking fleet attacking at any time, could well come all too soon.

It was whilst practising his skills that Edward was called over by Oswald and, at Lord Osric's suggestion, given a sword to try.

Oswald questioned why his uncle was so insistent that he should let a stable boy try his hand with a sword, the value of which was so far beyond what he could ever hope to afford that he was never likely to get the chance to wield one. True, he was by then more impressed with the boy and was beginning to think he might yet make a useful member of the fyrd, but he remained adamant that Edward would never become a fully fledged warrior. Nonetheless, he did as his uncle requested, if only to humour him.

'I've seen that you can handle a staff well enough and your strokes with the axe were well intended even if lacking in power, so let's see what you can do with one of these.' Having loaned Edward his own sword to try he stepped back a few paces. 'First, feel the weight of it in your hand,' he advised.

Edward did as he suggested and was surprised to find how heavy it was. He tried a dozen sweeping strokes through the air but already his arm was aching.

'You're gripping it too tight,' advised Oswald. 'Your grasp must be firm but you need to let your wrist flex so that you can present the edge of the sword cleanly to your target.'

Edward relaxed a bit and began to feel the sheer power of the weapon.

'That's right,' said Oswald. 'Let the weight of the sword do the work, that way you won't tire so easily. Your target is not your opponent's shield nor the edge of his sword for that will serve only to spoil your blade by blunting it. Worse still, it might become embedded in his shield leaving you at his mercy. Therefore use your shield as a weapon as well. It's not just to protect you. You can thrust it hard at your opponent to bring him down or you can use it to sweep his weapon aside and thereby open up his defence. But remember, leather and mail are hard to breach even if the blade is keen, so look for any areas which are exposed and then drive your weapon home with all the force you can muster.'

Having promised his uncle to give the boy a fair chance, Oswald allowed Edward to actually face an opponent, albeit using wooden replica swords. The boy did well, the exercises

Osric had suggested using the heavy bags of feed having made a difference so that he found that he could control the blade if not with ease then at least with some confidence. Even so, he found the session hard and very tiring, but he remembered what Osric had told him about keeping the contest short. '*Strike and prevail.*' Edward realised that it applied even more to sword craft than it did to combat with the staff, for the swords were so heavy that no man could wield one for long. 'And remember,' Osric had warned. 'A tired warrior becomes a dead one soon enough.'

After watching him, Oswald seemed impressed. 'I think you now have the feel of it,' he said. 'But you need a lot more practice. What you've learned will be difficult to remember when confronted by a screaming Viking intent on lopping off your head or ripping out your guts. Therefore you must stay calm. Oh, and one other thing. You will have to learn how to kill. It may sound easy, but you wouldn't be the first warrior to die because he hesitated before slaying a man he thought was beaten. Learning how to take a man's life is the hardest lesson of all – but it's one which we learn only for ourselves.'

Chapter Thirteen

No one troubled to look for Coenred. In fact, few people even noticed his absence and those who did simply assumed that he'd gone to find somewhere where he could lick his wounds in private, unable to endure the shame of having been publicly beaten by a much smaller boy. In truth, there was much more to it than that. Although he knew little of such matters, he had begun to suspect that Mildred might be with child. There were no outward signs to suggest as much – or at least, none that he recognised but, nonetheless, he had detected a subtle change in her which he could not otherwise explain. He'd also begun to realise that all the hints she'd been making about getting married might well be for that very reason. Either way, the prospect of being forced to wed a girl who meant nothing to him and who would do little to advance him beyond his lowly station in life was not something he was willing to countenance. He therefore resolved to leave the settlement as soon as he could. Given that he was indentured to serve Governor Osric, it was a serious decision to make – and one from which, once taken, there could be no turning back.

His first thought was to seek out and join the band of robbers which was known to frequent Wareham forest to the north of the settlement. There they preyed on travellers or were not above raiding a small farmstead if they felt they could get away with it, often letting Viking raiders take the blame. Coenred quickly decided against that for, if caught, they would surely face execution and if he was going to be hanged it was going to be for more than a share of the meagre pickings which could be had from some unfortunate traveller or a poor farmer. There was a better prospect but it would mean taking a fearful risk – and that was to join a Viking warband. Whilst it was something few men would even consider, Coenred believed that his father had been a Viking raider and reasoned that that might well explain why he felt so at odds with life in a Saxon settlement. If so, he might fare better with those of his own kind and, with so much now stacked against him, it seemed that it might well be the time to find out.

Whilst he had no intention of trying to join the large fleet of Viking longships ravaging somewhere along the southern coast, he'd heard others say that some of those ships might well leave the main force and strike out on their own, intent on securing plunder for themselves which they then wouldn't have to share with so many others. If that was so, then he might well be able to join one of them. Although he could claim no particular battle skills, there was still much he could offer, not least of which was information about the weak spots in the defences at Wareham which they could exploit if they were so minded. His only worry was that Viking raiders tended to be suspicious of anyone who approached them and, having a hatred of spies and traitors, would most likely kill him on sight. What he needed was a way to convince them that he had something to offer. It was then that a thought struck him. There was the pretty red-haired girl at the nunnery who was almost certainly a virgin.

Although not actually a nun, she was dressed as one and the Vikings wouldn't know the difference. If he arrived with her as a hostage, he was certain that he would at least get a chance to be heard.

He was tempted to tup Mildred one last time before leaving but the wounds to his back were much too sore and, besides, they would give him the perfect excuse to visit the nunnery on the pretext of needing Ingrid's help to tend them. Once alone with her, it would be easy enough to take her hostage; he was certain that a mere slip of a girl would offer little in the way of resistance. He therefore went to the nunnery without saying so much as a word to anyone.

* * * * *

The nunnery provided accommodation for an order of just twenty-five nuns, all of whom resided there under the guidance of an abbess. It was located just beside the quay and comprised a huddle of buildings set within a gated courtyard to which all but the sisters were precluded from entering. It was yet to be fully restored, having been ransacked by the Vikings when they occupied Wareham, and was not a prosperous enclave as its precincts were relatively small. In fact, they extended to little more than a field which was bounded by the river Frome on one side and by the earthworks and fortifications on the other, the rest being enclosed by a feeble wicker fence. Nonetheless, the nuns provided for their modest requirements by keeping a few goats, chickens and geese, plus a garden in which they grew vegetables and the like. They also had a dovecot and several hives of bees but most of what they needed came from charitable donations and gifts in return for which they provided medical assistance and offered prayers for the sick, the dying and the departed. Thus when Coenred appeared at their door, bleeding and looking as frail as he could contrive, he was admitted without question and shown through to a small chamber which was set apart from the other buildings and which served as a hospital for the benefit of all.

Ingrid was immediately sent for and, when she arrived, she had him strip off his tunic and lay face down on a cot so that she could examine the weals on his back and the bruises he'd suffered. She was intrigued by the fact that he had the same red hair as her, though said nothing as she bathed his wounds with salted water before applying a balm to soothe them.

'So why were you beaten so harshly?' she asked him quietly as he dressed himself, her voice sounding full of concern.

'I was falsely accused,' he lied. 'Then the real culprit accosted me to make sure I didn't tell on him.'

'He must have been a brute to inflict those wounds,' she said. 'You should report as much to Ulrich, though I shudder to think who among us could do such a thing.'

Coenred thought for a moment. 'It was that new stable boy,' he said. 'Not content at having taken my place tending the horses, he beat me with a staff then, having knocked me to the ground, whipped me with a birch twig.'

'What, young Edward? Surely, he's not capable of such a thing? He's such a caring and good-natured lad.'

'Do you know him then?' asked Coenred, surprised that she should.

'I tended him when he was attacked by some bullies who

set about him with a stick on which a vicious spike had been affixed. Others here also know him from when he brings gifts of food from the Vill. All say he's a pleasant and well-mannered boy.'

'Well, he attacked me whilst I was unarmed,' lied Coenred. 'He took me by surprise and you've seen the fearful wounds he then inflicted.'

'There are other wounds to your back as well,' said Ingrid suspiciously. 'Some of them are partly healed which suggests that you've been whipped before. Did Edward inflict those as well?' Even as she said it she recalled that the boy who had attacked Edward had been flogged and at once realised the truth of the matter. 'Was it then you who struck him with that awful stick? The one you'd used for killing rats. Were you not punished for that and…?'

At that Coenred knew the game was up. 'What's it to you?' he demanded, grabbing her tightly by the arm and twisting her wrist painfully.

'Stop it you're hurting me!' she screamed knowing others would soon hear her and come to her aid, for one of the nuns always stayed nearby for that very purpose whenever someone was being treated.

'Shut up! You're coming with me!' he insisted.

She tried to free herself from his grip and made to call out again but he pressed his hand firmly over her mouth to silence her.

Ingrid was having none of it. She writhed and wriggled as he started trying to push her back on to the cot. As he did so, she bit his hand so hard that he cried out in pain, then lashed out angrily with his fist, striking her hard across the face.

Ingrid reeled away but Coenred was not done with

her. He grabbed her by the arm again, this time managing to almost throw her on to the cot before ripping at her vestments. She continued to resist him and, in a moment of black fury, he pulled out a knife to threaten her, ordering her to be quiet. Frightened, Ingrid tried to get up intending to push past him and thereby escape his clutches but, in the desperate struggle which followed, she somehow became impaled on the blade.

At first neither of them were quite sure what had happened. In fact, it was only as Ingrid looked down at her shift and saw the pattern of blood rapidly spreading that she realised she'd been stabbed. For his part, Coenred stood there aghast, holding the knife and hardly daring to believe what he'd done.

It was then that Ingrid began to feel faint. There was little in the way of pain after the initial piercing but she suddenly found it difficult to stand so, clutching her wound, she tried to steady herself against the cot but instead sank first to her knees and then to the floor where she lay as blood oozed freely from her wound.

Coenred had not meant to kill her, merely to silence her, but he knew that would count for nothing. Another of the sisters burst in at that point and, seeing him standing over Ingrid's body whilst still holding the bloody knife, turned away quickly meaning to secure the door whilst she went for help. He gave her no time for that. Instead, he grabbed her and struck her as hard as he could. As she still resisted and was blocking the doorway, he struck her again, then, stepping over her, made his bid for freedom.

* * * * *

'And you say that Coenred did this?' asked Osric as he and his nephew looked at the body of poor Ingrid. She had been lifted from the floor by then and laid out on the cot on which she'd tended Coenred, her eyes covered and her torn clothes arranged to preserve her modesty. The other nun who had come to her aid had been knocked almost senseless by Coenred and was, by then, being cared for by others.

The abbess nodded. 'She was a sweet-natured child who wanted nothing more than to tend those who are ill or impaired,' she said sadly.

'So what was his intent?' asked Osric. 'Did he come here to abuse her or had he some other mischief in mind?'

The abbess crossed herself. 'Who can say? But either way it means that no woman is safe even in this Holy place whilst he's at large,' she warned.

'She was a very striking girl,' suggested Oswald who had joined Osric at the nunnery when he'd heard the alarm bell being sounded. 'He'd taken quite a beating earlier so perhaps came here for his wounds to be dressed but then his urges got the better of him. These things can happen.'

'Perhaps that's so,' said the abbess. 'Whilst Ingrid had a gift for healing, I fear that her beauty was the cross she had to bear. It was the same for her poor mother. She too had a rare beauty and was killed in this very chamber whilst giving birth to...' She stopped at that, recalling that she had vowed never to speak of what she knew about Ingar – or indeed about Ingrid and Coenred being born to her as twins.

'We'll know for sure when we find him. Which we will, you can be assured of that,' promised Osric. 'We'll set all to the task and hunt him down so that he can be brought to justice. And when he is he'll surely hang, for a crime such as this warrants no mercy.'

Once outside, Oswald summoned two guards. 'You go that way and you the other,' he said to them. 'Circle the defences and speak to all on duty. If he's intending to make a run for it he'll have to find a way to leave the settlement, in which case someone is bound to see him. Go quickly and return as soon as you have anything to report. He cannot yet have got too far.'

As the men set about following his orders, he went next to the Vill where others who had heard the alarm bell had gathered, including those members of the fyrd who had only just been released from training. He told them all what had happened and ordered everyone to help search for the boy, albeit they had no way of knowing where to start looking.

* * * * *

Coenred had to think fast. He'd also heard the alarm bell and so knew that everyone would be looking for him in earnest. That meant that both the North Bridge and the West Gates would be on full alert and therefore he couldn't use either to make good his escape. He briefly considered clambering over the earthworks but knew there was a risk of being seen by someone if he did. Besides, there was nowhere for him to go from there even if he managed it. Then a thought occurred to him. He remembered the small gap in the fortifications at a place known to all as Bell's Orchard. It led to a path which was considered too narrow to pose a significant threat but was nonetheless protected by a stout gate which was guarded at all times, albeit by just one man. It was sometimes used as a shortcut by guards who were to be posted at the watchtower positioned where the rivers join the harbour.

Whilst he knew that the guard at Bell's Orchard would also have heard the alarm, at least it would mean that he'd have only one man to deal with. He therefore made his way there as quickly as he could, then watched and waited long enough to be sure that the man was still alone before casually sauntering forward.

As soon as the guard saw him he turned and raised his spear.

It was not someone Coenred recognised but at least it wasn't one of the permanent guards so wouldn't be too difficult for him to deal with. 'Any sign of him?' he asked calmly.

The guard immediately relaxed and allowed Coenred to get closer.

'All quiet here,' he said. 'No sign of anyone. Do you know why the bell was sounded?'

'It seems one of the nuns at the nunnery has been attacked,' explained Coenred, keeping up the pretence. 'No doubt the charms of that little red-haired minx who works there proved too hard for someone to resist! I've been sent to relieve you as you're needed for the search.'

The guard looked surprised. 'But I've only been on duty for a short while.'

Coenred shrugged. 'Exactly. That's why you're needed. They're setting up a search party and everyone on duty is ordered to meet at the Vill. Looks like you're in for a long night but you know how it is, orders are orders.'

With that the guard cursed and left Coenred to cover the remainder of his watch as he made his way back to the

Vill. Coenred waited till he was out of sight before opening the gate and slipping away from the settlement as quietly as he could.

* * * * *

Oswald was giving orders to all who had gathered at the Vill in response to the alarm bell, sending them off in groups of three or four to search every corner of the settlement. He was convinced that Coenred could not have got past the guards – or at least he was until the man who had been on duty at Bell's Orchard returned.

'Sir, who is it we're looking for?' enquired the guard.

'That idle wretch Coenred,' Oswald replied hastily, still preoccupied with organising the search.

'But sir, I've just seen him! He told me he was sent by you to relieve me and would take my place on duty at the gate!'

Suddenly all became clear. Oswald ordered the bell to be sounded yet again to summon all to return and then interrogated the guard further.

'How long ago was this?' he demanded.

'Not long, sir. I came straight here. When I left him he was standing guard, just as I was.'

'Then as like as not he means to use the path there to reach the harbour,' suggested Oswald.

Wulfric, Oswald's second in command, looked doubtful. 'Why would he do that, sir? I mean there's nowhere for him to go from there and with scarce an hour or so of daylight left, only a fool would risk crossing the marsh in the dark if that's what he intends.'

'Does he have kin anywhere nearby?' demanded Oswald.

Wulfric was slow to answer. 'None that I know of, sir. In fact, so far as I'm aware he has no kin anywhere.'

'Then perhaps he'll try to reach the road to Twynham from there to make good his escape.'

'That's a possibility, sir. Or given that he'll soon have a price on his head, perhaps he'll try to join that band of robbers in the forest,' suggested Wulfric.

Oswald acknowledged that possibility as well. 'Then we must stop him before he does,' he said.

With that Governor Osric, who had been watching all that was being done but had thus far not intervened, went across and took his nephew aside so they could speak in private. 'There's something more you should know,' he said. 'The boy has Viking blood in his veins. As I recall, his mother was raped by one.'

'How do you know this?' asked Oswald clearly stunned by the revelation.

'There's yet more, but this is not the time.'

'Then do you think he'll try to join a warband somewhere along the coast?'

'I do. At least, it's a possibility we have to consider. As like as not they're the only folk he has and as you and I both know, bad blood will always out. God knows we've seen that happen often enough.'

'Then I wish him good luck with that, for I doubt they'll recognise him as kin,' said Oswald.

'Any more than he knew that the girl he killed was his half-sister.'

Oswald looked shocked. 'What! How can that be. They barely knew each other!'

'It's true, believe me.'

'Are you certain of it?' he demanded.

Osric nodded. 'I am, though for now it must remain a secret. I can say only that they were born as twins to the same mother but of different fathers and were separated at birth.'

Oswald looked at his uncle. 'Are you then saying that he murdered his own sister?'

'So it would seem. Though whether it was an accident or something he intended I cannot say, but their mother was named Ingar – a very wise and talented healer. She predicted that one twin would one day kill the other which is why they were reared apart. It now seems that events have proved her right.'

'Why did we not know of this before?' demanded Oswald.

'Because it was of no concern of yours.'

'But the Vikings will know none of this! They'll kill him on sight!'

'Aye, most likely they will. And maybe that would be for the best. But my fear is that he knows the defences here all too well and will doubtless try to use that to trade with them for his life and for the chance to join them.'

Oswald said nothing at first as it was a possibility almost too terrible to contemplate and certainly not something he'd even considered. However, with his uncle having raised the point, he realised what an extremely dangerous position they were in, particularly with the prospect of an attack by the Viking invasion fleet at any time. 'Then we have to stop him!' was all he managed to say.

'Exactly,' said Osric. 'The question is can we do so in time?'

* * * * *

The path from Bell's Orchard was narrow and had marsh on either side of it. Even as he followed it, Coenred had still to decide where best to go from there, though, as he realised quickly enough, his options were limited. He could strike north and, with any luck, reach Wareham forest. Once there he wouldn't have to look too hard to find the band of robbers for, as a man travelling alone, they'd surely find him readily enough. The question was whether they'd let him join their band or, when they realised he had nothing for them to steal, would simply kill him to avoid their whereabouts being discovered.

Having already decided against that course, his only other option was to risk travelling through the marsh but that carried the danger of either falling foul of the many bogs and pools of quicksand to be found there – or being spotted by those on duty at the watchtower. However, if he could avoid all that and reach the higher ground to the east, there would then be plenty of places where he could hide and from where he could also watch from the cliffs for any sign of a Viking band he might be able to join. They were almost bound to come ashore at some point, if not to raid then to take on fresh water and supplies, so all he had to do was follow them along the coast and go down to meet them when they did. After that his fate would be in the lap of the Gods. He no longer had the hostage to offer them as he'd planned, but he did have information about the defences at Wareham any raiding party would be pleased to learn. In particular, the path from Bell's Orchard he'd used was a weak spot which, although narrow, might enable a small raiding party to enter the settlement unseen under the cover of night, complete their havoc and be gone before anyone could stop them. It didn't trouble him that it meant many people there could well be slaughtered. By his reckoning, they'd treated him badly so deserved all they would get. Besides, there was no one there who meant anything to him.

* * * * *

Oswald hurriedly formed a plan of his own. 'We have to catch the little runt before he betrays us,' he said. 'Collect weapons and war gear and prepare to come with me. He can't yet have got too far.'

It sounded like a good plan but all knew that finding a lone boy on the marsh or on the heath beyond would be far from easy. Both would offer countless places for him to evade them, especially once it got dark.

It was Osric who pointed out the flaw in Oswald's plan, taking him aside once more. 'So many men to catch a single boy?' he queried. 'Besides, you daren't risk men in the marsh until it's light and even then it'll be dangerous enough.'

'So what would you have me do?' demanded Oswald, offended that his uncle should try to meddle with the arrangements he was making.

'Take your elite squad, ride hard and try to overtake the boy. That way you'll travel more quickly than those of us on foot and if you leave at once you may be able to intercept him before he reaches the marsh. If you can't find him, wait at the ford. I'll have Wulfric join you with a contingent of thirty armed men at first light. They can then bring you supplies for several days at least.'

'Thirty men?' said Oswald. 'Why so few? You said yourself how important it is for us to catch the little bastard before he betrays us.'

'Don't forget the bigger threat,' warned Osric. 'There's a hundred Viking longships somewhere between here and Exeter which could strike at any time. Therefore we must keep most of the men here just in case.'

Oswald realised that his uncle was right, so agreed to the plan. 'Very well, but make sure the men you're sending tomorrow come in haste, for we've no time to lose.'

* * * * *

Coenred found a shallow ford just before the river widened before reaching the main harbour. He used it to cross and then continued northwards, hoping to find a way through the marsh in order to reach the heath which lay beyond it. There was a risk that those manning the watchtower might see him at that point, particularly as they would have heard the alarm bell and would thus be on full alert. However, he reckoned there was a good chance that fearing the Viking fleet had been sighted, their eyes would be fixed on the harbour itself, watching in case the beacon on Haven Point was lit.

As far as he was concerned, it was a gamble worth taking, particularly as he couldn't go back or even remain where he was for fear of being caught sooner or later. Thus all he could do was to keep moving and hope that the search party would not even attempt to follow him into the marsh until morning. If so, then with any luck he could put even more distance between himself and them. He had never been to the marsh before so had no idea what to expect but decided he would go as far as he dared, then lie low until morning, hoping to reach the heath by the end of the following day. Once there he would be safe enough as being on much higher ground he would be able to see his pursuers long before they could see him. More importantly, if he could find a place to hide somewhere on the cliffs he would be able to keep watch for any sign of a Viking longship as well.

* * * * *

Oswald sent Edward to help the members of his elite squad to get their horses. In the end they took them all, including the two farm horses.

'Am I to come with you, sir?' he asked.

'No, remain here and come with the reinforcements tomorrow. You can then use the mule to carry the extra supplies we'll need as the track is too narrow for a cart.'

Edward did as he was ordered and, as soon as all the horses were saddled, Oswald and the rest of the squad mounted up and set off for the gate at Bell's Orchard with all possible haste. Once there, they followed the path towards the harbour, by then needing torches to light their way.

They reached the ford quickly enough but were already too late. Oswald immediately despatched a rider to speak with the guards at the watchtower in the hope that they had seen the boy but he already knew it was unlikely they would as their job was to watch the harbour in front of them, not the path to their rear.

'We'll stay here for the night,' Oswald announced. 'I'll not risk lives by trying to cross the marsh at night. God knows it's dangerous enough even in daylight.'

'What of the others?' asked Sigbert.

'They'll come at first light bringing supplies and

provisions for three days at least, plus whatever else they think we'll need.'

'So it's a cold night for us whilst the others take to the comfort of their own beds,' moaned Sigbert quietly to one of the other men.

Oswald overheard him and was not impressed. 'We stay here in case the wretch tries to double back,' he snapped. 'He'll no more want to brave the marsh than we do as he doesn't even carry a torch. Drowning in some putrid bog is no way to die, particularly alone in the dark.'

Sigbert acknowledged the point.

'Besides,' continued Oswald. 'Come tomorrow we can rest as the others spread out to search for the little toad. We can't afford for him to get away for he already knows too much about our defences and could therefore betray us all.'

It all seemed reasonable enough, so the men settled down to make a crude camp, huddled round the fire for both light and warmth whilst taking turns to guard the ford just in case Coenred did try to double back and cross the path somewhere behind them.

* * * * *

Coenred began to wish he'd gone the other way as he quickly found that the marsh was every bit as difficult and as dangerous as he'd feared. Whilst looking sound enough, parts of it were actually quicksand which could devour a man whole by sucking him down into the bowels of the earth. There were also several deep pools which he narrowly missed stepping into.

He therefore dared move only very slowly, creeping

forward step by treacherous step as he tried to avoid any area which felt too soft or wet underfoot. He had no idea how far he'd travelled any more than he knew how much further he had to go. Whilst he'd heard that Twynham, the next settlement along the coast, was reckoned to be a full day's march from Wareham, that would be by using the road, not trudging through the marshes. With nothing to guide him, his only option in the dark was to keep the harbour to his right to ensure that he was at least going in the right direction, though in such poor light even that was far from easy. After about an hour he realised that to carry on was both foolhardy and extremely dangerous so decided to rest knowing that he'd make better time in the morning. He could by then see the glow from the torches of the search party in the distance and, so far as he could tell, they were getting no closer. He reckoned that they'd probably made camp for the night and, confident that he had at least put some distance between him and his pursuers, he decided to do the same. He therefore found a patch of reasonably firm ground and settled down for the night as best he could. He dared not risk a fire for fear of it being seen and, besides, the ground was so damp that he doubted he could get one to light anyway. All he could do was try to rest then make good his escape as soon as it was light enough for him to safely see his way.

Chapter Fourteen

As the additional men who had been selected to join the search for Coenred prepared to set off from Wareham at first light the following morning, Wulfric ensured that they'd each drawn weapons from the garrison store. It seemed unlikely these would be needed as their job would be to form a search party to scour the marshes, not get themselves involved in a fray but, nonetheless, it seemed a sensible precaution. The remainder of the fyrd were to remain at Wareham under the command of Governor Osric in case there was an attack on the settlement whilst the others were away.

Marching in single file along the narrow path from Bell's Orchard, the search party comprised thirty men, all of whom were on foot but with Edward leading the mule which carried the supplies. They quickly reached the ford across the river Piddle where they found Oswald and his men waiting, all of them having spent a very uncomfortable night on the fringes of the marsh with little in the way of food or shelter. Even so, they'd stirred themselves early and one of them had already ridden down to the watchtower again to ensure that there'd been no sign of the boy overnight. Oswald was not surprised when the rider reported back that there hadn't, so the assumption was that he'd crossed the river the previous evening ahead of them and risked travelling through at least part of the marsh in the dark.

'The chances are the poor sod has got himself drowned or, worse still, sucked down into the stinking mud,' suggested Wulfric when he heard that.

'Well, if he has we'll be wasting our time here,' said Oswald. 'For unless he's stranded in the mud somewhere we'll find neither hide nor hair of him. But I need to be certain. He knows too much about our defences.'

Edward was concerned to find that the horses had been left saddled all night and went across to attend to them.

'No, leave them be!' shouted Oswald. 'They have to remain ready at all times in case the wretch is sighted!'

Edward started to explain that the horses needed the chance to rest properly but Oswald would have none of it. 'If Coenred betrays us and word of any gap in our defences reaches the Viking fleet, we'll all be slaughtered,' he stressed. 'What does the comfort of a few horses matter compared to that?'

He gave Edward no time to answer. Instead, he started to brief the men. 'It's my guess that if the boy still lives he'll try to make for the higher ground to the east of the harbour. He'll then find a vantage point on the cliffs from where he can keep watch for Viking raiders.'

'Why the hell would he do that?' asked Wulfric, knowing nothing of Coenred's Viking blood.

'Because it's my guess that he plans to join them,' said Oswald. 'He'll use what he knows about our defences to secure a place in their ranks.'

With that he sent two men on ahead of the main group to check for signs of a trail, though he doubted they'd find

197

any. All the rest were ordered to strap their shields to their backs and secure their weapons and such like to one of the horses or the mule, though some kept a spear to use as a staff with which to probe the sodden ground. The plan was for them to fan out so they could sweep as large a section of the marsh as possible.

'For God's sake, everyone watch where you tread,' ordered Oswald. 'You all know how treacherous this place can be so stay within sight of the man nearest you and call out if you discover anything or if you need assistance. Those with horses must also travel on foot and lead their mounts by the reins,' he added. 'Keep back behind the line and follow those in front so you know where it's safe for the horses to tread.'

'Are we to take him alive, sir?' asked Wulfric.

'Dead or alive it makes no difference. Just find the little sod, for I fear all our lives are at risk if we don't.'

* * * * *

Coenred woke feeling very stiff and was still sore from the beating he'd taken. He tried to check the cuts on his back as best he could, wishing that before he'd left the nunnery he'd stolen some of the balm Ingrid was using to treat them. Having done what he could to soothe them with cold water taken from one of the many pools, he set off, continuing his way through the marsh by parting the reeds whilst taking care not to leave anything by way of an obvious trail. It had been a perilous journey in the dark and although waiting for daylight had delayed his escape, he knew it had been a wise precaution. In fact, even once light it proved to be a long and treacherous journey which took much longer than he'd hoped. Skirting around the many pools meant that he made only very slow progress and it was actually beginning to get dark again by the time he reached the far edge of the marsh, or at least, that part of it where the ground seemed firmer. From there he worked his way up towards the higher ground, looking for a place on the heath where he could safely spend the night – ideally somewhere from where he would have a good view of the open sea yet would also be able to see his pursuers if they began to close on him. All he had to do from there was remain hidden and, as soon as he sighted a Viking longship, follow it along the cliffs and go down to meet it if and when the raiders came ashore. Then one of two things would happen. What he hoped was that they would allow him to join them. If not, he knew they would kill him – and the agony of even a hundred lashes of the whip was nothing compared to that of being butchered by a Viking warband, for they knew all there was to know about inflicting pain.

* * * * *

Oswald's men also made painfully slow progress through the marsh and however much he urged them to hurry, there was nothing they could do to speed up the search. Not only was it treacherous ground, but they also needed to be thorough as there were so many places where a boy could hide among the tall reeds which seemed to circle every pool. By the end of the first day they had pretty much completed their sweep of that area and knew that the heath beyond would bring problems of its own. It was a vast expanse of gorse and scrub, all of which would provide excellent cover for someone not anxious to be seen. Oswald's one consolation was that if he was right and Coenred was indeed intending to join a Viking warband, the boy would need to watch for sight of a longship. Thus all he had to do was to concentrate his search on the edge of the cliffs which was where he was all but certain he would find the fugitive. However, he dared not risk missing the boy in the dark so was obliged to instruct his men to make camp once they reached the heath, eat some food and settle in for the night so they could resume their search the following morning, the better for having rested. Most were grateful for that but with little in the way of shelter and only meagre provisions, many found it hard to actually sleep.

Matters were made worse when just before dawn there was a fall of torrential rain which forced everyone to take what shelter they could and try to wait out the weather. It was whilst doing so that one of the men spotted the smoke from several beacons which had been lit to the west. Fearing a raid on Wareham in their absence, Oswald sent two men to ride on ahead of his main group to see what they could from the cliffs. When they returned they reported that they'd seen two ships with their sails set, both moving slowly eastwards but yet some way out to sea.

'Sir, as far as we can tell, they've already sailed past the harbour entrance so present no danger to Wareham,' they assured him. 'In any event, it looks as though the settlement has already seen them as they've lit the beacons there as well.'

Oswald looked relieved. 'Then our best course is to leave matters to them and resume our search for Coenred,' he said.

In fact, sighting the longships was exactly what he needed, for doubtless the boy would see them as well and give some sort of signal to attract their attention. When he did, he would surely give away his position.

* * * * *

Coenred had indeed seen the ships, just as he'd also seen the columns of smoke rising up from the beacons all along the coast. Like Oswald and his men, he also realised that the Vikings had seemingly ignored Wareham and slipped past the narrow harbour entrance. That meant that all he had to do was wait for them to eventually come ashore. With that in mind, he was forced to ignore the rain and set off at once, grateful that the ships seemed to be making very slow progress as they ploughed their way through a particularly heavy sea. At that point they were still too far away for him to see what was on the banners which flew from their masts but he knew at once that they were raiders, not traders, for the hulls of both ships were decked with shields.

* * * * *

Oswald also had his men set forth at once, despite the weather. Whilst he had still seen no sign of Coenred, he was certain the boy was not far ahead of them and would have to reveal himself sooner or later.

In fact, neither had long to wait. The two longships had not progressed far along the coast before they lowered their sails and took to their oars instead as they turned and headed towards the beach. Once close enough, men leaped ashore and, in a well-practised manoeuvre, hauled both vessels clear of the shore break and secured each of them by means of a long rope which they tied to a stake driven deep into the sand.

Both vessels were of a type which was designed for speed rather than carrying goods and livestock. Having a shallow draught, they were ideally suited to raiding as they could be sailed along rivers and thus strike deep inland. They were also equally well suited for coastal attacks as, having a prow at each end, they could be beached and then relaunched again in a hurry without first needing to be turned around. All the crew had to do in order to sail away was to move the steering oar from one end to the other, then push the ship out to sea again and row for all they were worth. With each ship being manned by as many as fifty hardened warriors, they were thus a force to be reckoned with.

* * * * *

When Coenred eventually reached the point where the ships had come ashore, he knew that his fate then rested in the hands of God – not that he placed much store in the Christian faith. For him, the pagan deities who offered tangible signs of their divine power such as thunder, lightning and stars which flew across the sky at night were much more believable. He'd therefore practised what he'd been told to practise and ostensibly believed what he'd been told to believe but left to his own devices he, like many others at that time, had not entirely forsaken his pagan roots.

Gods or no Gods, at that point he began to think his luck had changed. He could see no sign of his pursuers and realised that the Vikings had chosen a good place to come ashore. It was one of the many chines along that part of the coast – places where there was a gently sloping beach and a narrow cutting through the cliffs which led to the hinterland beyond. All he had to do was go down through the chine to meet them. After that he would either be allowed to join them or face being brutally butchered.

* * * * *

Oswald also recognised the place where the ships had come ashore when he reached it, though had no idea why the raiders had chosen it. The beach at that point was a stretch of fine sand which would offer a good mooring and the gap in the cliffs would make it easier for the Vikings to access the heath but, apart from that, it seemed to offer nothing that would interest them. There were no churches nearby for them to raid and whilst there were some farmsteads on the edge of the heath to the north, they were all too far inland to make viable or profitable targets. If it was food they were after, it was true that many people left their livestock to graze on the heath but it was unlikely that the raiders would know that. The only other possibility was that they needed fresh water. That at least did make some sense as there was a small stream which flowed down through the chine to reach the sea.

Yet Oswald was still not satisfied. As he considered the position more carefully, it occurred to him that he might be missing the obvious. Further along the coast from there was the settlement of Twynham which, whilst smaller than Wareham, was also a fortified burh but was considered to be poorly protected even though it would offer rich pickings. He began to fear that the settlement there might be their intended target. If so, then it was clear that the Vikings knew exactly what they were about. Twynham also bordered a large harbour – nowhere near as big as the one at Wareham but significant nonetheless. The entrance to that was protected and largely concealed by a spit of land known as Hengistbury Head which would afford excellent cover and which the Vikings could use to their advantage, especially at night. However, there were two problems – the tide around the spit was fierce and the entrance to the harbour was narrow, difficult to navigate and easily missed in the dark.

'They could be planning to strike at Twynham,' he announced once he'd finished his deliberations.

'Surely there's not enough of them for that,' said Wulfric. 'They could be planning a lightning raid but they don't have near enough men to overwhelm the settlement completely.'

Oswald wasn't quite so sure. 'Agreed, but if they unstep the masts to keep their ships from being seen they could row their way around the spit at Hengistbury Head and take the settlement by surprise. They would then be able to unleash their havoc, seize as many captives as they could to sell as slaves and be gone before anyone could stop them.'

'Perhaps,' acknowledged Wulfric. 'But surely they'd be seen in time for the fyrd there to muster a credible defence?'

It was that last comment which made Oswald realise that there might be a chance for a much more favourable outcome. He reckoned that if his small force could combine with the fyrd from Twynham, they would stand a good chance of actually defeating the Vikings if only by sheer weight of numbers. He outlined the idea to both Wulfric and Sigbert but neither seemed overly impressed.

'Sir, we should just alert the settlement and be done

with it,' suggested Wulfric. 'We don't have near enough men as we are and who knows how long it would take those at Twynham to muster the fyrd and join us.'

'Nonsense, those at Twynham will have seen the beacons so the fyrd will have been alerted already,' said Oswald firmly. 'What's more, these bastards don't seem to be in much of a hurry to get on with their raid. It's my guess they'll want to attack under the cover of night so will spend tomorrow unstepping the masts and then resting. After all, it's a long way to row.'

Both Wulfric and Sigbert saw the logic of that but still had reservations.

'Look, we've nothing to lose,' said Oswald, trying to convince them. 'It'll take but a few hours for someone to ride to Twynham from here and alert them. He can then return with the fyrd and between us we can take these bastards by surprise before they leave tomorrow night.'

'And what do we do in the meantime?' asked Sigbert.

Oswald hadn't got that far with his plan but quickly thought of an answer. 'It'll soon be getting dark so we'll find somewhere safe to spend the night. I used to hunt here as a boy and if I remember rightly there's a river to the north of here which follows the line of the cliff before joining the sea some miles to the east. At one point it splits into two channels for a short distance before joining up again, thereby creating an island. That would be a good place to hide out until the fyrd from Twynham arrives.'

'How wide is the river?' asked Wulfric.

'Wide enough. And deep enough for the most part. Many people use the island to graze their cattle in order to keep them safe from rustlers. They've formed a narrow bridge there which should be easy enough to defend if we have to.'

Still neither Wulfric nor Sigbert much liked the idea and said so but Oswald was determined, thinking more about the glory he could achieve than the risks. In the end he ordered a man named Egbert to ride hard to Twynham to warn them of the Vikings' presence. 'But Egbert, I'll need you to return as quickly as you can with whatever force can be mustered. Until you reach us we'll remain hopelessly outnumbered and therefore at risk.'

'So, what do we do now, sir?' asked Wulfric as they watched Egbert ride off.

'Take the men and find the river. It's due north of here. If you then follow it downstream you'll quickly find the island and the bridge. You can remain there overnight. Sigbert and I will stay here and, once you've gone, will go down to the beach and hide within the dunes. We need to keep an eye on these bastards but will avoid confronting them until the fyrd from Twynham arrives to bolster our numbers.'

* * * * *

The heath was a desolate place, bleak and exposed and with just a few withered trees which were bent and twisted from the wind. At first, Wulfric struggled to find the island Oswald had mentioned and, with the light fading, he began to look for an alternative place to spend the night. His concern was that there were few places on the heath where all his men could safely hide, and nowhere where they could conceal the horses.

He therefore led the men further inland until he at last came to the edge of the river. Relieved, he then followed it until he found the island, which was actually a lot bigger than he expected and formed a natural pen which was being used to graze cattle, just as Oswald had said. However, there were still two things which worried him. First, there was no other viable crossing to the island, the bridge being the only way to reach it. Even that was a somewhat crude affair being formed from several trees which had been felled and then split to form a level surface and simply laid across the river from one bank to the other. Second, he realised that if they were attacked and the Vikings managed to take the bridge, his men would have nowhere to go. He shuddered at the thought of them being pursued and cut down as they tried to escape the slaughter which would follow. He resolved to raise this with Oswald when he joined them but, in the meantime, set about doing what he could to establish a camp for the night, posting guards so that the remainder of the men would at least get a chance for some much needed rest.

* * * * *

Oswald and Sigbert took up a position within the dunes. From there, they were able to make a rough count of the raiders and found that they actually numbered less than they'd feared. In all, they counted not more than eighty men.

'So, do you still think they're here purely to rest before attacking Twynham tomorrow?' asked Sigbert.

'Well, they've been here for what, several hours at least,' explained Oswald. 'All they've done so far is use the stream to replenish their supply of water and set up a makeshift camp. They've made no attempt to leave the beach to forage for food or go off in search of plunder.'

'Aye,' said Sigbert. 'Nor have they made any attempt to protect themselves with temporary fortifications so presumably they're not intending to stay here long. Also, none of them are armed having all left their weapons aboard the ships. Surely they should be worried lest they encounter the fyrd? After all, they'll have seen the beacons just as we have so will know they've been sighted.'

'Well, whatever it is they're planning, at least Egbert will warn the settlement at Twynham in time,' said Oswald. Yet even as he spoke there was something which worried him. Whilst his plan was working well enough with everything falling into place exactly as he wished, he still wasn't entirely satisfied as to the Vikings' intent. 'My worry is that there's more to this than meets the eye,' he admitted at last. 'It's almost as if they're waiting for something.'

'Waiting?' asked Sigbert. 'Waiting for what?'

'I don't know. But raiders usually strike hard and fast, not sit around resting on a beach where they might be seen.'

Oswald was still considering that when Sigbert pointed out a solitary figure walking down towards the beach, his arms spread wide to show he was unarmed. They both recognised who it was at once.

* * * * *

It seemed that having given the Vikings time to settle, Coenred had at last plucked up enough courage to make his move. He'd emerged from where he'd been hiding and was walking slowly towards where they waited.

Sigbert raised his bow. 'Let me shoot the little runt and be done with it,' he suggested.

Oswald shook his head. 'No, if you do that they'll know we're here. I don't want to engage them before the reinforcements arrive. Besides, he'll die soon enough. The Vikings will see to that and ensure that he meets a much less merciful end than you planting an arrow in his chest.'

Sigbert needed no reminder of how much the Vikings hated spies and traitors. They reasoned that such men were cowards who, without actually risking their own life, could cause the death of many. Thus they would devise a very bloody end for Coenred if it suited them.

When he was within about twenty paces from the Vikings' camp, Coenred stopped and held his breath as he waited to see what they would do. At first they made no attempt to speak with him, they just watched as if not sure what to make of the fool who was so calmly walking to his death. He then tried calling out to them but, not surprisingly, they didn't understand what he was saying. Instead, they started jeering and cajoling him, daring him to get closer. Then one of them got up and went over to the ships to collect his daneaxe before returning to where Coenred waited.

'I would join your band if you'll have me,' pleaded Coenred, shouting to make himself heard. 'I will pledge myself to fight beside you and will swear allegiance to your Lord.' With that he fell to his knees and bowed his head invitingly.

The Viking, who Oswald assumed was a chieftain of some sort, called for one of the others to come forward. The man who joined him was tall with long fair hair and blue eyes but looked much older than most of the others. However, he at least seemed to understand what Coenred was saying. As he translated this the chieftain simply laughed then raised his axe as though intending to strike.

'Wait! I can help you,' pleaded Coenred.

Again the fair-haired warrior translated. The chieftain looked doubtful but stayed his hand whilst he waited to hear what else the fool had to say for himself.

'The Saxons will be here,' advised Coenred. 'They'll have come on horses to intercept you and will delay you long enough for the rest of the fyrd to arrive.'

As that was repeated the chieftain lowered his axe completely.

'They could already be here,' continued Coenred imploringly, hardly daring to look up. 'Surely you've seen the beacons?'

The interpreter replied on the chieftain's behalf, speaking with barely any trace of an accent. 'My Lord wants to know why he should believe you?'

'Would I risk my life to tell you lies? You'll see all too quickly that what I say is true. If not, you can kill me then.'

The Viking chieftain looked around but could see nothing untoward which might suggest a Saxon ambush. Nonetheless, he gestured to a few of the men to carry out a quick sweep of the beach and the chine itself to see if there were indeed any Saxons hiding there.

'The little sod has done for us!' warned Oswald. 'They'll see us if they come any closer!'

It was then that Sigbert realised that it was already too late as one of the raiders was headed straight to where they were hiding. Seeing the danger in that, he raised his bow and shot the man, then turned his attention to others on the beach as well, killing two of them with perfectly judged arrows.

As they were unarmed, the Vikings on the beach scattered, looking for cover wherever they could find it, most of them seeking shelter beside the hull of one of the ships. Coenred ran to join them and although Sigbert loosed an arrow with which he intended to kill the boy, he was too far away by then so it passed wide of its mark.

Sigbert continued sniping at anyone who dared to show himself and, although he did well enough in keeping the Vikings pinned down, both he and Oswald knew they could never hold off that many men for long. They also knew that as the light continued to fade those opportunities would become fewer and fewer.

'Sir, if they attack us in the dark we'll both be slaughtered,' warned Sigbert.

Oswald could see he was right. The darkness should have been their friend but it would also aid the Vikings as well, for it would enable them to creep up on them unseen. 'We've done all we can here,' he said. 'Let's fall back to join the others.'

'Then what?' asked Sigbert.

'Then we'll have to pray that the men from Twynham get here soon.'

'And what if they don't?'

Oswald looked at him. 'Then God help us, that's all I can say. We've now roused these bloodthirsty bastards and if that means we're forced to confront them whilst still outnumbered, this won't end well for us, that much is certain.'

Chapter Fifteen

By the time Oswald reached the island, he was all too well aware of the dire position in which he'd placed his men. In having alerted the Vikings to their presence, he and Sigbert had awoken a sleeping beast and he'd need to find a way to subdue it or risk his entire force being brutally slaughtered. He hurriedly considered his options. His small contingent numbered just forty men if he included Edward, though he knew the boy would hardly rank as a warrior having had so little training. Most of the rest were drawn from the permanent guard and were thus able enough but he doubted whether even they would stand much chance against twice their number of hardened Viking warriors. All he could do if the Vikings did attack was to try to hold the bridge until the fyrd from Twynham could reach them with reinforcements, albeit he knew that was unlikely to be before morning at best.

As he and Sigbert joined the rest of the men he explained what had happened. 'We had no choice but to kill a few of them in order to get away,' he told them. 'I fear we'll now have to make a stand here.'

Having already made his own assessment of their position, Wulfric could hardly believe what he was hearing. 'But if they attack us here, sir, there'll be hell to pay,' he warned. 'There's nowhere for us to retreat to. Surely we

212

should use the cover of night to withdraw whilst we still can?'

Oswald dismissed even the thought of retreating. 'If we do that they'll cut us down like dogs in all that open ground on the heath.'

'Not if we head north,' suggested Wulfric. 'There are places in the stream behind us which look possible to ford and, once across, we can then head inland. If we destroy the bridge before we leave they'll either have to repair it or find another place at which to cross before they can follow us. That should buy us enough time to get away.'

Oswald was still intent on glory, anxious to try anything which would enhance his own reputation as a warrior – and that certainly didn't include withdrawing. 'No,' he insisted. 'We were sent here to either kill or capture Coenred and those orders still stand.'

'But what can we do against so many?' asked Wulfric.

'For one thing we can stand our ground,' said Oswald. 'The bridge is narrow so they can cross it only three or four abreast and therefore can't use their numbers to any real advantage. We'll form a shield wall to hold them back whilst our bowmen pick off others as they wait to cross. That way we can even up the odds and hold out until the fyrd from Twynham arrives.'

Wulfric was speechless at first. He could see at once that what Oswald was intending was not only foolhardy but also misguided. 'Sir, is that wise?' he managed, questioning the order as tactfully as he dared. 'There's no point in dying defending a worthless heath. Why not let them take whatever it is they've come here for? There are no farmsteads or settlements nearby and we've alerted the people at Twynham so they can muster their own defence. That means there's no one at risk so…'

'You have your orders!' snarled Oswald dismissively. 'Organise a rota of men to guard the bridge until morning. Start with Aelwyn, he's wide enough to block it on his own.' His last quip was intended to lighten the mood but it fell a long way short of the mark.

* * * * *

The raiders were well used to situations such as the one in which they found themselves. That being so, they waited before breasting the dunes, knowing there could yet be more Saxon bowmen lurking nearby waiting to pick off anyone they could see. Their chieftain, a man named Borg, had already decided that the slaughter of a few Saxons could wait at least until dawn. That prospect didn't worry him unduly even though it meant that his men would need to spend the remainder of the night cowering beside their ships with some warriors even sleeping on board. He sent for Coenred and had him kneel before him. Then, through his interpreter, he demanded answers.

'My Lord wishes to know who these fools are who have come up against him, and who leads them?'

'My Lord, they are led by Oswald,' said Coenred. 'He's the Garrison Commander at Wareham. His men are trained and of good intent, but mostly pressed to serve in the fyrd.'

When that was translated, Borg clearly didn't recognise the name of Oswald.

'My Lord asks whether this man Oswald is the son of Osric, for he was told that the old war horse is the one who commands there.' He didn't say as much, but Osric's reputation was one reason why Borg had decided to sail past Wareham and raid elsewhere instead.

'He is. Osric is Governor at Wareham but now too old to fight.'

When that was translated, Borg was by no means ready to believe that Osric would be anything other than a worthy opponent just because the fool of a boy said he was getting too old. To his mind, the reputation of warriors like Osric had been earned the hard way and deserved respect.

'My Lord asks whether he is then to fight the son of Osric? If so, then he wishes to know whether the son is as good as the father?' asked the interpreter.

'No, my Lord. He is not a patch on Governor Osric. Besides, Oswald is not his son, he's a nephew and commands the garrison and the fyrd only with his uncle's help.'

Borg grinned when he heard that. He relished the chance to kill Osric's nephew, particularly knowing that the fyrd comprised of men who were not seasoned warriors. That would mean that they'd have no particular thirst for blood so would be easier to deter, though he knew better than to underestimate the courage of the Saxons, whether they were trained warriors or not.

'How will they form up?' demanded the interpreter.

Coenred looked worried. 'They'll choose their ground and form a shield wall, my Lord and...'

A warrior such as Borg needed no explanation about what that entailed. He'd faced those tactics many times before and knew well enough how to deal with them.

'But my Lord, they came here in pursuit of me, so will number no more than a dozen men,' added Coenred, not realising that more of the fyrd had already joined the search. 'I've seen the watch beacons lit to the west so most will have remained within the settlement to defend it in case you strike there. Once they realise that you've sailed on beyond the harbour entrance the main force may well be deployed, but they won't have arrived as yet. My Lord, if you attack now you can take these fools easily enough, for you have six warriors at least for every one of them,' offered Coenred. 'And once you've slain them, my Lord, Wareham will be yours for the taking. I can show you how to enter it via a secret path which is guarded by just one man. It leads right into the heart of the settlement.'

When that was translated Borg beamed his approval and then laughed out loud. He wasn't convinced by what the poor fool of a boy had said but, whether true of not, it was of little consequence. He hurriedly revised his plan, forming one which would provide more booty than his men could carry and enough killing to satisfy even their voracious appetite for blood. It would start with the slaughter of the small band of Saxons and, after that, the fools at both Wareham and Twynham would learn what it was to face a Viking warband.

* * * * *

As soon as Egbert arrived at Twynham he quickly gave his report to the Garrison Commander, a man named Cedric. 'Sir, there are two ships with perhaps a hundred men in total,' he warned. 'Oswald has them pinned down on the beach between here and Wareham. I'm to urge you to make all possible haste as until you get there he'll be hopelessly outnumbered.'

'Where is this?' demanded Cedric.

'A short way along the coast, sir. The Vikings have come ashore at one of the chines and beached their ships there, probably to rest and take on fresh water before attacking you. Oswald plans to hit them before they have the chance to strike.'

Cedric looked worried. 'We cannot offer assistance or support for we have word of another ship sailing towards us from the east. I can only assume they were planning to meet with those you've seen already and attack this settlement together.'

'A third ship, sir? Surely that can't be so?'

Cedric looked to his second in command, a man named Dunstan. 'Are we certain of this news?'

Dunstan nodded and pointed to the east. 'It's now too dark to see but yonder is the beacon at Chichester, sir. When it was lit a few hours ago it was plain enough.'

Cedric considered this. 'So is their target here or Wareham?' he asked aloud.

'Sir, Wareham is too well defended,' suggested Dunstan. 'My guess is they intend to meet up at the chine and then sail back together to attack us here, using the spit at Hengistbury Head as cover.'

'Then if we march to relieve Oswald we'll leave this settlement undefended!' stormed Cedric.

'But, sir,' protested Egbert. 'Oswald may have already engaged them and…'

'Then he's a fool! He should have withdrawn if he's outnumbered!' he said sourly. 'Besides, we have only a small contingent of our men mustered here at present, the rest will come in from nearby settlements and farmsteads but they'll not be here till morning at best.'

'But Oswald will know nothing of the third ship, sir. He'll have assumed that your beacons are to warn of the ones he's already holding at bay!'

'So what would you have me do? I can't leave this settlement undefended to support him, not with a ship laden with warriors headed towards us!'

'But Oswald is relying on you!'

Cedric was still not convinced. 'Then ride back at once and warn him. Tell him about the third ship and say that I advise him to return to Wareham with all possible speed in case the attack is there. With God's good grace he'll not yet have engaged them and therefore it won't be too late for him to withdraw.'

Egbert looked at him, knowing that Oswald would have no intention of retreating. 'Then God help us all,' he said. 'For if the fray has already started then come morning all who stand with him will be slain. What's more, with three longships to contend with, the settlements both here and at Wareham will be at risk. God knows which of them will be the Vikings' intended target but I fear whichever one it is will be sorely tested.'

* * * * *

Egbert rode hard to reach Oswald and the remainder of the fyrd, praying he would be in time. He reached the chine just before dawn and was relieved to find that the Saxons had moved on. The Viking raiders were still there, their boats pulled up on to the sand as they had been before but now with most of the warriors donning their war gear and preparing themselves for battle. He knew that Oswald and the fyrd would have gone inland to find somewhere to make a stand, so headed off to find them. He was surprised how easy that was even in the half-light of dawn as the path they'd trodden through the gorse and scrub still left an obvious trail. He was concerned as that would mean the Vikings would also have little trouble in finding them.

As soon as he reached the river, he followed it until he came to the bridge then rode across it, dismounting from his tired horse even before it had stopped. 'Sir, the fyrd from Twynham won't be coming,' he warned breathlessly. 'A third ship has been sighted sailing from the east. The Garrison Commander fears an attack on the settlement and says he must keep all his men there to defend it.'

When Oswald heard that news his heart sank.

'A third ship!' exclaimed Sigbert. 'Then you were right! They were waiting for something!'

It was Wulfric who then spoke. 'Sir, if they combine it will mean we could now be facing a force of perhaps a 150 men! Can't you see that this is all a ruse? By sailing in from both directions they've contrived to cause beacons to be lit all along the coast so we've no way of telling where or when they'll strike! We must withdraw now, not just for the sake of our own lives but also to reinforce those at Wareham in case that's the intended target. Surely it's our duty to bolster those defences if we can?'

Oswald still seemed to be questioning what Egbert had said. 'No, this is madness. We should unite and beat the bastards whilst we can,' he insisted. 'A force of 150 men pose no significant threat to Wareham. In fact, my uncle should be able to see them off with ease but it's far better that we try to defeat the bastards here. Does Cedric not see the sense of that?'

'But sir, he fears he'll leave Twynham exposed if he comes

to join us,' explained Egbert. 'The defences there are not as secure as at Wareham.'

'So would he leave us exposed instead?' he demanded. 'He must come! It's his duty to support us! That way both settlements are rendered safe.' Even as he said it he must have realised the enormity of his error yet he still refused to acknowledge it openly in front of the others. Instead, he turned away and went to stand beside the bridge. Wulfric followed him and dutifully waited for orders.

'The raiders will expect us to retreat so we'll not give them the satisfaction,' announced Oswald at last. 'They'll plan to attack whichever settlement is weakest. Those at Twynham are already on their guard and my uncle will have mustered the defences at Wareham. They should both be able to hold out well enough and if we remain here we're midway between the two of them so can relieve whichever one the Vikings deign to attack first.'

Wulfric could hardly believe what he was hearing. Like all the other men there he was prepared to die defending his home and his family if he had to, but not some pointless bridge. 'Surely that's not the way of it,' he pleaded. 'From here we can help no one and should they decide to attack us first we'll all be slaughtered anyway!'

Oswald took no offence but instead explained his logic. 'Look, we can hold this narrow bridge for several days if we have to,' he assured him.

'Perhaps,' agreed Wulfric. 'But our supplies won't last that long. We have enough for one more day at best.'

Oswald laughed. 'We have water in the river and can slaughter some of those cattle to feed ourselves if we must. What more do we need?'

Wulfric looked at him long and hard. 'More men,' he said simply. 'If we are to take on 150 Viking warriors we're going to need more men.'

* * * * *

The next morning it seemed that very few of the men had slept so all were tired and most were very frightened as the prospect of meeting an overwhelming force of Viking warriors loomed large in all their thoughts.

Not surprisingly, many took a few moments to kneel in prayer before waiting for their orders whilst Oswald set about trying to improve their position. He began by posting new guards on the other side of the river to warn if and when an attack was imminent, thereby relieving those who Wulfric had stationed there. Beyond that his plan was simply to kill any Vikings as they tried to cross the narrow bridge, leaving those that did make it to be forced back by the shield wall. It was a dangerous ploy and not much of a plan but they no longer had the option of retreating as, in broad daylight, it would be far too risky. As Wulfric ushered the men who were to form the shield wall into position, Oswald considered how best to use the bowmen who had formed his elite squad. In the end he stationed them along the banks of the river either side of the bridge and had them set their shields into position in the soft ground to provide some measure of cover. 'Keep shooting,' he ordered. 'Loose your arrows into the midst of those Vikings waiting to cross thereby reducing their numbers. Also, shoot any who try to wade across for we dare not let them get behind us.'

All there knew it was a brave but futile plan. Even so, the

men made themselves ready by sharpening their weapons and praying some more. As for Edward, he was ordered to herd the cattle close together and then tether the horses and the mule. As they were unused to the din of battle, the fear was that the beasts could be easily frightened – and large animals running loose on the battlefield could cost lives if they distracted any of the men who were fighting.

Having all checked their war gear several times at least, there was then little for the others to do that had not been done, except to wait. They'd trained hard for days like that, practised until every move was instinctive, but still the prospect of dying etched at their guts. Most had fought before, but none had ever faced an enemy that was likely be at least three times their number.

* * * * *

The raiders greeted their comrades as the third ship was beached and secured alongside the other two. Coenred could hardly believe what he was seeing but remained quiet, not wishing to draw attention to himself. It was then that the tall, fair-haired man who had acted as an interpreter came across and spoke to him direct.

'You're a fool boy,' he said. 'They'll kill you as soon as you've told them all they need to know. And believe me, they'll not only take their own sweet time in doing so, they'll relish all the pain they can inflict upon you. Either that or they'll sell you for a slave.'

Coenred swallowed hard. 'But I want to join them,' he said.

The man laughed. 'What the hell do they need you for?'

222

he asked. 'It would mean that each of them gets even less from whatever plunder can be secured if they have to give you a share as well. Why would they do that? After all, you're not even a warrior so add nothing to their numbers.'

Coenred was not sure what to say.

'If I were you, I'd make a run for it whilst you can,' continued the interpreter. 'They're planning to kill the fools here just for the pleasure of it. After that they had intended to attack Twynham which they reckon is poorly defended but, given what you've told them, they'll now change their minds and attack Wareham instead, using you to show them how to get within the fortifications.'

'But there's not enough of them to take it!' said Coenred.

'They don't want to take it. All they want is to seize as many slaves and as much booty as they can and then be gone. If you still have kin there then I should pray for them. Borg is not known for showing mercy and these men have a thirst for blood like none I've ever come across before.'

Coenred was suddenly quiet, perhaps regretting what he'd done or more likely fearing for his own life. 'What will they do with me?' he managed.

The man laughed. 'Who can say what these bastards are capable of. But as I said, if it was me I'd take the first opportunity to get away from here. At worst, they'll cut you down with an arrow as you try to escape but believe me, that's a better death than whatever else they'll devise for you.'

'What about you?' asked Coenred. 'How did you come to be among them. For you're a Saxon are you not?'

The man hesitated for a moment. 'I was once. But that's another story.'

With that it seemed that Borg had summoned all

to attend him. The horde of warriors from all three ships formed a ring around him as he outlined his revised plan. He was no longer a mere chieftain – he now commanded a significant force with three longships at his disposal. On that basis he ranked as a warlord, elected by his men all of whom were sworn to follow him to the very gates of Valhalla if he asked them.

Whilst Coenred couldn't understand a word of what he was saying to them, they all clearly liked it, cheering and shouting as they waved their weapons in the air – not so much an army, more a rabble of angry men all of whom were baying for blood.

Chapter Sixteen

There were several good reasons why the Vikings elected Borg as their warlord. For one thing, he certainly looked the part, being a huge bear of a man with a shaven head and a long black beard which he'd vainly combed and plaited. More importantly, he was said to have all the guile and cunning of a wolf, which was probably why he didn't immediately believe what Coenred had told him about the number of Saxons ranged against him. Instead, rather than rush headlong into what he feared could be a trap, he sent half a dozen warriors on ahead of his main force to both locate the Saxons and also to assess their true strength and numbers.

Using what limited cover they could find, the small advance group followed the trail left by the Saxons across the heath and quickly found the river which they then followed downstream as far as the bridge. The two sentries Oswald had set to watch for any signs of an imminent attack were easily spotted and quickly overcome. Having been taken unaware, their throats were cut and their bodies then dragged aside to where they wouldn't be seen by anyone.

From there the Vikings could see the Saxon defences, such as they were. They realised at once that Coenred had lied, for there were far more men than he'd led them to believe – though that was of little consequence.

It was as they prepared to leave in order to report all they'd seen that they noticed Oswald frantically directing men to where he needed them to stand. Realising he was probably the leader of the small Saxon contingent, one of the Vikings produced a bow and, crawling forward on his belly, got as close to the bridge as he dared. Taking careful aim from there, he loosed a single arrow and, whilst his aim needed to be better than it was, it still struck home and embedded itself in Oswald's thigh. The Saxon leader cried out as he fell, cursing the pain whilst desperately trying to pull the arrow free.

As some of the men saw the Vikings off, Wulfric went to Oswald's aid and urged him to leave the arrow, knowing that once removed there would be nothing to staunch the flow of blood from the wound.

'Then leave me!' screamed Oswald, still grimacing as he endured the pain. 'Get the men to their positions! The bastards are here!'

Wulfric didn't need telling twice. Assuming command and fearing that the full attack was imminent, he barked orders of his own. 'Take your positions!' he shouted. 'Form up! Ready yourselves!'

Oswald was sorely wounded but far from finished. He snapped off the shaft of the arrow, then, relying on one of the men for support, limped to a position beside his bowmen who had already taken shelter behind their shields. 'I'll use that log over there for cover,' he insisted, in too much pain to hobble any further. Then, once settled, he drew his sword and laid it on the ground where he could reach it more easily when needed.

All the men who were to make up the shield wall hurriedly grouped themselves together. Edward joined them, though was not entirely sure where he was supposed to stand. As they all waited anxiously for the Vikings to show themselves, he plucked up courage to ask Sigbert who explained that at some point everyone would have to take a turn in the front row. 'No one will want to serve there longer than he must,' he warned. 'But we each take our turn so as to share the risk.'

* * * * *

Having managed to set the Saxons on high alert, it was several hours before Borg deigned to arrive, bringing his force with him. He knew that any delay would fuel the fears of those in the Saxon ranks and wanted to test their resolve to the limit. He therefore had his men take their time, knowing he had the advantage both in terms of numbers and position. Certainly he was in no particular hurry, unlike the Saxons who, seeing what they were up against when the Vikings eventually arrived, immediately raised their shields and formed up much sooner than was needed.

As always, Aelwyn was in the centre of the front row of the shield wall and seemed almost fearless. 'Stand easy!' he urged. 'The bastards are just toying with us!'

Wulfric realised that Aelwyn was right. Yet he could see the danger of being caught whilst unprepared. 'He's right,' he shouted. 'Stand down but hold yourselves ready to form up again when needed. They could attack at any time!'

'Don't worry,' boasted Aelwyn, puffing up his huge chest. 'They can play all the games they like but they'll not get past me whilst I've breath in my lungs and blood in my veins.'

His bravado went some way towards settling the others but most of them were still very frightened.

With that Oswald called Edward over. 'Remain with the horses,' he ordered, his voice etched with the pain from his wound. 'Hold them ready. We may yet need to leave this place.'

Edward knew better than to argue, though wondered where they could go if they did retreat, particularly as they didn't have anywhere near enough horses for everyone. Nonetheless, he did as he was ordered, making sure that the horses were all securely tethered for fear they might bolt when the battle started in earnest. There were nine horses in all, plus the mule and about twenty long horned cattle. He went between the beasts, giving them all water from a pail whilst trying to calm them.

It was Aelwyn who then made the first move. 'Pah! I'll not wait here to be slain like a dog!' he shouted, seemingly impatient to get on with the fighting. 'We need to kill a few of these bastards and leave their bodies on the bridge to impede the others. Maybe they won't be quite so keen to cross it if they have to step over their friends to reach us!' With that he broke rank and shouldered his blacksmith's hammer. Armed with that and his shield, he strode out on to the bridge and stood there, alone but defiant, daring anyone to cross as he voiced his challenge.

The Vikings responded by taunting him but eventually one of them was unable to resist the challenge any longer. He broke rank and moved on to the bridge only to be cut down by one of the Saxon bowmen. Another man followed and was also killed but after that a group of half a dozen warriors rushed towards Aelwyn and quickly had him surrounded, clearly intending to settle the matter with blood. Aelwyn killed the first to reach him, his hammer first splitting the man's shield then cracking his skull wide open. Several others also fell as he struck them and the Saxons cheered loudly as he looked ready to kill yet more. But whilst impressed with his courage, all who watched knew that he couldn't hope to survive for long. Sure enough, he was eventually killed by a spear driven deep into his side but even as he fell his huge body all but blocked the bridge. It took two Viking warriors to roll it into the river, one of whom was slain by the Saxon bowmen.

That should have been the cue for the Vikings to surge across the bridge but, anticipating that, the Saxons made ready to receive them by closing their rank. As they did so, Oswald cursed, for although Aelwyn's courage had been an example to them all, with him slain they'd lost one of their best men for very little advantage. It had been a brave but futile effort on his part but it left the Saxons still hopelessly outnumbered and even more dejected having seen what was almost certainly in store for them all. Hurriedly he called out to encourage his men but his voice was lost to the din of the Vikings shouting their defiance as Borg at last ordered them to attack.

Screaming their abuse, the Vikings surged across the bridge. Wulfric had already given the order for the Saxons to brace themselves but, even so, the force as the enemy slammed into them was as much as they could manage. Moments later, both sides were locked in deadly combat, hacking at each other where they could, probing with their spears and striking out with whatever weapons they had. At first, the small Saxon shield wall held well enough, though it cost the lives of several men to do so. Whilst defending themselves, they even managed to slay several of the Viking attackers yet all knew they wouldn't be able to hold out against such overwhelming odds for long. Sure enough, the shield wall eventually began to falter when two men in the front row were killed at the same time, forcing the Saxons to break away whilst relying on the bowmen to cover their retreat.

The Vikings, whose lives were steeped in combat, knew better than to follow as the Saxons withdrew. Instead, they calmly remained on the bridge taking what respite they could as they readied themselves to charge again.

Oswald could only watch helplessly from where he lay but was, by then, all too well aware of what he'd done. His stubborn pride, his arrogance and his pointless ambition would result in the slaughter of every member of the fyrd, himself included. With utter defeat but a heartbeat away, all he and his men could do was to prepare themselves to die as best they could.

As Wulfric looked across at Oswald, they both knew there was only one option but, before Wulfric could give the order to form a new wall ten paces further back, all in the Viking ranks were suddenly silent. Then, for no apparent reason, they began to slowly withdraw back to their side of the river.

Mystified, Oswald hurriedly tried to count the bodies of the dead which were strewn across the bridge. There were many more than he expected, but he could hardly believe it was enough to deter a Viking warband. Then he realised that lying among them was that of a young boy who, despite having been shielded by others, had been killed by an arrow.

With that Borg stepped forward, passed his daneaxe to the man nearest him, then walked out on to the bridge unarmed and with his arms spread wide. Realising that the boy was of some significance to him, Oswald shouted for everyone to let him be, hoping that by showing respect they might earn some respite from the fray or at least a more merciful death. They then watched as Borg retrieved the body of the boy, scooping it up and carrying it back in his arms.

Wulfric went across to speak with Oswald. 'What now?' he asked.

'They'll come again and once across the bridge will spread out and then try to engulf us from all sides at once. Have the bowmen stand behind the shield wall to prevent them as best they can. When that fails or they run out of arrows, have all the men form a shield circle. That won't protect us for long but it's the only chance we have.'

Wulfric acknowledged the order. 'What about you and young Edward?'

'Have someone help me to join you. I'd rather die with the men than here on my own. As regards the boy, tell him to take a horse and ride back to Wareham to fetch help. He should be able to find a place where the horse can cross the river and from there reach the road and follow it.'

'Even if he does, he'll not get back in time to save us,' warned Wulfric.

'No, but he won't know that. There's no point in him dying here as well for he adds nothing to our numbers.'

Wulfric did as he was ordered. He sent Sigbert to help Oswald and then went to speak with Edward. 'We're all but lost,' he told the boy mournfully. 'Oswald has ordered you to mount up and ride back to Wareham for help. Cross the river, then find the road and follow it to the west. Can you manage that?'

Edward simply nodded.

'Good. Get back here as quickly as you can with all the men who can be spared.'

As Edward singled out Knave, what surprised everyone was that the Vikings seemed reluctant to press home their advantage. It was as though they were waiting for orders, yet, instead of finishing the battle, Borg seemed to have lost all appetite for the fight. He stood there, cradling the dead boy in his arms whilst glowering at Coenred accusingly, realising that the Saxons were more than just a few farmers forced reluctantly into battle. Good sense suggested that he should not bother with them further lest he lose more men for no advantage. It would be better for them to return to their ships and sail off but by then his blood was up, not least because the boy who'd been killed was his eldest son whom he loved dearly. According to his creed, that demanded vengeance – and blood could only be answered with blood.

Stirred by that, Borg realised that the longer he delayed the battle the more chance there was of reinforcements arriving to support the men he was confronting. Certainly he had no wish to be caught between the small Saxon contingent on the other side of the river and any fresh warriors who came to join them. Yet what impressed him was that it looked as though even whilst outnumbered, the Saxons would make a fight of it.

In the meantime, his men had formed up once more, this time into a proper file, packing themselves tightly on the bridge four abreast, waiting for orders to slam home their attack like a battering ram. Still silent, they stood for a moment, then all raised their weapons as if to acknowledge the respect the Saxons had shown to their warlord but all there knew that wouldn't last for long – nor would it count for much in the end.

As Edward mounted Knave and prepared to ride for help as ordered, he realised that all the animals were already unsettled by the din of battle. Then he suddenly had an idea. Seeing the Vikings packed so tightly on the bridge, he grabbed hold of the Saxon banner, then loosed all the other horses. Riding in behind them, he drove them and the cattle towards the bridge, shouting for the Saxons to part and let him through. At first, they were not sure what he was doing but when they saw him coming they had no option but to hurriedly step aside as Edward, still screaming as loud as he could manage, stampeded the terrified animals towards the Viking ranks.

At first, those on the bridge were not sure what to do as the herd closed on them. Some hesitated, others turned and tried to run but Edward, still mounted, yelled and shouted so loudly that the horses and the cattle were more afraid of him than of the men blocking their path, most of whom were cowering with their faces unseen behind their shields. As the solid wall of terrified beasts crashed into them, there was little the Vikings could do. Some warriors were knocked senseless whilst others were gored or trampled underfoot as the huge animals barged their way through. Others were pushed or jumped into the deep, murky water on either side of the bridge where, weighed down by their war gear and their weapons, they sank like stones and drowned. Still Edward drove the herd onwards and, once across the bridge, it crashed into the massed ranks of those Vikings who were still waiting to cross, the beasts forcing their way through and splitting them asunder. By then the Vikings were in such disarray that they made easy targets for the Saxon bowmen, though Edward knew nothing of that. He simply charged on, holding the banner aloft whilst still screaming to keep the frightened beasts moving. He was actually part way across the heath before he fell, unseated when Knave was struck by an arrow. The horse stumbled, then fell, taking Edward with her and hurling him to the ground.

He lay there for a moment, realising that he'd hurt his shoulder in the fall but was otherwise not seriously harmed. As he got to his feet he saw the one person he least expected – Coenred, holding a daneaxe in both hands, grinning at the prospect of exacting the vengeance he so badly craved.

'You'd best go whilst you can!' warned Edward. 'They'll hang you if they catch you now!'

Coenred just grinned. 'Not before I've settled my score with you! I'm minded to hack off your arms and legs with this axe, then leave you to squirm like a helpless worm until someone puts you out of your misery!'

Edward looked round for a weapon but found none he could reach, at least not in time. He therefore had no choice but to hold himself ready to die. It was then that he recalled all that Osric had told him about a daneaxe being a terrible weapon to come against but little use in defence. He also quickly assessed his attacker and realised that Coenred looked unsteady – almost as if the axe was too unwieldy for him to manage. He remembered how he'd struggled with the axe he'd been given to try by Oswald so waited and, as Coenred lurched towards him, managed to dodge the first blow when it came. As he did so, he noticed the banner which he'd dropped when his horse fell. Whilst Coenred struggled to free the axe and raise it again, Edward picked up the banner intending to use the shaft of it like a makeshift spear. Sure enough, Coenred came at him again, wielding the axe as though meaning to hack Edward's head from his shoulders, but he never got the chance. As the bully closed on him, Edward thrust the shaft forward, impaling him on the point of it, then driving it home with all the force he could muster.

Coenred looked down at the shaft still protruding from his stomach then again at Edward, hardly able to believe what had happened. He tried to say something but the blood which welled up from his throat stopped him from getting the words out. With that he let the axe fall from his hand, then dropped to his knees, clutching the shaft before falling forward, driving it in even deeper as he did so.

Edward was horrified at what he'd done. He stared at Coenred's twisted body for a moment, then turned away and vomited. He remembered what he'd been told about learning how to kill a man and, having now claimed a life, knew the truth of it. He then looked back at the carnage from the battle which included not only men but also most of the horses and cattle, many of which were dying in agony from all manner of wounds. Yet the tide of the battle had turned in the Saxons' favour. Having re-formed their rank, they'd charged across the bridge with their shields raised and their spears ready. Those Vikings who still struggled in the river were shot by the bowmen as were any who had managed to reach the banks, but even that was not enough. The slaughter continued as small groups of Vikings tried to re-form into viable units but were cut down where they stood. By then the Saxons had slain at least half the Viking force and left many more dying or seriously wounded.

It was then that Edward realised he was isolated until the rest of the Saxons could reach him. He therefore picked up the axe which Coenred had been using but found that with his wounded shoulder he could barely raise it high enough to use as a weapon. He quickly cast it aside and looked round for something better but, as he did so, he became aware that none other than Borg himself had been watching him.

At first, Edward thought that the Viking warlord had come seeking vengeance for the young boy who'd been killed. Despite having bettered Coenred, he knew that he was no match for such a seasoned warrior as Borg but there was no time for him to feel afraid. Instead, he simply accepted his fate and readied himself to die – but it wasn't him Borg had come for, it was the traitor Coenred whom he held to be responsible for the death of his son. Seeing that Edward had killed the wretch for him, Borg nodded as though to acknowledge his respect for such a brave young warrior, then turned away and walked towards the beach, still carrying the body of his son.

* * * * *

It seemed that without Borg the Vikings lacked any proper cohesion. In truth, enough of them survived to make a fight of it but instead of regrouping and forming into a credible force, they tried to follow their warlord back to their ships, thereby retreating even though having been so close to victory. The Saxon bowmen had already shown how well they could shoot so when they reached the ships, the Vikings were forced to scramble aboard one of them and take what cover they could find.

In the meantime, Borg made no attempt to join them. Instead, he stood at the water's edge, still mournfully cradling his son's body. Two Saxon warriors approached him with their bows raised but he still made no attempt to escape. It was as though he was so lost in his grief that his own life no longer mattered – he simply wanted to die as well, preferably in combat as was the Viking way, and thereby take his rightful place in Valhalla, along with his son. The Saxon bowmen duly obliged and, as their arrows struck home, he sank to his knees but still had strength enough to lay his precious son down gently on the sand. With that another Saxon went forward, shield and spear in hand to finish him. He despatched Borg easily enough but the warlord died bravely and without complaint, his body then lying beside that of his son as though reunited with him in death.

* * * * *

At that point Oswald limped down to the beach, helped by Sigbert. He ordered his men to ignore the chance of plunder and to make sure they finished what they'd started. 'All booty will be shared,' he ordered. 'When we finish this there'll be enough for all but keep these bastards from sailing away.'

As it turned out they didn't have to wait long for reinforcements to arrive but it wasn't the fyrd from Twynham which came to help them to complete their victory, but Governor Osric. Those watching on the cliffs to the east of the harbour at Wareham had seen the third ship and lit both beacons. Fearing it was the start of the invasion, people flocked into the settlement seeking shelter only to realise it was a false alarm. Osric then selected a small force from those who had arrived and marched to his nephew's aid. When he got there he could scarce believe that Oswald's men had not only survived the fray but had actually emerged victorious.

On seeing those reinforcements arrive, the Vikings cowering in the ship decided they had no option but to risk making good their escape. With a sudden rush, some of them slipped over the side and, as one man set about cutting the mooring rope with an axe, they used their shields to protect him. That done, they heaved the longship back into the water and pushed it off between them. Having managed to refloat the ship, the survivors then leaped back on board and set about rowing away from the shore.

As soon as Osric saw this he knew he had no choice. He had hoped to take all three ships intact so they could be reused but quickly realised that was no longer an option. He therefore gave the order for fire arrows to be made. This was done by tightly wrapping strips of cloth around the arrows then dipping them in the pitch buckets they found aboard the remaining ships. The arrows were then lit and loosed into the retreating longship as it struggled away from the shore, some of the men running down the beach to get close enough to ensure that as many as possible found their mark.

The Vikings on board had no chance. The pitch-coated timbers and the sail which was rolled up on the deck began to burn and the fire quickly spread. As it did so, the flames gave off a thick and noxious smoke that engulfed them all and left them with just two options – burn, or more likely choke to death, or leap overboard where they would surely drown. Most preferred the latter, hurriedly stripping themselves naked before leaping into the sea. By that time they were already a good way from the shore and, with the tide against them, those in the water struggled to make much headway. Most simply drowned, but several who could swim made it back to the shore where the Saxons were waiting to finish them with spears. Only one man was spared, the tall man with fair hair and blue eyes who had been the one to translate for Coenred and who spoke without any trace of an accent. It was that which saved him.

'Wait!' he pleaded as Sigbert made ready to finish him. 'I'm a Saxon taken hostage by these bastards!'

Sigbert was not immediately inclined to believe the man but the accent was enough for him to stay his hand long enough to hear him out. Besides, the prisoner was going nowhere. He lay in the surf, naked and stranded like a beached seal as the waves crashed over him, his hands held up imploringly.

'Name yourself!' ordered Sigbert, his spear still poised. Several men came to see what was going on, having brutally slain any others who had made it ashore.

'I was christened Edmund, son of Lord Edwulf who was an Ealdorman known to the King in person.'

The name of Lord Edwulf meant nothing to Sigbert or to any of the others with him but, given that many men had been taken as slaves over the years, nobles and ceorls alike, it was enough for him to be given a chance to explain himself further. He was therefore allowed to get up and taken under guard to where Oswald waited. Mercifully, he ordered the man to be taken away and detained until they had time to deal with him.

Meanwhile, the Saxons all watched from the shore as the longship was finally engulfed in flames and sank, taking with it all those who had stayed on board.

* * * * *

With the fighting over, the Saxons showed no mercy and put all the wounded Vikings to the sword then, ignoring Oswald's orders, began stripping what they could from the dead. This included silver armbands, jewellery and such like which they saw as a reward for all they'd endured, plus weapons and any war gear which could be reused. Most valued of all was a sword which had belonged to one of the Vikings and been dropped as they retreated. It was offered to Oswald who, as commander, had every right to receive it.

As he examined the sword, he noted that it was a very fine weapon with a well-forged blade. The grip had been gilded with a silver pattern of a serpent's tail with the pommel shaped to form its head. There were also runes etched into the blade which he knew would be the name of the sword but which he couldn't read.

* * * * *

During this time, many men began to speak of Edward's courage and quick thinking but the boy was more concerned with the remorse he felt for the part he'd played in so much slaughter. It was not just that he'd actually killed Coenred, it was more that he mourned the loss of so many horses, especially Knave who had been badly hurt not only by the arrow but also in the fall which followed. He knew she had to be put down but had not the heart to do it himself. Instead, he tried to calm the poor creature as one of the other men mercifully despatched her for him.

That done, he managed to instruct the men on how to round up the two frightened horses which had survived. All the others lay dead or, like Knave, were so badly injured that they needed to be destroyed, as did many of the cattle and the mule. Whilst Edward bitterly regretted that, he knew it was for the best given the horrific injuries the beasts had sustained.

Meanwhile, some of Osric's men clambered aboard the two remaining longships and searched for whatever loot they could find. It amounted to little more than some furs, a few weapons and a modest store of supplies and plunder. However, at least having taken the ships intact, they could be reused by the Saxons, perhaps forming the basis of the fleet at Wareham which Osric was so keen for Alfred to assemble.

With Oswald wounded, Osric had assumed overall command of the entire field. He ordered a few men who had some sailing experience to row both ships back to Wareham, taking their dead and wounded with them, including Oswald himself. As they prepared the ships to leave, the prisoner was also placed aboard one of them where he was made to help row, albeit with his feet securely bound and his hands tied to the oar.

Once they'd gone, Osric turned his attention to disposing of the Viking dead.

'Send word to Twynham,' he ordered. 'As we've done their job for them and killed the bastards, the least they can do is come here to dispose of what's left.'

The dead he referred to, of course, included Coenred

who, because he was a Saxon in name at least, caused them something of a dilemma.

'Leave his body here,' decided Osric. 'He was keen enough to join them so let him rot with them as well. I pray only that God will have mercy on his troubled soul.'

With that the fyrd marched back to Wareham, all looking tired, though no doubt relieved to be alive. Edward in particular was very dejected, so much so that Sigbert went to walk beside him.

'You did well,' he said. 'All here now regard you as a hero, for you saved the lives of us all, not to mention Oswald's reputation.'

Edward stared at his feet as he walked, still looking very morose.

'Is it the loss of your horses which troubles you or the fact that you were forced to kill that traitor Coenred?' asked Sigbert.

Edward looked up. 'It was all such a waste,' he moaned.

'Which? The horses or the men who died?'

'Both,' replied Edward. 'But at least the men knew the risk. The horses didn't deserve to be killed and I bitterly regret my part in it.'

'What even killing Coenred? Surely you can't regret that, for the little sod deserved to die and would surely have killed you if he could.'

Again Edward was silent.

'Don't worry, all men feel bad about taking another man's life. They say it gets easier, though I've not found that to be so.'

'Did he? Deserve to die I mean?' asked Edward.

'Well, he murdered that girl at the nunnery for no good

cause. If you hadn't killed him he'd have been hanged for that even if he'd survived the battle. He was also intent on taking your life with that axe he got hold of.'

'Somehow that doesn't make me feel any better.'

'No, and nothing will. Though I think your conscience should be clear enough, for you did only what was required of you. In fact, it seems to me you are one of the few who acquitted themselves with honour in all of this. It's Oswald who should be made to answer for all the blood that's been shed for so little purpose, not you.'

Chapter Seventeen

The two Viking longships which had been salvaged were rowed back along the coast and into the main harbour, but such was the level of alarm that they were made to wait before being allowed to sail into the river Frome and thence to the quay at Wareham. Once there, they were beached on the muddy riverbank and the dead were taken off to be returned to their families for burial. Oswald, together with all the other wounded, was taken to the nunnery for treatment, although with Ingrid having been murdered there were none there with anything other than very basic skills with which to tend them. Nonetheless, the arrowhead was removed from Oswald's thigh and the wound then cauterised. Afterwards he lay exhausted, dreading his uncle's return knowing that he'd be sternly rebuked for having risked the lives of his men.

'By rights we should be picking up your bodies from the battlefield,' scolded Osric angrily when he and the rest of the fyrd at last arrived back at the settlement. 'When you knew what you were up against you should have withdrawn, not engaged an enemy with the odds stacked so firmly against you. You had no right to risk so many lives just to enhance your own reputation.'

'I didn't knowingly risk anything,' argued Oswald. 'I expected support from the fyrd at Twynham but that never came thus leaving us to stand alone. Cedric, who is the

Garrison Commander there, should be made to answer for leaving us to face three Viking longships unaided.'

'Cedric's first duty was to the people at Twynham. Only once he could be sure they were secure should he have risked sending men to join you.'

'That's not the way of it as well you know!' argued Oswald. 'He should have at least sent word about the sighting of a third ship!'

Osric struggled to keep his temper. 'He did!' he stormed. 'As I understand it he sent your own man back to warn you. At that point you still had the chance to retreat yet you chose instead to put all those within your charge at risk, not to mention this settlement as well.'

'This settlement was far more at risk from all Coenred could have told the main Viking fleet about the defences here than it was from a raid by just three Viking ships. I therefore saw it as my duty to carry out your orders and try to kill or apprehend the little wretch, not withdraw,' insisted Oswald defensively. 'Besides, I was proved right for we gave a good account of ourselves and—'

His uncle didn't let him finish. 'Your plan worked only because a stable boy saved your lives,' he said harshly.

Oswald offered nothing in response to that, for there was no denying the truth of it.

'That same boy you once said would never make a warrior,' continued Osric. 'Yet his courage was such that he rode headlong into a band of Vikings who were all armed and baying for blood. To my mind that took more guts than you'd expect from even a seasoned warrior.'

Put like that, Oswald could see that he'd misjudged the boy. 'I agree that we owe him much,' he managed.

'You owe him your life and that of all your men,' said Osric flatly. 'Those who stood with you can speak of nothing else. I've therefore sent for him so we can acknowledge his quick thinking and his courage.'

'I confess there is something about the boy,' admitted Oswald. 'We recovered a very fine sword which must have belonged to one of the Vikings. I plan to give it to him as a reward, for he's shown an interest in learning how to wield one.'

'Good. Then you must teach him. Now what about this prisoner? I hear there's something about him as well.'

'He's just a man bargaining for his life by claiming to be a Saxon. We should put him to the sword and be done with it.'

'I've never known a Viking to plead for his life. They don't fear death, they welcome it! Have you yet spoken with him?'

Oswald shook his head. 'I thought I'd leave that to you. He claims to be the son of a man named Edwulf who was an Ealdorman in Wessex some years ago. Apparently he and his sister were taken for slaves following a Viking raid.'

Osric was suddenly taken aback. 'Does he by God!'

'Why, do you then know the man of whom he speaks?'

'I do. Assuming it's the same Lord Edwulf I once knew, then he's claiming to be the eldest son from a very noble family indeed. In fact, a bloodline which is perhaps second only to that of Alfred himself.'

'Surely that can't be so?'

'Well, Lord Edwulf and his wife were both killed in a Viking raid and their eldest son and daughter were indeed taken as slaves.'

'And you knew Lord Edwulf?'

'I did. He was also a personal friend to the King and a great supporter of the Saxon cause.' With that he noticed a sword which had been placed in one corner of the chamber, still unsheathed. He immediately went across and picked it up, then stood for a moment, cradling it with an almost curious reverence. 'Is this the sword you mentioned?' he asked. 'The one which was found on the battlefield?'

Oswald nodded, glad for the chance to change the conversation. 'Aye, it is. There are some runes on the blade which I take to be the name of it.'

'The runes say that it's called "Red Viper",' said Osric.

'How do you know that? You can't read runes any more than I can,' protested Oswald.

'I don't need to read them,' said his uncle. 'For I've seen this sword before. It was once taken from a Viking warrior by another friend of mine, the renowned Lord Edwin. He in turn passed it to his younger brother, a man named Matthew but who was christened Edward. But here's the rub. Both Edwin and Matthew were also sons of Lord Edwulf so if this wretch you're now holding as a prisoner is telling the truth, they would have been his brothers.'

'So what has all that to do with the sword and how did it come to be here?' asked Oswald.

'Heaven only knows. As I recall, Matthew returned it to a Viking boy named Arne whose father had once owned it. He also offered to adopt Arne as his brother as part of the treaty of peace Lord Alfred agreed with the Vikings following the battle at Edington. After that I can say no more of what became of it; the last we heard was when it was discarded by Arne as he ran away after the battle at Leatherhead where he'd used it to slay Matthew.' He stopped short of saying that Edward, the young stable boy, was almost certainly Matthew's son. 'There are reasons why it would not be an apt gift for the boy,' was all he managed. 'In fact, he may prefer to see it destroyed.'

Oswald looked confused. 'What? Surely it's too fine a weapon for that!' he protested. 'But there's more to this, I can tell. What is it that you're not telling me?'

'All in good time,' said Osric. 'Lord Alfred himself will need to be told of these things and will have much to say about both the prisoner and this sword.'

'In what way?' asked Oswald.

Osric shook his head. 'There are things I am not yet at liberty to speak of,' he said. 'Things of such consequence that when Alfred hears of this he'll no doubt wish to come here in person.'

* * * * *

The following day word arrived by messenger to inform Osric that Lord Alfred and Lord Ethelnorth would indeed be visiting Wareham, though not in response to the matter Osric had referred to. In fact, at first it was not clear what had happened to warrant the visit, though Osric suspected that in part Alfred was coming to look at the captured longships to see what use could be made of them. Either way, such visits from the King were not unusual given that he and selected members of his court constantly travelled throughout the realm, administering justice and signing charters and such like.

The royal party arrived the day after that, accompanied by members of Alfred's personal guard. Alfred and Ethelnorth were accommodated within Osric's Vill whereas the other members of his escort were found places within the fortifications, leaving the rest of the army camped just beyond the marshes.

Alfred and Ethelnorth were, of course, taken direct to the Vill where Osric waited to receive them. As they exchanged greetings, the Hall was cleared of all except a few servants and even they were not allowed to remain once the table had been set with refreshments. Even though still nursing the wound to his leg, Oswald was permitted to join the meeting and took his place at the table as well.

'So my Lord, how goes your campaign?' asked Osric once all were seated.

'The Viking fleet has lately put to sea so we can no longer follow their progress,' said Alfred. 'No doubt they'll strike somewhere when we least expect it. As like as not the first we'll know of it is when they're next sighted but until then all we can do is to watch and wait.'

Osric was not sure whether to be troubled or relieved at the news. 'What about elsewhere, my Lord?' he asked.

'You're aware that we've been fighting on several fronts since last we met?' said Alfred.

'I am indeed, my Lord. Word came that you trapped a faction at Farnham but they managed to escape and took shelter on an island on the river Colne.'

It was Lord Ethelnorth who replied. 'Aye, the bastards there proved to be as slippery as eels! Our men could not contain them long enough for us to arrive with reinforcements and hence they managed to escape. We then moved to attack others who were besieging Exeter but once again they were gone by the time we arrived.'

'I heard tell that at one point you held Jarl Haesten's

wife and two young sons captive but released them?' queried Osric, mystified as to why the King should have done so. 'Is that true, my Lord?'

Alfred hesitated before answering. 'It is. We are a Christian realm and his family had all been baptised so I therefore allowed them their freedom. Just because we're at war with these heathens doesn't mean we should stoop to their brutal ways.'

Osric nodded knowing that an act of mercy such as that was typical of Alfred. 'So what now?' he asked.

Lord Ethelnorth got up and poured mead from a pitcher. He drank deeply, then spoke. 'We fear that the worst is yet to come,' he warned. 'We believe that those who threatened Exeter came in ships from both Northumbria and East Anglia. We can only assume that their intent is to ravage the coast of Wessex, hoping to establish a viable foothold from which to launch their invasion, then use the rivers and trackways to strike deep inland from there.'

Oswald, who had remained quiet until then, could barely contain himself. 'An apt warning, my Lords but it comes too late. Already we've faced an attack from three ships which were intent on taking whichever settlement seemed weakest, Wareham or Twynham – or perhaps both.'

'I doubt that was anything more than a warband out to take what they could for themselves,' noted Alfred. 'We have word of many such attacks all along the coast as the ships which make up the invasion fleet seek fresh water, food and supplies. Needless to say they don't eschew the chance for plunder whilst they're about it.'

'Even so, it was a cleverly devised ruse and would have worked but for our swift response and…'

'And luck,' added his uncle solemnly. 'We were saved thanks only to that stable boy you sent me.'

Alfred was immediately interested in how the boy had managed to secure their victory and seemed pleased when an account of the battle was explained to him.

'So he drove the beasts directly at them across the bridge and thereby split their ranks!' said Ethelnorth, clearly impressed. 'Now that took guts!'

'But for him we might have all been slain,' admitted Oswald.

'Then I would speak with the boy,' said Alfred. 'It seems it's time for him to be told something of his true lineage.'

'I'll send for him,' said Osric. 'Though I warn you he's not easily lured away from looking after his precious horses – or at least the two which were not killed in the battle or put down afterwards.'

As they waited, Oswald realised there was much he didn't know. When he asked about that he was told only that all would soon be revealed.

When Edward eventually arrived, he was shown through to the Hall where he seemed bemused by all that was going on. Recognising Alfred and Lord Ethelnorth at once, he bowed as he entered, unsure of what he should say or how he should conduct himself.

'Don't worry, Edward, you're not in any trouble,' said Alfred to reassure him. 'In fact, the opposite. I hear you've done well and I see your father in this, for it was the sort of thing he'd have done when alive.'

Edward looked shocked. 'My father? You also knew him, my Lord?'

Alfred smiled. 'Aye, I did. And like Lord Ethelnorth and Governor Osric, was proud to have fought beside him.'

'Then who was he?' asked Edward anxious to at last learn about matters which seemed to have eluded him all his life.

Alfred looked at Lord Ethelnorth who in turn looked at Osric.

'Your father was christened Edward but took the name of Matthew when he entered the Church as a boy,' ventured Alfred at last. 'He was the third born son of a very noble Saxon called Lord Edwulf, an Ealdorman of Wessex and one of my most trusted Councillors. His brother was Lord Edwin, a warrior of whom many Saxons still speak of with great respect. You may well have heard of him.'

Edward looked incredulous. 'But, Sire…' he stammered.

'Wait, there's more,' said Alfred, picking up the sword. 'This weapon was found following the recent fray and Oswald has deemed that you should have it in recognition of your courage and quick thinking which saved the lives of so many. However, I must first warn you that I believe it to be the very same sword which was used to kill your father. It was first taken by your uncle who gave it to your father to use. As a gesture of peace, your father then returned it to a Viking boy named Arne, a treacherous little wretch whose father it had once belonged to. As like as not it was Arne who then used it to slay your father after a battle at a place called Leatherhead. He then discarded it as he ran away but I cannot say for certain how it came to be here. There is much more to say about these matters which we shall tell you in time. For now, suffice to say that the sword is yours. It's called "Red Viper".' With that he took the weapon, still without a sheath, and handed it to the boy. 'Take care, for it's a very fine sword and worth a great deal, certainly more than its weight in silver. However, I must insist that you have the blade bent and thereby rendered useless, for there's probably much Saxon blood on the blade and, as I say, quite possibly that of your father. I have another sword which I shall give you in its place, equally as fine and also yours by rights, for it's been wielded by members of your family for several generations.'

It was Osric who spoke next. 'My nephew Oswald here will teach you how to use it as soon as his wound allows. I need hardly say that as you saved his life along with others, you have my thanks as well.'

Edward looked shocked. 'My Lords, it's more than I deserve but I'm truly grateful. But why was I not told about my father before? I have asked many times but have never been told anything...'

'We will tell you more over the next few days but for now, I would like to set matters right regarding your mother. I believe you are aware that she was a whore but there is much more to it than that. She was not so inclined by nature but rather was forced to become one, so you should therefore feel no shame on that account. Yet, because of that, I could not be sure that you were indeed of Matthew's blood and thus swore all to secrecy until we could be certain,' explained Alfred. 'As his son, you stand to inherit lands and great wealth, all of which I've resolved to return to you now that I'm convinced of your bloodline.'

Edward laughed. It was a nervous laugh because he could hardly believe what he was hearing. 'But how can I be worthy of such an honour, my Lord? I'm a stable boy and have been so all my life...'

Ethelnorth smiled. 'Don't worry, if you're truly Matthew's son you'll prove yourself worthy soon enough, of that I'm certain. In fact, I think that so far as most of us are concerned, you've done as much already.'

* * * * *

As Edward left the Hall he noticed the prisoner who was waiting to be taken in to be questioned. The man was by then dressed in a simple loincloth but his hands remained bound and he was closely guarded. He looked tired and drawn after several days of confinement and ill-treatment by the guards and his head was bowed. As they passed each other, he glanced up at Edward and perhaps saw something in the boy's features which seemed familiar, but then quickly looked away.

The prisoner was then led into the Hall and forced to his knees in homage. Alfred stared at him for a moment but said nothing, preferring to let Ethelnorth conduct the interrogation. The old warrior got up, drew his sword and walked over to stand behind the man.

'The only reason I have for not killing you here and now is that I would not wish to despoil this place with your heathen blood,' he threatened.

'My blood is every bit as Christian as your own,' said the prisoner quietly. 'I was christened and have proof of it, for Lord Alfred's brother stood sponsor for me at the font.'

Ethelnorth looked at Alfred who simply raised an eyebrow and then nodded to confirm that his eldest brother had indeed been Godfather to the eldest son of Lord Edwulf.

'You remember me, my Lord,' said the prisoner, looking up at the King but taking care not to hold his gaze. 'My father was both friend and Councillor to you. He and my mother were both slain in a Viking raid on our Vill and I and my sister, Edwina, taken for slaves.'

Alfred had intended to remain silent but the detail was enough to intrigue him. 'You had other brothers,' he insisted. 'Name them.'

The prisoner proudly straightened his back and spoke up. 'I am Edmund, the eldest son, my Liege. Then there is Edwin a warrior in your service, and also our youngest brother christened Edward but who took the name of Matthew when he entered the Church. He was named for one of the Apostles as I recall. Either will speak for me.'

Ethelnorth returned to his seat. 'Then what became of your sister?' he demanded.

The prisoner lowered his head as if ashamed to speak of it. 'Edwina was ill-used like all the other women who were taken,' he managed. 'The last I heard of her was when she was sent to the cold lands in the far north of the Viking homelands where she was forced to become a whore and died riddled with the pox some years ago.'

'And you did not avenge her?' said Ethelnorth, incredulous that he had not done so.

'How could I, my Lords?' he pleaded. 'I was a slave myself, sold to an evil bastard named Borg who beat the shit out of me if I so much as looked as though I might try to escape.'

'You endured all that yet you still have blood in your veins? How do you explain that if you claim to be a noble Saxon?' demanded Ethelnorth.

Edmund looked up at him. 'Yes, I survived. I was taken to Borg's farmstead where it was found that I knew something about farming for, as my father's eldest son, it was left to me to manage his estates. I laboured there for many years but the winters were long and cold and there was little to be done during those months which needed my skills. Thus, when Borg decided to join Haesten's warband, he didn't trust me to be alone with his wife and daughters so made me come with him. When we arrived here I waited, hoping for a chance to escape.'

'Was that the same Borg who led the attack on us a few days ago?' asked Osric.

The prisoner nodded. 'It was. And the boy who was slain was his eldest son.'

'We also found a very valuable sword among the dead,' said Osric. 'We believe it belonged to a boy named Arne.'

Alfred laughed. 'He'd be a boy no more, for it was near fifteen years ago that we last came across that treacherous little toad,' he said.

The prisoner nodded knowingly. 'Aye, he was there right enough. But as you say, he's a cowardly wretch so I wonder how it was that your paths ever crossed?'

'We'll speak more of that later,' said Ethelnorth. 'As Lord Alfred said, it was all a long time ago.'

'Aye,' said the prisoner. 'Fifteen long, hard years, and every day I woke longing for my freedom – sometimes even praying I would die rather than endure more years of bondage.'

'Yet you carry wounds from the fray,' observed Osric. 'That suggests that you fought beside the Vikings against us. Doubtless you killed at least one of our men if not more.'

Edmund shook his head. 'No my Lords, I held back intending to break free when the chance arose. But there was such chaos when the beasts and the horses were driven through the ranks that I was caught in the melee that followed. I went with the others as the Saxons advanced lest I be slain before I could reveal myself.'

'And you expect us to believe this crap?' said Ethelnorth sternly.

'My Lord, it is the truth, I swear it.'

Alfred also remained suspicious. 'You had your chance to escape during the battle but returned instead to the ship. That doesn't seem right to me. Also, no Saxon would fight alongside men who had killed his parents and forced his sister to become a slave and a whore.'

'There was nothing I could do on either count, my Lord. What other option did I have?'

It was Ethelnorth who answered. 'You could have died like a Saxon should and, in so doing, avenged all the wrongs which were done to you and your family.'

'My Lords, I implore you to ask my brothers to come here. There are things I can speak of which only they will know the truth of.'

'Both your brothers are dead, as by rights should you be,' said Ethelnorth.

Alfred summoned the guards to approach. 'I agree with Lord Ethelnorth in this but there are questions which have yet to be answered. Take him away. Give him food and water and there are to be no more beatings until we determine the truth of his claim. We shall debate this matter and, if his story is found wanting, he'll then suffer more pain than anything you can inflict, be assured of that. For the man who he claims to have been his father was a good friend to me and a loyal Saxon. I'll not tolerate anyone taking his repute in vain.'

Chapter Eighteen

Alfred had decided to remain within the relative safety of the fortifications at Wareham for several days at least, thereby taking the opportunity to deal with various administrative matters which demanded his attention. Whilst taking a much-needed break from those deliberations, he and Lord Ethelnorth stood together to watch as Osric at last attempted to ride Fleet, his prized stallion.

Osric started by first petting Fleet before mounting him whilst Edward remained beside them, holding the reins of the horse securely. At first, he just sat there for a few moments, almost as if afraid to move.

'As you say,' said Ethelnorth. 'That boy has a way with horses.'

'And loves them dearly,' replied Alfred. 'I'm told that despite his newfound status he continues to sleep in the stables.'

Ethelnorth laughed. 'Aye, but I've no doubt that Osric's great-niece will put an end to that soon enough.'

Alfred saw the joke at once. 'And do you know, I think even Oswald is now keen to see his daughter betrothed to a stable boy. I wonder how long it will take for the boy to pluck up enough courage to suggest courtship?'

'Ha!' said Ethelnorth. 'If he's anything like his father,

once he gets a taste for it there'll be no stopping him!'

'Which reminds me, there is yet something more we need to tell young Edward.'

'As I see it, there's much we need to tell him but what in particular do you have in mind?'

'The truth about Coenred for one thing. For if what Ingar told me all those years ago is true, that would make the boy Edward slew some sort of a blood relation, would it not?'

Ethelnorth considered that for a moment before replying. 'As I recall, what Ingar said was that Matthew had sired her daughter whereas her son was the spawn of that Viking slaver. On that basis, I don't see how Coenred can be regarded as being of Matthew's blood, thus he and Edward weren't actually related.'

Alfred seemed to accept that. 'But her daughter Ingrid would have been Edward's half-sister as they had the same father, albeit different mothers. Is that not so?'

'It is, Sire. Or at least, that's as I understand it,' agreed Ethelnorth. 'Though it assumes that what Ingar told us is correct and I still wonder how she could have known such a thing for certain given that she carried both babies in her womb at the same time.'

'Either way, Edward will still need to be told.'

Ethelnorth didn't seem to agree. 'I think the boy has endured enough surprises for now. Besides, there's no rush as both Coenred and Ingrid are dead so what good would come of spoiling Matthew's reputation with something which cannot be proved and may well be untrue?'

Alfred simply nodded to acknowledge the point.

With that Edward coaxed Fleet to take a few steps forward as Osric sat up straight in the saddle. When they reached the gate to the pasture, Edward opened it and handed over the reins. For a moment Osric seemed to hesitate before looking back at Lord Ethelnorth and at his King proudly, clearly enjoying a long-awaited moment. As he did so, Edward whispered something to Fleet and the horse moved off, slowly at first to allow Osric to gain his confidence. Within a few minutes they were trotting and then finally the horse broke into a steady canter.

'So what will you do with this rogue who claims to be Edmund?' asked Ethelnorth as they continued to watch Osric. 'If you acknowledge his claim, then being the eldest son, he would rightfully be entitled to inherit all Lord Edwulf's estate.'

Alfred was ahead of him on that. 'Yes, which makes this a very complicated matter indeed, for it means that Edwin should not have taken title to their father's lands all those years ago if his elder brother was still alive. Matthew's claim to that fortune would therefore have been similarly denied so young Edward could now inherit only that which was his father's by right.'

'That would still be a goodly amount,' said Ethelnorth. 'Don't forget that Matthew donated a significant amount of treasure to your cause for which you promised him lands of equal worth. He would also have been entitled to a share of the spoils we took when we liberated Chippenham. All of that should now pass to young Edward as of right.'

'I've not forgotten my promise to Matthew,' Alfred assured him. 'And I shall make good my pledge. The question which remains is whether this man really is Edmund as he claims to be, or an imposter.'

'He looks like Matthew and Edwin,' said Ethelnorth,

saying aloud for the first time what Alfred had been thinking. 'The likeness is uncanny and had they lived they would all have been of a similar age by now.'

'True,' admitted the King. 'In which case, deciding who should inherit what will need the judgement of Solomon.'

'There must be some way to resolve matters between them,' mused Ethelnorth.

'Perhaps I won't have to,' said Alfred. 'If they are truly kin they should be able to come to an amicable arrangement if I allow them to settle matters between themselves. Also, there's enough to share and dividing their wealth will also serve to dilute the power of them both; that way I may at least sleep a little more soundly in my bed.'

'Surely you don't suspect that young Edward would seek to usurp you?'

'No, not him. Though others might use him to that same end. As for Edmund, much has happened to turn him against us. Hence dividing their wealth and power might well be a wise precaution.'

Ethelnorth sneered at the suggestion. 'As always you find a pearl in every oyster,' he said.

Alfred laughed. 'Well, not everything can be solved with a sword.'

'I'll remind you of that when the Viking hordes next confront us, as they surely will soon enough.'

With that Osric returned and dismounted. He then petted the black stallion, letting it nuzzle his hand before leading it across to where Edward waited. 'With Alfred's permission, I would that you would accept this fine horse as my gift in recognition of a favour your father once did for me,' he said as he offered the reins to Edward.

'But my Lord, what favour did he do to warrant such a gift?'

'As I told you, he cleared my name and my reputation when many thought I might be guilty of treachery against my King and against the Saxon cause. Besides, thanks to you I've had my wish and now ridden this fine animal. Having done so, I fear my nephew is right. He is so fleet of foot and such a powerful beast that my old bones would not survive a fall. No one is better placed to ride him than you.'

'My Lord,' said Edward feeling very unsure of himself. 'Surely this is all too much? '

Alfred and Lord Ethelnorth both went over to join them. 'You must be the strangest stable boy in all the realm,' remarked Ethelnorth. 'For you have a fine sword, a magnificent stallion and the prospect of great wealth. Not only that but you've earned the respect of all, including your King even though so young and as yet untrained as a warrior.'

Alfred smiled knowingly. 'And we still have much to discuss. I would have you come to see Lord Ethelnorth, Governor Osric and myself tomorrow that we may answer all that which still bemuses you. Also, there's another matter of which you should be aware.'

Edward hesitated. 'Of course, my Lord. But I'll first need to tend to the horses…'

All three men laughed heartily. Then Osric replied on behalf of them all. 'Edward, I think your duties at the stables can wait. What we have to say to you is of much more import.'

'Even so, my Lords, they'll need…'

Lord Alfred seemed more than pleased with the boy's commitment to his duty. 'So much of your manner reminds me of your father who was very dear to me. I can see that your bloodline is not to be denied and nor in this time of such great need should it be ignored, for there is much that you can bring to our cause. You have the blood of a true warrior in your veins and that's something I shall surely need – and probably much sooner than many might wish.'

* * * * *

Alfred, Ethelnorth and Osric next went with Oswald to examine the two captured longships. They found them beached on the muddy bank beside the quay where Sigbert in his role as carpenter was checking them over to see what repairs might be needed.

'Are they sound enough to be reused?' asked Alfred, calling out to him.

Sigbert bowed before answering. 'Sire, they are in need of some minor repair for which I'll need timbers and nails and such like, but I'll soon have them rendered worthy.'

'Good,' said Alfred, then turned to Osric. 'Perhaps now you'll stop asking me for ships. You have a fleet of two, which is twice as many as most of the burhs can manage.' Even as he said it, he smiled so that Osric knew that he was teasing him.

'Thank you, my Lord. Then all I need now is men who are able to sail them.'

Alfred laughed. 'Worry about that when they're fully mended. Though I suspect there'll be no shortage of men willing to learn, for most will much prefer to take to the water rather than serve in the shield wall.'

* * * * *

Ida was up early the next day as usual but when she went through to the kitchen, she was surprised to find that Mildred wasn't there. It was the maid's job to help with the preparation of food for all those staying at the Vill, and with two such important guests and the retinue of armed men they'd brought with them, there was much work to be done. She set about looking for the girl and found her outside where it was clear she'd been vomiting.

'Lord love us,' she said. 'Don't say you're unwell when there's yet so much to be done!'

Mildred, who was sitting with her knees drawn up to her chin, looked up pitifully. 'I'll be all right in a moment,' she said, wiping her mouth with the back of her hand. 'It's just this sickness which makes me feel so wretched in the morning.'

Ida knew at once what was wrong. 'How long has this been going on?' she pressed.

'Just this week. But it quickly passes…'

'How long since your last bleeding?' she demanded.

Mildred shrugged, pretending she had not given that much thought. 'A few months or more.'

'You stupid girl. You're with child, don't you know as much?'

'No, it can't be that. For I'm not yet wed and…!'

Ida shook her head. 'I think you know the answer to that without me telling you! 'Tis that fool Coenred's, I'll be bound. And him run off like a frightened dog and now got himself killed! Well, you're not the first foolish girl to find herself with child and you won't be the last, though Heaven help you, for you're not much more than a child yourself.'

Mildred started sobbing. 'If what you say is so, what then will become of me?' she cried.

264

'That's not for me to say. You'd best pray that Ulrich takes pity on you but most likely he'll turn you out lest you bring disgrace upon us all.'

'What then?' she asked almost pleading.

'Well, you're spoiled so no man will take you to wife, particularly once there's another mouth to feed. Most men find it hard enough to provide for theirselves, never mind the bastard child of some fool boy, particularly a treacherous murderer.'

'How then will I manage?'

'You'll have to learn to fend for yourself, you foolish girl.'

Mildred needed no explanation of what that would entail.

* * * * *

Later that morning, Edward went to see Alfred as arranged and waited outside the Hall until summoned. Once called in, he bowed respectfully and stood before the three great men, not sure what to expect. In the end he was ushered towards a seat which was, in itself, a privilege, for few were allowed to sit in the presence of their King except Ealdormen and other nobles.

'How's your shoulder?' asked Alfred kindly. 'I gather you were hurt when your horse was killed from under you?'

'My Lord, it's much improved, thank you.'

'And what of that wound to your leg?' asked Osric. 'Is that now fully healed?'

'It is, my Lord. I still carry the scar but can now walk as I did before.'

'Good,' said Alfred. 'We've summoned you here where

we can speak in private because it's time you learned more about your kin. Some of what I'm about to say you will already know or may have gleaned from others but it bears repeating, for I wish to ensure that you know as much as I can tell you. I won't dwell upon events which stretch back beyond my reign, except to say that your bloodline traces back for many generations and that your forebears include many great warriors who have served our cause with honour and distinction. You'll doubtless learn more about that in time but, for now, suffice to say that your grandfather, Lord Edwulf, was a very dear friend of mine, both as an Ealdorman and a loyal Saxon. He and his wife were cruelly slain in a Viking raid and their eldest son and daughter both taken for slaves. Lord Edwulf had two other sons, Edwin and your father, who both remained steadfast during the difficult days as we sheltered at Athelney, a time about which I'm sure you've heard tell. There they both served with great courage. Edwin was rated one of the finest warriors in the realm but was slain at Edington. It was a great loss to our cause and even now his name is mentioned whenever men speak of that great triumph. That leaves us with your father. As I said, he was christened Edward and it was for him that you were named but, as the third born son, he was given to the Church where he was renamed for one of the Apostles and came to be known as Matthew.'

Alfred hesitated there, as if not quite sure how to continue. 'In truth, I doubt that he was ever suited for a religious calling and, having been caught up in the battle at Chippenham, was obliged to become a warrior. I and these two Lords can tell you more of what transpired there but all in good time. For now, suffice to say that he soon showed himself to be a brave young man with sense beyond his years and he quickly became much respected by all who knew him.' Alfred then paused again. 'That brings us to the part of which I am least proud,' he said at last. 'There was a girl with us at Athelney who was the daughter of a traitor. As such, all she owned was forfeit to me and I set her to work satisfying the men's baser needs. It was not in her nature to sell her body thus but she had no choice. In the end your father fell in love with her and would have wed the girl had I let him. It was, of course, unthinkable that he, the son of an Ealdorman, should marry a girl who was both a whore and the daughter of a traitor but he insisted. To give him time to reconsider, I sent him on what should have been a simple mission but in the course of that he was wounded in a surprise attack. By some miracle he survived the wound and became known as the Warrior with the Pierced Heart. By the time he was able to return to us, the girl had told me that she was with child. Your father was still determined to wed her but I again sent him off to prepare the defences at a place called Leatherhead which I believed would come under threat. My fears were confirmed and he perished there amid a desperate battle to save my realm. From all we know he died at the hand of a cowardly rogue called Arne.'

Alfred paused yet again. 'The girl was named Emelda. She was, as well you know by now, your mother who died giving birth to you. Because of what she'd been forced to become I could not be sure of your heritage but took you in and watched you grow. I am now certain of it, as are we all.'

Edward listened spellbound. 'Then am I definitely Matthew's son?' he queried.

Alfred nodded. 'I believe that to be so, just as I believe he would now be very proud to recognise you as such. I propose to issue a decree formally acknowledging that your bloodline is that of Lord Edwulf. What's more, your father amassed a small fortune which he lent to me and which I pledged to repay. I intend to honour that promise in full. Meanwhile, I would have you remain here under Lord Osric's charge so that you may learn what it is to be a nobleman. Whilst here, Oswald will teach you how to use the family sword I mentioned which has been wielded with such pride by many great warriors before you. That's on condition that you destroy the one which I believe was used to kill your father, for its mere existence offends me.'

'I will, my Lord, but I can hardly take all this in,' said Edward.

'There is one problem,' said Alfred. 'You would stand to inherit your family' lands as well, but another with a prior claim has come forward.'

'Another member of my family?' asked Edward excitedly.

'Yes. He claims to be your father's elder brother, the one who, following a raid, was taken by the Vikings for a slave.'

'So where is he, Sire? I would meet him if I may…'

Alfred looked at the others. 'All in good time. For now he's in bonds until his claim can be confirmed,' he said. 'For he's the Viking who was taken prisoner at the recent skirmish on the heath between here and Twynham.'

* * * * *

Alfred allowed enough time for Edward to leave before calling Edmund to the Hall. He arrived, fully dressed in a simple tunic but with his arms still bound, accompanied by two guards.

'Release him,' ordered Alfred. 'But remain here for our protection, for I doubt that he'll much like what I'm about to tell him.'

The guards undid the bonds and then stepped to one side but kept their spears poised.

'So, have you more to say on your account?' demanded Alfred.

Edmund looked concerned. 'Sire, have I not already said enough to prove my claim? Is it not sufficient that my father was a noble Saxon who was ever loyal to your cause?'

'If you are indeed who you say you are then that's true enough, though you have offered nothing beyond hearsay to prove you are the son of that great man.'

Edmund thought hard. 'There was a ring,' he announced suddenly. 'A ring which he said was a gift from you, my Lord. He showed it to me often and was proud of it, assuring me that as his eldest son it would one day be mine. It had a band of woven gold and a bright green stone as I recall. He only ever wore it on important occasions for he valued it so much that he was afraid lest it be lost or stolen.'

'I recall the ring you mention. It was indeed a gift from me. So what became of it?'

'It was taken from his dead hand by one of the raiders but after that I never saw it again. Surely my knowing of this is enough to prove my claim?' said Edmund. 'Will you now believe that I am indeed the eldest son of Lord Edwulf! If so, his title should by rights be mine.'

'No man can achieve that status by birthright alone,' said Alfred. 'True, it's often bestowed on the eldest son, but they must first show that they warrant such trust. You have not yet done so.'

'How could I?' demanded Edmund. 'I was held prisoner by our enemies against my will!'

'Any true Saxon would have died rather than let himself be taken. Also, you did nothing to avenge your dear sister. Instead, you took up arms with those who wronged you and even came with them to fight against your King. There are those who think you should be hanged for that alone but, in deference to the memory of your dear father and all that he did to serve me, I am inclined to mercy.'

'Then what of my lands? Am I to be deprived of those as well?'

'Your lands were all forfeit to me and, besides, they've already been given to others who've served me. There is also one who has a similar claim to your own.'

Edmund was intrigued. 'Who can that be?' he asked. 'You said that both of my brothers are dead and I know that all the other members of my family have been killed as well.'

'Not all,' said Alfred coldly. 'Your brothers both gave their lives for our cause but Matthew didn't die without issue. He had a son who is called Edward.'

'But Matthew was a monk, given to the Church!'

'Not all his life he wasn't.'

'So what of his wife? Does she still live?'

Alfred shook his head. 'He had no wife. And the woman who bore his child died giving birth to him.'

'You mean he's a bastard? You'd recognise the bastard son over that of a legitimate heir?'

'In the circumstances I would. For there's justice in that, all things considered.'

'So who is this ill-born wretch who takes my lands and

my birthright? I would meet him, for there's much he should know which only I can tell him.'

Ethelnorth laughed. 'You've met him already. He led the charge which broke the Viking ranks at the battle.'

Edmund was suddenly very quiet. 'The boy on the horse? He had more guts than all the other men there put together. Does he yet know of my fate?' he asked.

'He does,' confirmed Alfred. 'Though I shall ensure that the two of you do not meet until such time as you can do so as friends. For there's no room for malice between you in these difficult times.'

'And that's it? My fortune is lost through no fault of my own and I'm confined to a more lowly status than that to which I was born. Is there nothing I can do to resolve my position?'

'There are ways you may yet redeem yourself and prove your loyalty to your King and to our cause,' suggested Ethelnorth.

'How?' demanded Edmund.

'To start with, tell us what you know about Jarl Haesten.'

Edmund shook his head. 'I've never met him but, by all accounts, he's a very ambitious man and they say he has a heart as cold and as hard as ice. It's also said that if you cross him you can expect no mercy.'

'So, what's his intent?' demanded Alfred.

'How would I know? I was just a wretched slave, remember? Manacled to my oar and beaten if I refused to row.'

'But you must have heard something!' insisted Ethelnorth.

'Word was that he plans a full invasion, recruiting those of his kind who have already settled here.'

'That much we know already,' said Alfred. 'Hopefully we'll soon dissuade them of that.'

Edmund laughed. 'Then how little you know of the Viking ways, my Lord. They fear nothing, least of all death. To die with a sword in their hand is like going to Heaven for them hence they embrace it willingly, even rejoicing in the pain which follows! If indeed you are to face him then you'd best be ready for that. For if he prevails we'll all die soon enough, myself included.'

'Exactly, which is why we need to know what numbers he has at his disposal, where they will strike next and when,' said Ethelnorth.

'I don't know all that,' pleaded Edmund.

'Then you'll have to find out.'

Edmund could suddenly see what Ethelnorth was leading up to. 'If you're suggesting that I return to their ranks and be your spy, then you can think again! Do you know what Vikings do to spies?'

Ethelnorth needed no reminder of that and realised they would get little information they could rely on from him. He decided to try a different tack. 'Then tell me this. You mentioned that Arne was among the Viking ranks which were defeated here.'

'Aye, he was there right enough, though what became of him I cannot say. I didn't see him fall and usually he's minded to skulk away when it comes to a fray so he may well have escaped alive.'

'Well, he left his sword behind if he did,' mused Ethelnorth. 'And we have cause to know the weapon, for we recognise it well enough.'

Edmund laughed. 'It seems he has a habit of doing that!

It was said that he lost it after another battle many years ago and had to buy it back from the man who found it. The others made much of him having to barter for what was his by rights like some pathetic merchant.'

'Then what should he have done?' asked Alfred.

'Pah! Any true Viking warrior would have just taken what he deemed was his! I gather from what you said last time that you've crossed paths with him before?'

'We have. And if he lives we shall do so again, be assured of that. There are things which remain to be settled between us.'

Edmund said nothing at first. 'If I agree to spy for you I would need coin to cover my expenses,' he managed at last, having clearly changed his mind.

Ethelnorth agreed. 'We would see that your purse is filled, though it would pain me to deal with one whose hand has been raised against us.'

Edmund was far from sure how he would do what was being asked of him but didn't look beyond the promise of coin which he badly needed and, much more importantly, a chance to secure his release. 'All right,' he said at last. 'Then it seems I have no other option but to agree.'

Chapter Nineteen

Mildred stood in the kitchen, sobbing and with her head bowed in shame as she waited for Ulrich to speak. Having discussed the matter, both Osric and Oswald had decided to let him deal with the girl in his capacity as Reeve and he was in no mood to be lenient.

'You've brought shame to our master's door,' he said sternly. 'You've behaved no better than a bitch on heat and will now have to suffer the burden of your wanton ways.'

'Sir, I'm truly sorry. I was taken advantage of by Coenred who's the father of my child. He promised much but instead died without even knowing of my condition.'

'I doubt that!' said Ulrich. 'It's my guess that your "condition" as you call it was one of the reasons he left. That and the disgrace he'd brought upon himself by killing an innocent girl who tried only to help him.'

Mildred fought back the tears as she waited for him to finish.

'You've made your bed so must lie in it,' he stormed. 'Our masters will not have the bastard child of a treacherous murderer reared under their roof. So you're to take what's yours and be gone from here.'

'But I've nowhere to go!'

'You should have thought of that.'

'Sir, I beg you. Let me stay. I'll work harder to make up

for it. I'll do whatever you ask. Please don't make me leave. You know what will become of me if you do!'

Just for a moment Ulrich considered the position but then turned away. 'You have my decision. I expect you to be gone by morning.'

* * * * *

Despite the fact that Alfred had intended to keep it a secret until he'd issued his decree, word of Edward's true lineage somehow seeped out and quickly spread. Some claimed not to be surprised, saying they'd been able to see that he was more than just a simple stable boy right from the start, whilst others suddenly sought to befriend him by taking small gifts to the stable, anxious to curry his favour. Only one, Sigbert, seemed to have a genuine concern for the boy.

'I'm glad for you,' he said as they leaned on the gate to the pasture and watched the horses contentedly grazing. Having finished surveying the captured longships, he'd been sent by Osric to also look at the possibility of adapting the stables to accommodate more horses, for they planned to replace those which had been killed in the battle so that Oswald's plan could be put into effect again when needed.

'Thank you,' said Edward. 'Though it's all come as a great surprise to me.'

'And to that uncle of yours, I'll warrant. You must watch out for him, for he came here intent on reclaiming what he will see as his just inheritance only to find that he's likely to be denied.'

'But not by me,' explained Edward. 'I'm to be given only that which was my father's due.'

'I doubt he'll see it that way so watch your back. You've learned a little of the ways of men but I doubt you'd prove a match for the likes of him.'

It was a timely warning and one which Edward appreciated, for he knew he still had much to learn – and even more to lose now that he was set to become a nobleman.

'Now, what about these horses? We can't have a noble personage such as yourself shovelling their shit, now can we?'

'But I want to,' said Edward. 'It's the only work I know.'

'Well, I'll speak to Ulrich to see if there's another lad who might be given the task. You can teach him but at least then you won't have to sleep in the stables.'

Osric had already offered Edward proper lodgings at the Vill and, whilst he appreciated the gesture, he'd declined to accept it as he felt he would find it hard to settle given that apart from the night at Aelfric's Vill on the way to Wareham, he could scarce remember one he hadn't spent in a stable.

It was then that Sigbert noticed that Odelia was waiting nearby. 'I think you have another visitor,' he said grinning.

Edward looked across and was delighted when he saw who it was.

'I've a feeling you'd rather speak with her than with the likes of me,' said Sigbert tactfully. 'Besides, I've work to be getting on with.'

'Thank you for your advice,' said Edward.

'You be sure to heed it,' warned Sigbert. 'And remember, watch your back at all times. If you're worried, send word to me. It was my life you saved that day as well as others.'

Once Sigbert had left, Odelia went across to speak with Edward. 'I hear you're not a simple stable boy any more,' she said. 'Rather you're now a great warrior and from a bloodline even more noble than my own.'

'I'm hardly a great warrior,' he replied, protesting shyly. 'I did only what was needed, that's all.'

'Well, everyone seems very impressed. Not least of all my father who appears to have formed a very different opinion of you.'

Edward looked up hopefully. 'So, you're no longer forbidden to see me?'

'I was never "forbidden" to see you,' she said. 'It was just made clear to me that I was not to encourage you in any way.'

'What does that mean?' asked Edward.

'It means that I was not to waste my time with unsuitable boys.'

'But I'm now thought suitable? Suitable for what then?'

She giggled girlishly. 'I'll show you,' she said, then took him by the arm and led him towards the river. Keeping her arm tucked in his, they walked together along the bank but said nothing.

'What were you going to show me?' he asked, breaking the silence.

'That depends.'

'On what?'

'On whether you like me or not.'

'I do,' he said a little too quickly. 'But do you like me?'

'A bit,' she teased.

'How much is a bit?'

'Well, I might let you kiss me. Except...'

'Except what?'

'Except that you smell of horse sweat and worse. I think before I let you kiss me you need to bathe.'

'Bathe!' exclaimed Edward, astonished at the very thought of it. He could never remember bathing beyond occasionally sluicing himself down with cold water from the horses' trough.

'Now you're supposed to be a nobleman, it's something you'll have to get used to. And probably at least once a month.'

'But how do I bathe?' he asked.

'Well, you could try the river, though deep and wide as it is I doubt there's even enough water there to get someone as smelly as you are properly clean...'

With that she ran back to the Vill, laughing and clearly expecting Edward to follow her if only with his eyes.

* * * * *

Mindful of all Odelia had said, Edward took himself to the river and, finding a place where he couldn't be seen, stripped off all his clothes. The garments he wore had been given to him by Osric so that Ida, who now recognised him as more than just a stable boy, had willingly taken his old clothes away to be washed and mended.

The river was cold but he braved it nonetheless, wading out till he was near waist deep and then ducking himself under several times. It was not an experience he much enjoyed but if the rewards for enduring it included a chance to see Odelia again, he was more than happy to oblige. When he'd done, he turned to go back to the bank but then noticed something in the water which had got caught up in the reeds. He went across to see what it was and, to his horror, found it was the body of a young girl. He recognised at once who she was.

* * * * *

Finding Mildred had been a shock but he called others to assist, then left them to recover her body whilst he went back to the Vill to tell Osric. He met Ida first and couldn't seem to hold his tongue, blurting out that the unfortunate girl must have slipped and fallen in unnoticed.

Ida shook her head. 'The poor child,' she mused. 'Perhaps she saw no other way to end her plight what with Coenred now being killed and her having been turned away from the Vill.'

Edward didn't understand until she explained that Mildred had been with child. 'But surely they could have found a place for her?' he reasoned.

'No man would want her, nor the responsibility for a girl of such low repute. She brought it upon herself, though now there will doubtless be those who'll rebuke our masters for being so heartless.'

* * * * *

Later that day, a messenger from Twynham came to report that three Vikings had been found alive following the battle, two of them badly wounded and one who they said had fled the field but then returned to find a sword he'd lost during the fray.

Alfred, Ethelnorth and Osric were all intrigued by the news and insisted on seeing the messenger in private.

'How badly wounded are the prisoners?' asked Ethelnorth as the messenger knelt before them.

'My Lords, two them spent several days lying untended on the battlefield and have wounds they're unlikely to survive. In fact, one of them is already close to death.'

'What about the third one. You say he returned to find his sword?'

'That's what he claims, my Lord. He seems not to have suffered any injury but was fool enough to return whilst we were still disposing of the dead.'

Alfred could contain himself no longer. 'Describe him,' he ordered.

The messenger shrugged. 'Tall and fair, my Lord. He claims to be of noble Viking blood but we could well have taken him for a Saxon except that he doesn't speak our tongue.'

Osric turned to the others. 'Could it be Arne?' he asked.

'Who knows?' said Alfred. 'The sword we found was his, of that I'm certain. As to whether the man who went back to reclaim it is Arne, I cannot say. If it is him, then we at last have the chance to set matters right on Matthew's behalf but, until we're sure, we must say nothing of this to young Edward.'

The messenger looked confused. 'Is this man then known to you, my Lords?' he asked.

'Possibly,' said Alfred. 'Have all three prisoners brought here to me.'

'I will my Lord, but I fear that one of them may not survive the journey.'

'Then so be it. As like as not I shall have them all put to the sword anyway but I've questions I would ask them first.'

With that the messenger got up, bowed and then left. Once he'd gone the three men spoke further.

'How will we know if it is Arne?' asked Osric. 'It's been many years since last we saw him.'

'We could have Edmund identify him,' suggested Alfred.

'Pah!' said Osric. 'I wouldn't trust him further than I can throw him.'

Ethelnorth was more easily convinced. 'I agree we'll need to treat anything he tells us with caution but I'm sure he can be relied upon to identify Arne. As for any information he gives us about Haesten's intentions, we've nothing to lose, for what little we have at present is nothing but hearsay anyway, and much of that is based on fear.'

'That's as may be,' said Osric. 'But I'm still worried about Edward. Now that his true status has become known, he's much at risk from anyone who might try to use him. If Edmund is as treacherous as you fear, just remember that he has every reason to see his young nephew disposed of for he's all that stands between him and what he sees as his rightful inheritance. And there are men enough who would gladly oblige him if the price is right.'

Alfred considered all that. 'Which is why you must watch out for him,' he said to Osric. 'Teach him well, particularly sword craft, for that will surely be his best defence against the sort of low life who would kill a man purely for silver. Also, now is the time to begin to school him in what he needs to know to become a nobleman.'

'I will, my Lord,' said Osric. 'In fact, I've already asked Sigbert, the carpenter, to look out for the lad. He and Edward seem to get on well and he's a good man, one I'm sure can be trusted. He's working on repairing the ships down at the quay so is not too far from here. I've told him to look out for any strangers at all times, just in case.'

* * * * *

Wearing the new clothes which Osric had provided for him, Edward asked to speak with Oswald in private, saying that he had something personal to ask. Oswald was intrigued and so readily agreed to see him.

Edward began tentatively. 'Sir, as you know I am to be raised in station and understand that I may look to you for instruction in various matters.'

Oswald nodded, anxious to know what was coming next.

'There's much I need to learn so will value any help you can give me.'

Oswald was still not sure what to expect. 'You're welcome,' he managed. 'And deserve as much. But is there something which troubles you?'

'Not so much something which troubles me, sir. But something I scarce know how to mention.'

'Then speak plainly. That's usually the best way.'

Edward swallowed nervously. 'Sir, it concerns your daughter,' he said.

'My daughter? What have you to do with her?'

'That's the point. I believe that she and I might become friends yet I know you've previously not encouraged this. I would like only to persuade you to change your mind.'

'You mean you want to...' As his words trailed off he laughed aloud. 'Are you seeking permission to court my daughter? Is that what you're asking?'

Edward straightened his back. 'It is, sir. If you will allow it.'

Oswald could scarcely hide his delight. He went across and put his hand on Edward's shoulder. 'My daughter is young, though I suppose no father ever wants to admit that his precious child is old enough to consider such matters. Yet I now see you to be a worthy young man with excellent prospects so would not raise objection provided she's happy to return your approach. Because of your new position and the status of her family, Alfred himself will need to approve but, for my part, I freely give my consent.'

* * * * *

Following his conversation with Oswald, Edward could hardly contain himself. Plucking up courage, he went to see Odelia the following day to ask if she would deign to walk with him again.

'I think the tables are now turned,' she replied. 'I gather you will soon be a man to be reckoned with and even my father seems to fully approve of our meeting together.'

'He said that I could see you but only if that's acceptable to you.'

She looked at him, then sighed. 'Well, I suppose I shall have to agree. I mean, I gather you have bathed on my account so it's the least I can do.'

I should think so,' said Edward mocking her. 'Especially as I came upon the drowned body of poor Mildred whilst I was about it.'

Odelia was very quiet for a moment. 'Yes, that must have been awful. And such a tragic end for her.'

'Were you and she close?' asked Edward.

'No, we were never friends as such, though she had worked at the Vill for nearly a year.'

'Even so, it seems cruel that she should be cast out like that. I mean, she had nowhere she could go,' Edward replied.

'My father says she had only herself to blame,' explained Odelia. 'She was a foolish girl and would have brought shame upon our family, though I can't see how that would be. It seems more likely that the blame for her misfortune should rest with Coenred. Ida says he beguiled her and promised her much but brought her only disgrace. Finding her like that must have been dreadful.'

Edward was not sure what more to say. He remained bemused that so little had been done to ease the girl's plight and knew that her fate was even worse than it appeared, for, having taken her own life, she would be consigned to a grave outside the confines of their Minster. Like others, he was worried for the soul of her unborn child which would thus be similarly tainted through no fault of its own. 'In a way, I feel it's partly my fault,' he managed. 'For it was me who killed Coenred.'

'Yes, but he'd already left her by then so you can hardly blame yourself for that.'

Edward said nothing being still much troubled by what had happened.

'Well, I hope it hasn't put you off bathing for good,' said Odelia, trying to lighten the mood.

'No, but is it always so unpleasant?'

'It's actually supposed to be good for you,' she said, teasing him. 'But perhaps you need yet more practice at bathing before I let you kiss me.'

'I think I'm ready enough,' mused Edward boldly, then leaned across and gave her a light kiss on the cheek.

'I think you're going to need more practice at kissing as well,' she said. 'But we've time enough for that.'

* * * * *

Having been released on sufferance, albeit confined to the settlement until such time as Lord Ethelnorth had considered how best to use him as a spy, Edmund stood and watched two men who were playing dice whilst drinking heavily. Another man also watched but had no coin with which to join them.

'Are you not that traitor who fought against us?' asked the stranger.

The other two stopped playing when they heard that and looked up at Edmund suspiciously.

'I was a bloody prisoner,' said Edmund firmly. 'Alfred himself knows as much and has ordered my release.'

'But you were there?' pressed the man. 'Fighting alongside our enemies?'

Edmund didn't answer. Fearing things might get ugly and knowing that getting involved in a fight would not help his cause, he turned and began to walk away but the man followed him. Edmund turned to confront him. 'What do you want with me?' he demanded.

'A word,' said the man. 'We may have something in common.'

'And what might that be?'

The man laughed. 'A lack of coin for one thing. But there may be a way to remedy that for the both of us.'

Edmund walked on with the man beside him. 'I am not without coin,' he said.

'Aye. By all accounts you are man of some worth, albeit denied your full due by that little bastard stable boy.'

Edmund was suddenly all ears. 'That may be so. What of it?'

'Well, what if that little shit was to "disappear" or meet with an unfortunate accident? Would not your fortunes then be restored?'

'Who are you?' demanded Edmund.

'That doesn't matter. The less you know of me the better but suffice to say that I know of "ways" with which matters can be set to rights on your behalf. Do we understand each other?'

Edmund smiled knowingly. 'I think we are of one accord. How and when would you attend to my interests?'

'Like I say, the less you know the better, but soon. It'll have to be soon lest the boy is taken elsewhere. There are rumours that he may return to Winchester with the King.'

'And what will this "service" cost me?'

'Some coin now and more when the job is done.'

Edmund looked hard into the man's eyes but even then wasn't sure whether or not the rogue could be trusted. In the end he decided he had little to lose and a lot to gain so took out his purse and gave him a single coin, pressing it firmly into his hand. 'You may expect more when I know that you've served my interest. And ten times as much once my cause is fully satisfied.'

The rogue grinned. 'It'll be a pleasure doing business with you,' he said.

Edmund acknowledged the point, then, feeling he'd done well, turned and began to walk away, certain that one way or another his birthright would soon be restored.

Chapter Twenty

Two days later, Fleet had been turned out into the open pasture and was frolicking whilst paying a little too much attention to one of the surviving mares. Edward watched him for a while, then set about sweeping out the stables, contentedly whistling to himself as he worked. He no longer slept there but as they had yet to find someone to help him attend to the horses, he continued to look after them himself. He was so engrossed in his work that he failed to notice a man who was creeping towards him, carefully keeping himself to the shadows to ensure he wasn't seen. Suddenly aware of the man's presence, Edward turned to confront him.

'You seem happy in your work,' said the stranger.

'Who are you and what do you want here?' challenged Edward suspiciously.

'Nothing,' said the stranger. 'But it's always a pleasure to see a man enjoying his work even if it is just sweeping up horse shit from the stable floor.'

Sensing trouble, Edward remembered Sigbert's warning so put aside the broom and looked across to where he'd left his staff.

The man seemed to read his thoughts. 'What makes you think you'll have need of that?' he challenged.

The staff was too far away to reach quickly but Edward

knew he might well have to risk trying, particularly when the man drew a knife from his belt and began toying with the blade.

'Look, this is nothing personal, you understand,' said the man sounding almost apologetic. 'Unlike you I take no pleasure in my work but needs must.' With that he took a few steps towards Edward but stopped when he heard the sound of a dog growling somewhere behind him. He turned to look and saw the mongrel which seemed to be watching his every move, snarling and with its mouth drooling saliva. He hesitated for a moment but, having already shown his hand, he knew he would have to take his chances. Thinking that he had the means to kill the dog using the knife if he had to, he ignored it and took another step towards Edward. As soon as he did so, the dog sprang at him and quickly had one of his legs clamped between its jaws, ripping and tearing at it like some blood-hungry fiend.

The assassin screamed in pain as he tried desperately to shake the dog off, kicking it and even dragging it across the stable floor. Yet it seemed that there was nothing he could do to dislodge its vice-like grip on his leg so in the end he had no choice. Reaching down, he stabbed the poor creature repeatedly with the knife.

Edward was furious. He seized the broom again and immediately set about the man, using it to beat him off with a barrage of blows which was such that the man had no option but to turn and flee. Limping as left the stables, he ran down towards the quay, desperate to get away.

The poor dog lay on its side on the stable floor, bleeding and panting as it struggled for life. Edward knelt beside it and tried to soothe it as best he could and, just for a moment, it looked up at him, its sad eyes half closed. A few moments later it was finally still.

'It seems you made a friend of it in the end,' observed Ulrich who was the first to arrive having heard the commotion.

Edward just cradled the poor creature, tears in his eyes. 'He was not as bad as most people thought,' he said. 'All he ever wanted was kindness and for that he was prepared to offer his life in order to save mine.'

* * * * *

From where he was working on repairing one of the ships, Sigbert first noticed the assassin when he saw him hobble down to the quay and begin limping from place to place as if frantically searching for someone. He watched him for a few moments, then noticed that the calf of the man's leg was bleeding profusely. He realised at once that there was something amiss so hurried over to the quay but, by the time he got there, the assassin had already found who it was he was looking for and all but forced the man into a narrow alleyway between two of the sheds. Sigbert was not in the least bit surprised when he saw who it was.

'What, is it done so soon?' demanded Edmund sounding surprised.

'Yes,' lied the assassin. 'But I was seen so you must pay me now so I can be gone from here.'

'What, would you take me for a fool?' protested Edmund. 'I'll not pay you without proof. At least tell me how you did it and what you've done with the boy's body!'

'There's no time for that!' he warned, then pointed to the lacerations on his leg. 'As soon as they see these wounds they'll know it was me.'

'That's your problem,' sneered Edmund.

"No friend, it's your problem as well. If they find me you can be sure they'll find you, for I'll tell them of your part in this.'

Edmund grabbed the assassin by his throat and pushed him back hard against the wall, then stared into his eyes. 'If you do, it'll be your word against mine, do you hear me?' he warned. 'Besides, why should I pay you anything? The job's now done so you can whistle for your money and there's nothing you can do about it!'

'Don't be a fool,' warned the assassin. 'I'll hang, that's for certain. But there'll be room enough on the gallows for you, be assured of that!' Even as he spoke, he felt something being pressed against his belly. He followed Edmund's gaze downwards only to realise that he'd produced a knife.

'Think again,' said Edmund grinning. 'This blade will secure your silence once and for all. What's more, no one will blame me for killing the bastard who murdered my nephew.'

At that the assassin realised he'd been tricked and that Edmund had never intended paying him. He made a desperate attempt to grab the knife but, as he did so, Edmund drove it home with all the force he could manage, then twisted the blade.

Still leaning back against the wall, the assassin began to sink slowly to the ground. He was clearly in a great deal of pain but Edmund ignored his pleas for help. Instead, he just watched as the man died then moved out into the crowded quay. Only then did he realise that Sigbert had probably seen the whole thing.

* * * * *

Having been summoned, Oswald went across to speak with Sigbert whilst two of his guards lifted the assassin's body on to a hand cart. 'What happened here?' he demanded.

'I don't know exactly,' said Sigbert. 'But is Edward safe?'

Oswald looked confused. 'Why wouldn't he be?'

'Because I think that man was hired to kill him.'

Oswald looked shocked but hurriedly sent one his guards to check on the boy. 'So who is he?' he asked returning his attention to the body.

Sigbert shook his head. 'I don't know, but he was killed by Edmund, that prisoner we took at the battle,' he explained.

'How do you know this?' he demanded.

'Because I saw it. I was working on repairing one of the ships when I first saw this rogue. I knew something was up right away. I couldn't get here in time to stop it but saw what happened right enough.'

'So what had it to do with you?'

'Nothing, except that your uncle ordered me to look out for strangers who might intend to harm the boy.'

It was news to Oswald but he knew Sigbert well enough so was inclined to believe him. 'Very well, I'll speak to Governor Osric and if what you say is true, I'm sure that'll be the end of the matter so far as you're concerned. If not, he'll no doubt have questions enough of his own for you to answer.'

* * * * *

Meanwhile, back at the stables, Osric had arrived having been summoned by Ulrich. Glad to see that Edward was safe, he wanted to know how and why the dog had been killed.

'From what I can tell, my Lord, an assassin tried to kill young Edward but this dog died trying to protect him,' explained Ulrich. 'Edward then beat off the rogue and he fled towards the quay but fear not, he'll be easy enough to identify, for he carries the wounds the dog inflicted to his leg.'

At that, the guard sent by Oswald arrived and told them what he knew. 'A man has been stabbed, my Lord. Oswald is even now trying to ascertain exactly what happened.'

With that they left Edward to console himself over the death of the dog whilst they went to join those at the quay where Oswald was still trying to make sense of things.

'Uncle, as far as I can tell, this wretch was an assassin hired by Edmund to kill Edward. Having failed, he was afraid that the wounds to his leg would betray him. He therefore demanded whatever coin had been promised but Edmund refused to pay up and killed him instead. Sigbert saw the whole thing.'

With that Osric went across to examine the body which, by then, had been laid out on the cart. 'You're certain this is the rogue who tried to kill Edward at the stables?' he asked, turning to Sigbert.

'As far as I know it is, my Lord,' explained Sigbert. 'I didn't see what happened there but I believe he and Edmund had an arrangement between them to see the boy murdered, presumably to deprive Edward of his share of the inheritance.'

Osric nodded. 'Do we know the man by name?' he asked.

It seemed that nobody there had ever seen him before.

'Then do we know where Edmund has gone?'

'My Lord, he fled towards the West Gates,' explained Sigbert. 'I was too far away to stop him.'

'Then he's probably long gone by now but sound the alarm anyway, then search the settlement just in case he's hidden himself here. In the meantime, I'll report all this to Lord Alfred. In one respect, if Edmund has gone that may solve the problem of what to do with him but somehow I don't think Alfred will be best pleased. He had hoped to reconcile him and Edward but it's too late for that now.'

* * * * *

Osric found the King busy construing various documents of state which needed his attention. He stopped what he was doing when Osric explained all that which had happened.

'Having killed the assassin, Edmund has fled and there seems to be no sign of him, my Lord,' he said. 'There were others leaving the settlement at that time and the chances are that he hid himself among them to make good his escape.'

Alfred took the news well enough, though confessed that he was saddened to learn of it. 'I was minded to acknowledge his claim,' he said. 'But if he did indeed try to have Edward murdered, it only serves to prove that he was far from worthy.'

'We shouldn't judge him too harshly,' said Osric. 'All those years as a slave will have left him bitter and twisted. They were almost bound to turn his mind – as they would that of any man.'

'Aye,' agreed Alfred. 'But we must try to find him so we can put this matter to rest, once and for all.'

Osric looked doubtful. 'There's not much chance of that, my Lord. The wretch will be long gone by now.'

Alfred seemed reluctant to accept that. 'Then I fear for what will become of all this, for Edward can never be safe whilst Edmund lives. Our only hope is that he may not know that his assassin failed.'

* * * * *

The next day a small party arrived from Twynham bringing with them the Viking prisoners who had survived the battle, all three of them travelling by cart with their hands securely tied. As had been reported by the messenger, one of them was so badly wounded that he needed to be lifted down from the cart and carried into the Hall where he was laid on the floor on a blanket like so much baggage. The other two stood beside him, watched over by several armed guards.

Alfred stared at the prisoners, all of whom were dressed in rags and looked to be half starved and bedraggled, but he knew at once which one of them was Arne.

It was Ethelnorth who conducted the interrogation using an interpreter, leaving Alfred and Osric to watch.

'You're a treacherous bastard!' said Ethelnorth, looking directly at Arne.

As the interpreter repeated that, Arne just grinned and then replied.

'My Lord, he wants to know why you regard him as such,' said the interpreter. 'He claims he's the son of a noble Viking warrior and demands to be treated as befits his station.'

'Tell him he can demand what he likes. We know full well who he is and what he is. We also remember that he was offered the chance to be raised as a Saxon rather than be put to the sword after the battle at Edington. It was meant as a gesture of peace between our peoples but, having accepted that very generous offer, he then led Matthew into a trap in which he was all but killed. Worse still, after the battle at Leatherhead, he found Matthew and slew him whilst he lay wounded and was thus unable to defend himself. I wonder what his "noble father" would make of such treachery!'

Having been told that, Arne said something which the interpreter then repeated.

'My Lord, he says that he slew Matthew as an act of vengeance for the death of his father who was also killed whilst wounded. Matthew therefore deserved to die as he did.'

Ethelnorth reacted to that at once. 'You're a liar! For one thing your father was killed not by Matthew but by his brother, Lord Edwin. But it was an act of mercy, for your father was sorely wounded with no hope of life and was therefore slain so as to save him from a slow and painful death.'

Arne looked angry when that was translated and replied at once, almost spitting out the words.

'My Lord, he says you weren't there so how can you know what happened? It's true that his father was wounded but Lord Edwin tortured him before killing him. He wonders how you can regard that as an act of mercy.'

Ethelnorth was suddenly quiet.

'Then ask him whether he was there,' insisted Alfred, speaking for the first time.

The interpreter did so and Arne confirmed that he had indeed witnessed to whole thing.

'As always, there's fault on both sides,' mused Alfred. 'How many Saxons have been cruelly tortured and killed for no good cause? That being so, you can hardly blame Lord Edwin for doing the same. Certainly it didn't justify you so cruelly killing Matthew. After all, he'd caused you no offence.'

When that was translated, Arne just sneered then spat at the ground.

With that Ethelnorth picked up Red Viper, the sword which had once belonged to Arne and to his father before him. 'Tell him that if vengeance is to be the way of things between us, I can oblige him by using this sword to kill him – it was the one he used to slay Matthew, was it not?'

At that Arne looked anxious but said nothing so Ethelnorth continued.

'By all accounts you're a coward and the fact that you escaped from the recent battle unscathed is proof of that. In fact, all we know of you suggests that you deserve to die, for you bring nothing but shame on your father's name. As Lord Alfred has said, there's fault on both sides in all that's gone before but, for my part, I crave and demand vengeance for Matthew's death. He was surely a good man and a friend to us all. What's more, he never did you any harm and deserved no part in your quarrel with his brother.'

That was explained to Arne who swallowed hard, then protested that he was entitled to a fair hearing, if nothing else.

Ethelnorth just laughed. 'This is the only hearing you'll get from us! And I've heard nothing which might persuade me to stay my hand.'

When that was translated, Arne seemed to finally realise that his fate was sealed. Pleading to be spared, he fell to his knees and begged for mercy. When it was clear that was to no avail, he even offered himself as a slave.

Ethelnorth just ignored him and turned instead to the

other two prisoners. The one who was lying on the floor showed only the merest flicker of life. He was certainly beyond speaking and his body was quivering from the pain of the many wounds he'd suffered. 'What's this man's name?' he demanded. When it seemed that neither Arne nor the other prisoner knew him, Ethelnorth used his foot to turn the man on to his back but the effort proved almost more than poor wretch could manage. Ethelnorth could see little point in interrogating him so spoke to the other prisoner instead. 'And what are you called?' he demanded as the man stood tall and straight despite a severe injury to his shoulder. It had been bandaged but blood had soaked through to betray the extent of the wound.

The man told the interpreter that his name was Harald but in doing so made no reference to his lineage.

'Then tell me, Harald, what you know of Haesten's plans?' demanded Ethelnorth.

This time the man made no attempt to reply.

'I'll be minded to spare you if you tell us what you know.'

When that was translated the man still remained silent, though a flicker of a smile crossed his lips.

'What, would you rather die beside this cowardly wretch?' asked Ethelnorth pointing at Arne. 'Would you walk beside the likes of him to the gates of Valhalla?'

That was enough to arouse the man's interest.

'My Lord, he says he has no fear of dying,' said the interpreter. 'The wound to his shoulder has already started to fester so he knows he doesn't have long to live. As such, he'd as soon have you put an end to his suffering and be done with it but would prefer not to die beside Arne, for he agrees with you. The man is a worthless coward.'

Ethelnorth grinned when he heard that. 'Very well. If you tell us what you know we could arrange for you to die in combat and thereby find your way to Valhalla on your own. Would that not suit you better?'

When that was translated the man laughed and then replied that they could contrive what they liked, but he could never expect to enter Valhalla if he betrayed his warlord.

Ethelnorth nodded admiringly, realising that he'd get nothing more from the man, at least not like that. 'Take these two away. Let that one die in peace for he's suffered enough,' he said pointing to the man on the floor.

The interpreter looked concerned. 'My Lord, are you proposing to let them both live?' he asked.

'Yes, but only for now,' said Ethelnorth. 'That one will dead by morning and the other one has no fear of dying. In fact, he'd welcome death. It's living he's afraid of and, in exchange for a more merciful end, he'll tell us all we need to know once that festering wound starts to bite in a few days' time.'

With that the guards removed both prisoners leaving Arne alone.

'So, how will you die?' asked Ethelnorth pointedly. 'With honour or squealing like a stuck pig as we drag you to a place of execution?'

Arne looked frightened, as if trying to find courage where none was there to be had. He remained on his knees and continued to plead for mercy.

'Pah! Is that all you can manage?' said Ethelnorth disdainfully. 'All you'll get from me by way of mercy is a quicker death – and that only if you tell us all you know.'

Arne swallowed hard then spoke to the interpreter.

'My Lord, he says that he knows nothing of Haesten's plans. Although of noble birth, he was not treated as such by the Vikings and was therefore told nothing of their intent.'

Ethelnorth looked at Alfred. 'I can well believe that, my Lord. They wouldn't have trusted this snivelling coward with anything worth knowing. I suggest we just kill him and be done with it.'

Alfred considered that before speaking. 'This wretch has caused me trouble enough over the years,' he announced at last. 'I therefore agree and can see no grounds for mercy.'

'How would you have it done, my Lord?' asked Ethelnorth.

'At first light tomorrow, have him taken to the banks of the river and there have his head severed from his body. That may be a quicker death than he deserves so, to show our contempt for him, use his father's sword to do it.'

Ethelnorth acknowledged the order though would clearly have preferred for Arne to suffer a slower and more painful death than that.

'When it's done,' continued Alfred, 'I insist that Red Viper is destroyed for, as I said before, its mere existence offends me. Now, have the guards take him away. Tell them they can do with him as they will, for he deserves no better. But I want him alive in the morning, for I would see how he confronts his fate.'

* * * * *

Alfred next summoned Edward to speak with him in private.

'I regret to tell you that your uncle who also had claim to your family's lands and estates has now fled,' he said coldly, clearly much affected by all that had been said during the interrogation of the prisoners. 'It seems he was a treacherous soul who intended to see you killed and thereby secure your share of the inheritance for himself.'

Edward looked shocked. 'But was it then he who attacked me at the stables?' he asked.

'No,' said Alfred. 'But he paid the man who did. You'll find that such is often the way of treachery. He killed the assassin then ran like a craven coward rather than face up to his crime.'

'Even so, my Lord, treacherous or not, I should like to have met him.'

'Of course, but that was not to be. At least you now stand unchallenged to inherit all and are thus destined to become a very wealthy man indeed, for I intend to bestow upon you all that which is now rightfully yours.'

'Thank you, my Lord.'

'In the meantime, you must be wary. Edmund may not know that you're still alive but, once he learns of it, he may again try to kill you or pay others to do so on his behalf. There is also a risk from those who may seek to use you for ends of their own, so you must take care at all times. For that reason I would have you remain here at Wareham where you should be safe enough but learn who you can trust and be wary of strangers.'

'I will, my Lord.'

'Good. Now tomorrow, we shall execute the man who I believe killed your father. For that purpose, I shall use the sword which was found after the battle but, whatever its worth, it must then be destroyed and disposed of. As promised, I will replace it with one which has been wielded with pride by many generations of your family and is thus also yours by rights. Have you any questions?'

'I have my Lord, but none which cannot wait, for I can see that all that which has transpired of late now troubles you, so this is not the time for me to raise them.'

Alfred laughed. 'Already I see the wisdom of your father in you.'

* * * * *

At dawn the next day, Arne was dragged down to the quay. Having been stripped of his clothes, he was naked but for a loincloth so that the many cuts and bruises to his body could be seen by all. Although conscious, he had clearly been severely beaten to the point where two men were needed just to help him walk.

Once beside the river, he started desperately pleading for his life to be spared, though none there could understand what he was saying any more than he could understand the sentence which was read out by Governor Osric in person.

'By order of Lord Alfred who is both King and Bretwalda of all Wessex and other lands beyond this realm, you are hereby sentenced to die. There can be no clemency or mercy, for the many crimes you've committed against the Saxon cause are as treacherous as they are offensive. The sentence is to be carried out here, in this place, and with immediate effect.'

A murmur of anticipation went up from the crowd who had assembled there. Arne was then wrestled to his knees and held down whilst another man grasped him by the hair to keep his head up and his neck thereby fully exposed.

At that point he was shaking and his face looked almost ghostly.

Alfred then stepped forward and passed Red Viper to Ethelnorth who, given his seniority, was granted the privilege of carrying out the execution in person.

There was silence, broken only by the sobs from Arne as he still pleaded for his life.

'I strike this blow as vengeance for my friend, Matthew, christened Edward, third born son of the noble Saxon, Lord Edwulf,' said Ethelnorth loudly. 'I also strike it for all those other good men whose blood has soiled this blade.' With that he looked to Alfred for permission to proceed. As the King nodded his assent, Ethelnorth first showed the sword to Arne to make sure he recognised it, then raised and levelled it as he prepared to strike.

When it came, the blow was mercifully accurate, severing the head cleanly with a single stroke so that Arne's decapitated torso slumped to the ground like a sack of grain. The man who had held his hair still gripped it tightly, thus holding the severed head aloft, dripping blood. He looked towards Alfred who nodded his agreement and at that, tossed the head into the river. That done, the bloody sword was handed to the new blacksmith with orders for the blade to be destroyed, then returned to Alfred for him to dispose of in person.

* * * * *

Later that day, Alfred, Ethelnorth, Osric and Oswald stood beside the river, together with Edward and Odelia and various other persons of note. Alfred gave Red Viper to

Edward, the blade having been blunted, twisted and then bent almost double.

At first, the boy seemed unsure of what he was expected to do with it, then Alfred pointed to the river but said nothing. Edward held the sword for a moment and thought of the father he'd never known and of the mother who had given her life that he might live. He then hurled the sword as far from the bank as he could manage and they all watched as it sank into the murky depths of the river.

That done, he remained where he was, anxious to hide his tears as Odelia stepped forward then tenderly put her arm around his shoulders to comfort him.

It was Alfred who then spoke. 'With the disposal of this sword, so ends a sad and tragic part of our Saxon history,' he announced. He then looked at Edward and Odelia and seemed pleased at the prospect of their union. 'Such is the way of things,' he said simply. 'For I sense that with these two young people a new part of our history is already beginning. If that be so, then I pray that given all the blood which has been shed within my realm, God will grant that at least their children finally come to know a time of peace.'

However, even as he said it, Alfred knew that with Edmund still at large and the Viking fleet likely to strike at any time, peace was not something Edward was likely to enjoy for long.

To be continued…

Glossary

Whilst not all universally accepted, the following is an explanation of some of the terms as used in this story:

BERSERKERS Feared Viking warriors who were said to work themselves up into a frenzy prior to fighting, often by imbibing some form of hallucinogen. They sometimes fought bare-chested or wearing a symbolic bear skin and were said not to feel pain or fear anything, even death.

BRETWALDA A mainly honorary title given to a recognised overlord.

BURH A fortified settlement forming part of a defensive network of others, each sited close enough to reinforce the one nearest to it in the event of an attack.

CEORL The lowest rank of freemen.

EALDORMAN A high-ranking nobleman usually appointed by the King to oversee a shire or group of shires.

FYRD A group of able-bodied freemen who could be mobilised for military service when required.

LUR A battle horn.

JARL A Viking nobleman or chieftain.

REEVE An official appointed to oversee specific duties on behalf of the King or an Ealdorman. These included administrative and sometimes judicial responssibilities.

SEAX A short single-edged sword.

THANE A freeman holding land granted by the King or by an Ealdorman to whom he owed allegiance and for whom he provided military support when needed.

Acknowledgements

It seems hard to believe that this is now the fourth book in the series. For that I must thank my publishers who persuaded me to continue writing it even when I suggested that the series had probably reached a natural conclusion. They, and many other people who have been kind enough to support and encourage me, insisted that they wanted to know what became of many of the characters (in particular Matthew's two children) and also how the history of the era (such as we know it) continued to unfold.

Of course, history provides the backdrop for the series and so research continues to be an important and very enjoyable part of writing it. This inevitably took me to Wareham, where I met so many kind and helpful people who seemed interested in what I was doing and were keen to assist. With their help and input, I quickly amassed a significant amount of background information for which I am very grateful. I hope that I have used it to present a valid and realistic impression of what the settlement there was like during Saxon times but, of course, much of it still remains conjecture on my part. Likewise, I continue to be indebted to the many eminent historians whose work I have read and enjoyed, but not always slavishly followed, preferring to interpret events for myself. Therefore any mistakes, errors or omissions are mine, including the many 'liberties' I have taken throughout the series.

Many people say that writing must be a very solitary experience but I've not found that to be so. I enjoy the support of my readers, reviewers, followers on both my mailing list and on social media and, not least of all, the many people I meet at my various talks and such like. They all contribute a great deal to my work, probably far more than they realise.

Similarly, I must thank the team at my publishers, RedDoor – particularly Clare Christian, Anna Burtt, Lizzie Lewis and Heather Boisseau, not just for their professionalism in producing the books in this series but also for their help and guidance on so many aspects of my writing. I must also mention Carol Anderson who has the unenviable task of editing my work – I sometimes think she must have the patience of a saint.

Finally, I must once again acknowledge the support of my wife without whose help I could not have written even one book, never mind four! She has often been deprived of my full attention whilst I was 'away', first with Matthew and now with Edward on their many adventures.

I was once told that writing a book is like walking up a very steep hill. I can see how that might well be true but all I can say is that it's been a really enjoyable journey and one which I'm so glad I started out on (albeit a little late in life).

CJB

Author's Notes

As I stated in the author's notes at the end of Book Three (*The Final Reckoning*), one of the many challenges facing any author writing historical fiction is that of achieving a balance between 'fact' and 'fiction' whilst not losing sight of the need to tell a good story. This is particularly so when writing a novel set in Anglo-Saxon England where many 'facts' have become lost to the mists of time. Even those we do have need to be treated with caution as history is often written by the victor not the vanquished, giving us few unbiased contemporary accounts to rely on – after all, propaganda and fake news are nothing new. The mist thickens considerably where intervening generations have added their own embellishments and, in the case of such an iconic personage as Alfred the Great, there is the element of legend and folklore to contend with as well.

Given that I'm a writer and not an historian, my task has been to sift through all this information, thereby undertaking a huge amount of research. This was actually a labour of love for me as I have a lifelong interest in all things Anglo-Saxon, but it has given me the additional dilemma of deciding what to leave out rather than what to include. Therefore, whilst I must confess to having taken some 'liberties' with the perceived facts (such as they are), I must also 'own up' to some deliberate omissions as well.

However, in writing this latest book, I was fortunate in choosing Wareham as the principal setting. It was indeed an important Saxon settlement and one of Alfred's fortified burhs. In fact, it is one of the few places where considerable evidence of Anglo-Saxon occupation and influence remains, not least of which are the raised earthworks which you can not only see but actually walk around. These were probably much as I've described them, though they have no doubt been substantially modified over the years. For example, they would almost certainly have been 'topped' off with a fence, making them a very formidable defensive barrier indeed. Similarly, I've included reference to the nunnery in Wareham, though in fact this was largely destroyed when the Vikings took and held Wareham in 876 and was not fully restored until circa 915 (by Alfred's daughter). But it seemed to me that the nuns at that time would have been extraordinarily resilient so I've implied that its restoration was a work in progress at the time my story is set.

As with the earlier books in the series, almost all the characters in *Bloodlines* spring from my own imagination rather than from the pages of history. One of the few exceptions is Alfred himself about whom a great deal has already been written by others. For my part, I've elected to continue to portray him as a Churchillian figure, orator and far-sighted statesman, but with his share of human frailty as well. I hope I've done him justice in that respect.

With regard to the events depicted in this book, they largely follow the beginning of the Viking invasion in 892 and are based on the perceived historical facts. Against that backdrop, I've woven a plot that is largely fictitious and the battle depicted is intended to be representative of the many skirmishes and raids taking place at that time rather than a specific event.

I'm often asked about the detail which I've included in my writing and can say only that this is drawn from a store of useful 'snippets' which I seem to have accumulated over the years. In many cases I've long since forgotten how I came by them but they include such items as Alfred's stomach problems (thought to be Crohn's disease). Similarly, the story about Alfred actually capturing Haesten's wife and children and releasing them. This could well be true and, if so, it was an extraordinary act of mercy which tells us a lot about the great man himself. I've included these as a way of (hopefully) bringing the story to life.

My reference to the disposal of the sword, Red Viper, at the end of the book was inspired by the fact that the remains of a sword were found in the river Frome at Wareham whilst rebuilding the South Bridge in 1927. The sword is actually thought to be 'Saxon' rather than 'Viking' as I've suggested, but it was a remarkable find and it's now exhibited in Wareham Town Museum.

Throughout the first books in the series I tried to show the huge social divide between the nobles and the common man and have continued with this theme in this book. In reality, I suspect that for most people the struggle to feed themselves and their families would have been much the same whether ruled by the Saxons or by the Vikings and certainly my overall impression is that life for them must have been extremely hard and, at times, brutal.

With regard to the Vikings, I hope I've again portrayed them as something more than just the blood-crazed heathens they're normally depicted as being and given at least a glimpse of the adventurous and creative peoples I believe them to have been, albeit with some violent tendencies.

Finally, as I've relied on my own interpretation of events there are doubtless errors and inaccuracies for which I apologise and must acknowledge as my own. It was never my intention to write a history book as such but rather to relate a tale which initially came to me all but complete and continues to flow seamlessly from my pen almost at will. That's a rare and extraordinary experience for any writer and one of which I've often spoken and for which I'm extremely thankful. I've thus followed wherever that 'inspiration' has taken me even if it means that the series must inevitably sit on the fiction shelf of the bookcase rather than alongside the weightier tomes written by the many eminent historians whom I much admire but have not the capacity nor inclination to emulate.

Having completed *Bloodlines*, I realise that I've left scope for a further book to be written – a tantalising prospect, which I'm sure I shall not be able to resist for long. I therefore very much hope that you'll enjoy the series as it continues to unfold.

Coming soon, Book 5 in this exciting series

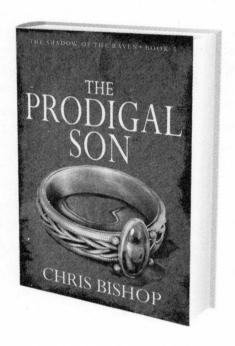

PRELUDE

WAREHAM FOREST

As Edmund stopped to drink at a small stream, he was all too well aware that he was not alone. He knew that at least one man had been following him since he'd entered the forest and was sure there would be others as well. With no proper weapon with which to defend himself, he checked that he still had the small knife he'd used to kill the assassin in Wareham, hoping he wouldn't need to use it again.

He remained kneeling beside the stream and waited until one of the men deigned to show himself. When he did, Edmund got up and turned to face him. 'Ah, so there you are,' he said, smiling benignly. 'It seems you're very hard men to find.'

The man who confronted him was a burly fellow with long black hair which was braided, suggesting he had once been a warrior. 'That all depends on who's looking for us,' he sneered, toying with a seax with just enough menace to suggest that he meant to use it. 'And, more importantly, why.'

Edmund stepped away from the stream. 'Well, there's me,' he said, cautiously. 'I've been looking to find you.'

'Have you now?' said the stranger. 'And why would that be?'

'Because I've a proposition for you,' explained Edmund. 'Something which may yet be of benefit to us both.'

Sensing no danger, the man stepped aside and signalled

for two others to join him, one of them carrying a spear and the other a bow. Both looked similarly dishevelled and, as they emerged from the trees, Edmund overheard one of them call the first man by the name of 'Byram', though was quickly rebuked by the others for doing so.

'A proposition is it?' asked Byram. 'Well given there's now three of us, my friends here think we should start by offering you something instead. How about you give me that purse you have tucked under your belt and in return we won't kill you?'

Edmund laughed. 'Oh, I had in mind something far more profitable for you all than the few coins I have in my purse.'

'And what might that be?' demanded Byram.

'Firstly, do you know who I am?' enquired Edmund.

'Should we?' said Byram.

'Not really, but it might help if I tell you. You may not yet have heard that a man was killed in Wareham a few days ago. A wretched fellow who had just murdered my nephew.'

'So, what concern is that of ours? We don't even know you, never mind your nephew.'

'Exactly,' said Edmund. 'Which is why you can help me.'

'And why would we do that?'

'Because it could be to your advantage. You see, in killing my nephew the rogue did me a great service. Which is why I paid him to do it in the first place. Mind, I then killed him as well.'

Suddenly the robbers were all ears. 'You paid a man to murder your nephew then killed him for doing so?' repeated Byram, clearly intrigued.

'Aye, that's about the strength of it,' admitted Edmund. 'But all with good cause, you understand.'

'That's as maybe, but like I said, what has it to do with us?'

'Well, you see I was then obliged to leave Wareham in haste and now have need of a place where I can lie low for a while. I've heard tell that you have a hideout in this forest, a camp which no-one has yet managed to find.'

Byram looked pleased with himself on hearing that. 'That may well be so,' he said proudly. 'And believe me, many have tried.'

'Which is why I want to join you.'

Byram laughed then looked back at his two men who were similarly amused. 'Friend, the pickings here are meagre enough as it is. Why the hell would we want to share them with you?'

'Because if you do, I can make you all very wealthy men indeed.'

Suddenly all three of them seemed interested. 'And how the hell would you do that?' demanded Byram.

Certain that he had their full attention, Edmund moved across to stand in front of a large tree, seeking protection in case there were others who might come at him from behind if they didn't like what he was about to say. 'Some fifteen years ago, I was taken captive by Viking raiders and then held by them as a slave,' he told them. 'When they decided to come here to raid, I was forced to come with them. Unlike most of their band, I somehow managed to survive the recent fray between here and Twynham but was taken prisoner and, in order to escape being put to the sword, revealed who I am. In so doing I thought that I might also reclaim my just inheritance but found it had already been dispensed to the bastard son of one of my dead brothers, a wretch who'd done

317

nothing to deserve it save being born of the same bloodline as myself.'

'So you had him killed?'

'Exactly. What else could I do for he was all which stood between me and a vast fortune? No one knows of my hand in his murder so all I need to do is lie low long enough for the dust to settle then set about reclaiming what is rightfully mine.'

'What sort of fortune are we talking about?' demanded one of the robbers.

'I am the eldest son of Lord Edwulf, who was a wealthy Ealdorman and a friend to King Alfred himself, thus it would amount to extensive lands and countless riches. If I can remain with you until such time as I can secure it, I'll share half of it with you all.'

The men all looked at each other, hardly daring to believe what Edmund was offering.

'How do we know you're telling the truth?' asked Byram.

'Well, you no doubt get news from Wareham from time to time so you'll soon learn that all I've told you is true. The fools there will be speaking of little else.'

'Even if we agree to let you join us, you'd need to prove your worth and also earn your keep,' said Byram. 'Or is that too distasteful for the heir to a great fortune?'

Edmund shrugged. 'I have no objection to soiling my hands. Believe me, to survive being held as a Viking slave for the past fifteen years I've been forced to do worse than rob a few strangers.'

The three men then drew closer together so they could discuss Edmund's proposal. Having finished their deliberations, it was Byram who then spoke again. 'Very well, we'll take you to our camp where you can tell us more. If all there agree, we may then come to some sort of arrangement. If not, we'll kill you – or perhaps drag you back to Wareham in chains and claim whatever price has been set upon your head.'

'And you'd do that?' asked Edmund. 'Even to a fellow fugitive?'

Byram just laughed. 'Oh yes my friend, make no mistake about that. From all you've told me so far I judge you to be a treacherous sod and that makes me ill inclined to trust you.'

Edmund looked him hard in the eyes. 'Then it sounds like I shall indeed be in the sort of company I'm used to.'

* * *

Edmund was blindfolded and, with his hands tied behind his back, was then led through the forest at spearpoint. He had no idea where they were taking him but so far as he could tell they were travelling roughly north and following a path which was not well travelled. He was certain he could hear running water from time to time so assumed they were following a stream or perhaps a small river but, apart from that, there was little to help him know where he was and even less that would enable him to retrace his steps. The latter didn't trouble him unduly. If all went as he intended, he'd join the band of robbers but, failing that, finding his way back through the forest would be the least of his worries.

They eventually stopped and, when his blindfold was lifted, Edmund found himself in a clearing which was encircled by a crude wicker fence. Looking around, he could see four more men, all of them busily going about whatever tasks had been assigned to them. That made seven robbers in total, though they were a mixed band, many of them carrying the reminders of wounds and all of them wretched and dirty from living rough in the forest. There was also a woman there who was presumably preparing food for them all as she was tending to a large pot which had been suspended over an open fire. He hurriedly surveyed the camp, noting that there was a cluster of seven or possibly eight crude hovels plus a makeshift shelter which was open at the front. The shelter contained a pile of firewood and a barrel but little else of interest apart from the carcase of a deer which had been hung up by its hind legs. The deer had been skinned and was being skilfully butchered by another man who was dressed in the shabby habit of a monk, his tonsure still shaven and with a large wooden cross hung about his neck. The monk stared at Edmund but otherwise kept his distance even as all the others crowded round, anxious to know why a stranger had been brought into their camp and, more particularly, why he had not been relieved of his knife – or indeed the purse which was still tucked under his belt.

Byram stepped forward to speak to them all. 'Well, what would you have me do with this wretch?' he asked aloud. 'He has a proposition for you but I insist that you hear it from his lips, not mine. Will you let him speak or shall I just kill him now and be done with it?'

There were several murmurs and mutterings but all there knew that Byram had already decided what they would do. 'So,' he said returning his attention to Edmund. 'It seems these good folks would hear more of what you have to say.'

If Edmund felt any fear at that stage he was careful not to show it. With his hands still tied, he started to explain his proposal but didn't elaborate any further than he had to. 'So, you have two choices,' he said once he'd finished. 'You can kill me now or you can accept what is probably the best offer you're ever going to hear. One which will keep you warm and well fed for the rest of your days.'

'Well, luckily for you, I'm not well disposed to killing men without good cause,' mused Byram.

'That's very noble of you,' conceded Edmund.

Byram laughed. 'Pah! It has nothing to do with being 'noble'. We have a good trade here from robbing travellers and such like who are using the forest paths. But if we go killing them Governor Osric will have something to say about it and would doubtless send the fyrd from Wareham to come looking for us. As it is, they leave us alone for they know full well how hard it would be to find us.'

Edmund simply nodded as if to acknowledge the point. 'So then, what's it to be?' he asked.

'How much are we talking about?' asked one man, raising the question others were almost itching to ask.

'A lot,' said Edmund bluntly. 'My father had lands and wealth beyond reckoning. Also, two of my brothers were warriors who both amassed a good stash of booty whilst they were alive. That should by rights revert to me as well.'

'Then how will you convince others that you are who you say you are?' asked a man who had only one eye, the other having no doubt been lost in a quarrel.

'Alfred himself has questioned me and was minded to acknowledge my bloodline,' lied Edmund. 'I don't think others will argue with that.'

'If that's so, then why do you need us?' pressed another.

'Let's just say that I left Wareham in haste,' explained

Edmund. 'Having fought against him, in return for a pardon Alfred required that I return to the Vikings as a spy but, having lived with the bastards for all those years, I know full well that only a fool would agree to do that. I've seen what they do to spies. They've devised some very brutal ways for dealing with any who are caught, inflicting agonies so dreadful that you'd not even want to imagine them!'

'Ha!' said Byram. 'Or is it because you now have a price on your head for killing that assassin and for plotting to have your own nephew murdered as well? If so, the fyrd could come looking for you and thus you could bring them down upon us all.'

'There's nothing to link me to my nephew's murder. As for killing the assassin, I could hardly be blamed for avenging what he did to my nephew. Besides, if they'd caught the wretch they'd have hung him anyway; all I did was save them the trouble. Certainly they won't bother to come looking for me on his account.'

They were all quiet for a moment, mostly trying to decide whether the risk was one worth taking given they knew nothing about the events in Wareham and had never seen Edmund before, nor even heard of Lord Edwulf. It was Byram who spoke. 'We'll see how this turns out,' he announced. 'We have friends in Wareham who will confirm what transpired there but if your story is found wanting...' he left the rest of his words to remain unsaid.

Edmund smiled to himself, by then certain that the greedy fools would not be able to resist the chance of earning a share of such a vast fortune. Not that he had any intention of honouring his promise in that respect. All he needed was a secure place in which to bide his time as he planned how best to restore himself. After that he would betray the robbers to Osric and, in so doing, reveal himself as a 'true and loyal Saxon'. Of course, they would pay with their lives for all the crimes they'd committed, and deservedly so. Doubtless they would curse him and try to embroil him as being part of their band, but they could say what they liked. No one would pay much mind to any accusations made by a few worthless robbers, particularly those they uttered before they dangled from the end of a rope.

WAREHAM, LATER THAT SAME DAY

Alfred had sent word to Governor Osric and to his nephew, Oswald, asking them to attend him at his lodgings. When they arrived, the place seemed a hive of activity. Two of Alfred's servants were busily packing the King's personal belongings into several chests whilst he remained seated, sorting through a pile of documents he had yet to construe. The King looked up and stopped what he was doing as soon as they arrived. 'My friends,' he announced. 'I regret that Lord Ethelnorth and myself have no option but to take our leave of you. We both now have more pressing duties elsewhere.'

'My Lord,' said Oswald. 'Has then the threat from the Viking fleet abated?' As Commander of the Garrison at Wareham, he had been much concerned with ensuring that they could deal with the anticipated invasion of over one hundred Viking ships should it deign to strike there.

'No,' said Alfred. 'I regret that's not the case though I wish it were. In fact, I fear we may all be sorely tested in the weeks and months to come. Ethelnorth is even now preparing my personal guard to break camp. We intend to rejoin my army which is still camped beyond the marshes and march out from there at first light tomorrow.'

'Where to Sire?' asked Osric.

'A warband of Vikings have left Essex and are raiding seemingly at will across my Realm. The fyrd should deal with them well enough but I would have Lord Ethelnorth command them. For my part, I shall remain in Devon to provide support where necessary. So, if you have any sighting of the invasion fleet then you need only send word to me and I will return in haste with reinforcements.'

Neither Osric nor his nephew took much comfort from that. 'But surely, my Lord, that will mean splitting your forces?' suggested Osric.

'That's true,' admitted Alfred. 'But I have no choice. I am obliged to cover both attacks as best I may.'

Having once been head of the King's personal guard, Osric had more he wanted to say about that but left it to his nephew to speak instead.

'My Lord, this arrangement worries me greatly given the size of the fleet,' said Oswald, his voice filled with concern.

Alfred got up and placed some of the documents in one of the chests. 'The fleet is most likely abroad at present, collecting supplies,' he assured them. 'After that it could strike anywhere and you're no more at risk that any of the other major settlements which have harbours large enough to accommodate them. They may even land on some isolated beach and fight their way inland from there or navigate along one of the rivers. We can't cover every possibility so just hold yourselves ready. In particular, I would advise that you train men to sail the two captured longships as they could be useful given the width of the harbour entrance here. It's narrow enough to be blocked completely if you have to.'

'Will you then return to Wareham, my Lord?' asked Osric.

'No, my friend,' said Alfred. 'I thank you for your hospitality, but must go where I'm most needed. After that I would return to Winchester as there's much there which demands my attention. In my absence, I am most anxious that you continue to look out for young Edward.'

'Of course, my Lord. As we agreed whilst in Winchester, I'll ensure that he learns the ways of a Saxon nobleman as now befits his new station.'

'I was thinking more of his personal safety,' said Alfred. 'I fear that his treacherous uncle doesn't yet know that the assassin he sent to the stables failed and that Edward is therefore still alive.'

Osric had to admit that it was something which greatly concerned him as well. 'So you think he'll try again?'

'I'm sure of it,' acknowledged Alfred. 'Either that or he'll have others do so on his behalf.'

Osric considered that for a moment. 'Then I'll alert the permanent guard to keep a lookout for any strangers,' he offered.

'Do that. But that won't be near enough. Don't forget that there could be other rogues who may try to use Edward to their advantage or relieve him of his fortune.'

Osric remembered all too well what Ethelnorth had said about how a fool and his money are soon parted. He also recalled what he and Ethelnorth had discussed about the risk of Edward being used to usurp Alfred, the consequences of which were too dire to think about. 'Then what more can we do?' he asked.

'I recall you said that the carpenter, Sigbert, gets on well with Edward and is a man who can be trusted?' said Alfred.

'That's true, my Lord,' agreed Osric without hesitation. 'He has served us well often enough and is also one of the most experienced members of the fyrd.'

'Good, then have him finish repairing the ships but after that charge him to continue watching Edward's back at all times. I have already advised Edward to confine himself to Wareham and warned him to be wary of anyone else who tries to befriend him.'

Osric looked worried. 'My Lord, all that should help to keep him safe from those who might seek to use or exploit him, but there's little we can do to guard against Edmund's murderous intent. A stray arrow loosed from behind a tree or an assassin who strikes when Edward least expects it – these are surely the greatest threats and yet are also the ones which we can do little to protect him against.'

Alfred didn't answer at first. 'Yes,' he managed at last. 'I fear that's true. But you can do no more than try. That and pray that God will see him safe, though with all that which now threatens this pious Realm, the good Lord may well have more immediate concerns than the plight of just one boy.'

To be continued…

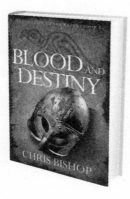
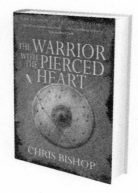

Set at the time of Alfred the Great when Wessex stands alone against the invading Viking hordes, this epic series tells the story of several members of one noble family who each play a crucial role as their King struggles to preserve his people's freedom and their religion… and their right to live as Saxons

Such troubled times demand courage, loyalty, personal sacrifice and, inevitably, blood if they are to survive under

The Shadow of the Raven

AVAILABLE FROM ALL GOOD BOOKSHOPS

About the Author

Chris Bishop was born in London in 1951. After a successful career as a chartered surveyor, he retired to concentrate on writing, combining this with his lifelong interest in history. This is the fourth book in The Shadow of the Raven series, the first, *Blood and Destiny*, having been published in 2017, the second, *The Warrior with the Pierced Heart*, published in 2018, and the third, *The Final Reckoning*, published in 2019.

STAY IN TOUCH WITH CHRIS BISHOP

Sign up to receive Chris's email newsletter at

www.chrisbishopauthor.com

FOLLOW CHRIS:

 @CBishop_author

Find out more about RedDoor Press and sign up
to our newsletter to hear about our latest releases,
author events, exciting competitions and more at

reddoorpress.co.uk

YOU CAN ALSO FOLLOW US:

 @RedDoorBooks

 Facebook.com/RedDoorPress

 @reddoorbooks

Red Door